ARDAN QUINN

Barnibus Jones and the Purple Man

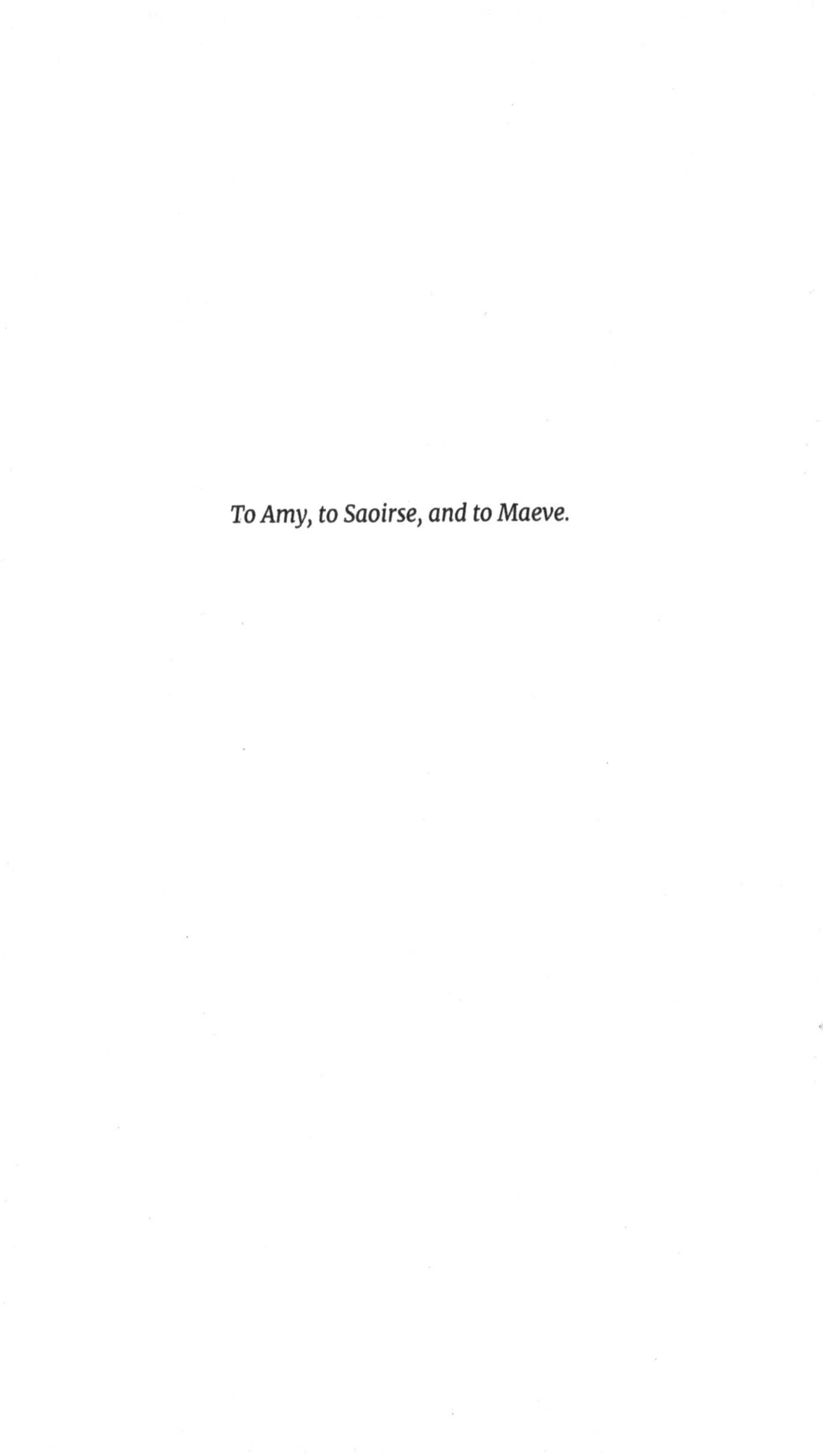

To Amy, to Saoirse, and to Maeve.

Contents

Prologue

Barnibus Jones was a boy who did not dream. Not in the night, and not in the day. Or perhaps one should say he was a boy who had given up on dreaming. For in his dreams he saw a world of storm. A world of endless pain and of murder, and of death that never ended, often not even when he awoke. So after much careful consideration, he swore off dreaming completely. Cold turkey. Because if you're going to stop dreaming, he reasoned, it would be best to make it a clean break.

Better not to drag on the inevitable, he told himself.

The next night, at an hour at which a boy his age ought to be exploring the untold reaches of his subconscious, he made his way out of his room, past the door to his parents' room, down the stairs and, quiet as a mouse, out the front door into the warm summer evening of his quiet cul-de-sac. This world felt alien to him. He had been out here countless times during the day and into the deep summer evenings, adventuring with his friends. But he could only imagine what wonders lurked beyond the shadows in the night. As he began to imagine, however, he realized that this folly of thought — this metaphysical walk-about, exploring the possibilities of what could lie beyond — was getting dangerously close to a dream. Thinking better of it, he quieted his mind.

And so, determined to put an end to his dreams once and for all, he left his home that night and made his way out to bury those dreams in a grave at the farthest reaches of the world. A place so far that no one else would be likely to happen upon them, and a place that he himself would not care to return. It took some time, but he was relieved to find that he had arrived at the far edge of the world in just under two hours. A fantastically quick commute, he thought to himself, smart as he felt to make the trek in the off-hours of the dead of night.

He picked a spot of no importance. A spot so unremarkable as to go completely unnoticed, completely devoid of any landmark or lodestar, so that he himself may never stumble upon this place again. Barnibus dug. In modest, even strokes, he pulled from the earth. And in time, when he grew fatigued, he'd stop and rest a spell, careful not to get lost in his thoughts as he sat. And when his thoughts would precede him, he did what any responsible person would do in his situation, and he wrote those thoughts down in his journal. After all, what makes a dream a dream is its ethereal nature; that fleeting lack of reason or of reality that makes dreams so impossible to pin down or contain. But Barnibus was smarter than his mind. That much he knew for certain. So, by writing his thoughts into his journal, he took them out of the world of the impossible and planted them in reality, where they would remain static. Locked in time and in scale. Easily controlled.

Before long, he felt he had dug far enough. Far enough that no light could reach. He deposited into the earth his dreams, his nightmares, his musings, his fancies, and, just to be safe, even his wonderments. And more easily than he had dug, he returned the earth back to where it had emerged, making quick work to amend the world whole again. When he was done, he stopped and searched his mind. Behind every curtain, deep into every corner, he searched. He saw a mind at peace. And all that remained was shadow.

After all, he reasoned, isn't that what everyone wants?

Barnibus' brother, Saga, unfortunately could not be so lucky. Where Barnibus had successfully rid himself of his dreams — cleared his mind's eye of all but essential reason — Saga saw everything that could be, and everything that would become. Three years Barnibus' junior, Saga was cursed with the Truth; cursed where his brother was not to see the world for what it was: darkness teeming with pain and immense suffering.

Saga's eyes held war. Death. Totality.

The two sons of Barnibus Sr. and their mother Carol had a simple life. Their home, much like the rest of their lives, was perfectly manicured; sculpted and refined to the point of sanitation, devoid of chance or variance that could cause what Carol had called 'uncommon notions detrimental to young boys'. They grew up on a quiet street, nestled among a jungle of similarly quiet streets, which themselves were in a town which was nestled among a jungle of similarly quiet towns. It was a dreadfully boring affair, which was not entirely unintentional. The son of an apprentice butcher, Barnibus Sr. had longed for a simpler life. When pressed further about what complications and preponderance of circumstance it was he wished to avoid, Barnibus Sr. would simply shake his head and chuckle lightly to himself, as if to say, *you wouldn't understand.* The inner machinations of a butcher's son are often without reason or comprehension, so it's best not to push the topic further.

Their mother, Carol, was of a simpler ilk. Born far from the limelight and dazzle of the meat trade, her backstory is without complication or note, aside from the very particular drive that seemed to dictate her approach to parenthood, which was as simple as it was exacting: *No Variation As Long As It Could Be*

Avoided.

And it could always be avoided.

This notion was the sole impetus behind every decision in their lives. Every opportunity — both those seized and those avoided — would trace back to their mother's dogged pursuit of unflinching uniformity. Each morning the boys would wake up and have breakfast at 6:30 AM sharp (traditionally in Pacific Standard Time, but conversion and adaptation would of course be necessary when the family vacationed abroad), then onto school at 7:15 AM. They would attend school from 7:50 AM until 2:45 PM, having brought with them identical lunches consisting of salami sandwiches — 5 slices of salami, 1 slice of American cheese on white bread — one mandarin orange and precisely 20 plantain chips. They would return home, arriving at precisely 3:30, where they would retire to their studies. Dinner was at 6 PM, and they would be in bed by 7 PM without fail.

No exceptions.

1

ONE EXCEPTION

At 6:38 AM, Barnibus awoke with a start to the gentle trailing light of dawn streaking in from the split in his curtain. His eyes frantically searched the room, his hands feebly sweeping about his bed in search of nothing in particular, until his gaze landed on his clock, now 6:39 AM.

What happened? Where is everyone?

He threw his legs off the side of his bed where his feet landed naturally into the pair of slightly-too-large-but-comfortably-so slippers that he kept parked next to his bed. He scarcely had the time and forethought to adorn his robe before he exited his room, but when faced with the possibility of not grabbing it, he thought better of his choices and snatched it off the coat rack next to his door, spinning around as he swooped it over his shoulders, his arms sliding into the sleeves as if he had rehearsed this maneuver several times (he had).

He pulled open the door to the hallway, but hesitated before he emerged. *Maybe she didn't notice,* he thought. *I might make it into the bathroom without anyone noticing my tardiness.* He peered sidelong up and down the hallway as he rested his tightly fitted glasses into the worn-in grooves on the bridge of his nose. Having not spotted his mother in either direction, he made a break for it, rushing in long, light strides directly down the hallway, practically leaping into the bathroom and swinging the door shut gently — but swiftly — behind him. He paused for a breathless moment, listening for any movement outside. When he did not hear the familiar sounds of anyone stirring in the house following his big break, he breathed a sigh of quiet relief. Barnibus had made it unnoticed, and his tardy rise would be just a footnote in his journal and nothing more.

"They're not here," Saga's voice cut through the morning silence like a small, prepubescent knife. Barnibus turned with a jolt, his heart planted in his throat, his knees locked under him. There was Saga sitting on the edge of the tub, one leg crossed over the other like a parent sitting in your doctor's waiting room.

"Holy Christmas!" Barnibus exclaimed.

"Yeah, that's what I said, too. Pretty much exactly like that, I said, 'Holy Christmas'."

"What do you mean they're not here?"

"They're not here. I woke up — on time, by the way — and the house was empty. Nobody here but you and me."

"That's not possible!"

"Sure it is," Saga offered by way of an explanation. Saga's direct explanations of his view of the world had long irritated Barnibus. When they were younger (*younger-still*, as they are, by most professionally accepted definitions, still quite young), he thought it was because they struck him as brusque, as if Saga sought to demean or dismiss his older brother. His blunt demeanor and curt tone seemed at odds with his slight build and diminutive stature, but his self-assuredness — to

Barnibus' mind — gave him the appearance of a much bigger kid, a more towering presence. But the longer he spent with that explanation, the more apparent the truth had become to him: this is his younger brother — his *little* brother! How can he see everything as a world of absolutes? So confidently he strides through life with this unabashed, unchallenged view of everything happening around him. Meanwhile, Barnibus stumbled, perpetually lost, dwarfed by the foreboding power of his little brother, who had only years earlier learned to ride a bike without training wheels. In the back of his undreaming mind, their dynamic stung.

Barnibus turned and slowly cracked the bathroom door open, just far enough to peer out of it, but not wide enough to be noticed from the outside. He studied the hallway. When he saw no motion, he turned his head a quarter turn and listened intently, confident that he'd hear his mother's hum as she prepared their lunches, or the gentle patter of her slippers (which match Barnibus and Saga's slippers, naturally) trotting from room to room getting everything ready for another day.

Nothing. Silence.

Barnibus closed the door, easing it back into the jamb gently before returning the knob and allowing the latch to engage silently. He hesitated for a moment before turning back towards his brother, allowing for any sounds that might have been late traveling down the hallway another moment or two to catch up. Nothing came. He turned to his brother, puzzled. He opened his mouth, begging his mind for an answer or, failing that, a question of any kind. Nothing. In the mind of an undreaming child there is frightfully more than questions and cravings, and while Barnibus was himself a naturally inquisitive young boy, this particular morning left him particularly aghast.

"I know," Saga reassured him as he arose, turning to squeeze between the bathtub and Barnibus. He pulled the door open confidently as Barnibus watched this daring act with a mix of awe and pure terror. Once again, he was struck by the confidence of his little brother.

Still nothing. Silence.

In the hallway they moved carefully, walking in unison to minimize the amount of noise they would make. *After all,* Barnibus reasoned quietly to himself, *if Mother really is home, she'll be none-too-pleased to find that we not only woke up late but also wasted time faffing about in the bathroom!* But alas, as he watched his brother, he knew this desperate hope to be untrue. And as that truth washed slowly over him, his gait eased and his steps fell out of sync with Saga's. Relieved to give up the charade and walk like a normal human boy, Saga relaxed as well, allowing himself to shift gears swiftly to his normal speed as he rounded the corner into the kitchen.

Barnibus entered the kitchen only a couple of steps behind his brother and was impressed to find that in the intervening two and a half seconds Saga had managed to get himself a bowl, pull down the cereal, get the milk from the refrigerator and was already diving headlong into preparing himself a bowl. It wouldn't be until much later in the day when he'd realized that his brother had likely pulled out at least some amount of those two key ingredients earlier in the morning, as Saga had been careful to note that he had gotten up on time, unlike Barnibus.

"Well, this is just great," Barnibus grumbled. "What are we supposed to do now?" He dropped into a chair at the table with a heavy thud.

"Right now I'm going to have a bowl of cereal," Saga said

absently around a mouthful of corn puffs. "After that, if there's time, I'll have another." He turned to look at the clock hanging on the wall. One of those cats with enormous eyes, whose tail swings back and forth with each passing second. It had been a wedding present to Carol and Barnibus Sr. from Barnibus Sr.'s father, Barntholomew. "But we should head to school pretty soon."

"School? Today?"

Saga nodded.

"I can't just go to school like everything is okay. My family is missing!"

"Parents."

"What?"

"Your parents are missing, not your family. I'm right here."

"Oh."

"See? Not so bad."

"Right..." Barnibus said as he regarded Saga's view. "Wait. No. That's just as bad!"

"It's a third less bad if you think about it," Saga reasoned.

"I don't want to think about it! I've got enough to think about right now without also considering how mathematically worse it would be if my entire family had gone missing, and not just our parents!" Barnibus' thoughts were getting away from him. When he realized he was starting to lose his careful grip on his imagination, he got up and shuffled around the junk on the counter, searching for one of the journals he keeps around the house.

"It would be 33.3% worse. I just said that. And for all we know, maybe they think that we're missing," Saga mused as he poured more cereal into his bowl. "Maybe they're right where they belong, and to them we're missing. We don't know what this is." Saga watched his brother mull over the facts in his head. He could see the gears moving, but could not decipher what thoughts were going through Barnibus' mind. The two brothers were close — very close indeed — but unfortunately telepathy had thus far eluded them, despite how often Saga urged them to practice.

Unsure of how to reach his brother at this moment, he offered, "I know a guy a couple of towns over, says he has one of those... What are they called? Quiji? Weejay?" He paused, hoping Barnibus would help, but he only stared back at Saga, eagerly waiting to hear what it was his brother was trying to say. After a moment, "Ouija! One of those boards that lets you talk to dead people—not that Mom and Dad are dead! I don't think. Hopefully. Yeah, I don't think so. That feels excessive." He took another bite of cereal, confident that he had smoothed over his minor misstep in implying that perhaps their parents were dead after all.

"Dead! You think they're dead?!"

"I knew that's the only part of this that you'd latch onto — no! I don't think they're dead. I'm just saying that I know of a guy — right? — lives a couple of towns over, and he might be able to help us at least try to talk to Mom and Dad, or try to put some feelers out there and see if they respond. It'll at least let us cross one possibility off the list." He studied his brother's face, hoping for a clue, or a glimmer of a hint that his brother was not spinning out.

But Barnibus was already beyond listening to his brother. He needed to get these thoughts down in his journal — and fast! Out of his mind, into his journal. Same as always. Out of the ether, onto the page. Once it's on the page, it's fixed. It cannot get away from him once it's in his journal, because it's there forever and unable to break free. *Can't change on the page*, he pictured his mother saying. Carol never said that, and in fact, he had been careful to keep his worries about his dreams far away from both his mother and his father. But alas, the voice in his head that told him right from wrong was invariably that of his mother. So now that she's gone, what is he supposed to do? How will Barnibus be able to tell right from wrong, or know when the path he's chosen — whatever it is he does now to get them back — is the right way? What if whatever he does now ends up putting them in worse danger, or, worse still, causes them never to come back? Will it just be Barnibus and Saga alone from then on? Or will—

No. Your mind is racing. Out of the ether, onto the page.

"I think we should give it a shot," Saga cut in. Barnibus looked up from his journal, bleary-eyed, barely keeping it together while writing.

"What?"

"Let's go put some feelers out there."

"Feelers?"

"Tendrils, some appendages, I don't know. Let's go see if we try to reach out to the other — whatever — the other side, other dimension, whatever — and see if we hear anything. At least then if we hear nothing back, we'll know that they're still around here someplace, probably."

"How are we going to get two towns over?"

"We'll walk," Saga shrugged.

"No. No, absolutely not," Barnibus fervently protested, as he tried to turn his attention back to his journal. "If we walk, it's going to take us the full day to get there, and we'll be completely out of contact if they try to reach us, or — worse! — if they get home and we're missing and didn't go to school today." He shook his head hard enough to almost lose his balance. "No way."

"It's just an idea. You said you didn't want to go to school anyway. I just thought I'd put it out there." It was not a common theme between them, but when it happened, albeit rarely, Saga hated the feeling of being defeated by his brother. Even though Saga was the younger of the two, he always tried to appeal to Barnibus on his level, and while most of the time he could keep his own, these occasional missteps always caused him grief. He thought for a moment about telling his brother this. About how it makes him feel when he shoots him down the way he does sometimes, but something in Barnibus' nervous shaking and bulging eyes made Saga think that right now might not be the best time. Once Carol and Barnibus Sr. return home and things have calmed down a bit, he will have a frank discussion with his brother. Probably. Hopefully.

By now, Barnibus had already moved on from Saga's suggestion — as nonsensical as it was — as he raced to catch up with his thoughts quickly enough to get them down onto the pages of his notebook. He had let his guard down for a moment, and he could feel his mind getting away from him as he scribbled. *Can't change on the page. Write it down. Write it all down now, before things get out of hand.*

And so he did.

2

OUT OF THE FRYING PAN, INTO THE SCHOOL

Like clockwork, the school bus arrived precisely at 7:15 AM. After all, it was the two Jones brothers who were running late that morning, not the fleet of district buses. There was a tight schedule to keep, and the district's Transportation Manager, Gregory Collins, had no intention of letting that slip, especially not on account of two young boys whom he had never met.

Barnibus trudged onto the bus with heavy feet. Every step felt momentous, taking every ounce of energy he had just to climb the steps onto the bus and down the aisle to his seat. Behind him, eager to keep moving, Saga eyed the bus and the other students already in their seats with some regard. He did not know what he was looking for, but he knew he was looking for something. Whatever it was they were experiencing this morning must be happening beyond just the two of them — beyond just their family — but he could not for the life of him figure out what it was, or why it was happening, or for that matter, to whom it was happening. As far as Saga was concerned, everybody was a suspect. A suspect of what, he was not sure. But he suspected each of them could be suspects, especially those who struck him as particularly suspect.

They climbed into their seats, Barnibus at the window, staring blankly at the seatback in front of him, and Saga on the aisle, still searching around the faces on the bus. Everybody else on the bus was entirely unfazed, simply going about their day as any other. And for most of them, Saga reasoned, it probably was a day like any other. For them, it was just another Tuesday.

* * *

Barnibus had one goal at school: make it through the day. It appeared much simpler on paper. He knew that to be true because he had spent the entire commute writing as much into the notebook he kept in his backpack. *Just make it through the day.* Line break. *Just make it through the day.* Line break, repeat.

Walking up the front steps of Anna Tuthill Harrison Junior High, Barnibus, lost in the vast, soundless chasm of his imagination, heard a familiar call from the sidewalk.

"Barney! Hey, Barney!"

Saga kept walking, but Barnibus turned with a grimace as the nickname shattered against his ear. There were very few things he hated more in this world than being called '*Barney*'. Not even his mother would call him Barney, and he would use it as an instantaneous way to know that someone was trying to pull a fast one on him; someone was trying to be too familiar with him to get something from him, or to get into his good graces. The perpetrator's intentions could only be inferred, but they were seldom wholesome. There are very few things on this green earth that filled him with greater frustration than that nickname, and Barney — sorry, *Barnibus* — turned on his heel, ready to unload on the poor kid that dared cross that line.

"Oh, hey man," Barnibus called out meekly. Now was not the time to ruffle feathers, he figured. All this tragic business with his parents was enough drama for the day; best not to create more trouble.

"I've been trying to get your attention for like 20 minutes, dude. What gives?" The nicknamer in question was Nathaniel, a kid from Barnibus' class. They'd known each other since they were six years old, and while they had been friends for quite some time, Barnibus was always careful to keep him at arm's length, as there were a few things that he did that annoyed Barnibus. The nickname, for one, was a bit much, and he made a mental note to make a real note about that in his journal when he got to class. But aside from that, Nathaniel was also an exaggerator. Case in point: Barnibus had only been off the school bus for barely three minutes before he heard Nathaniel calling. And Nathaniel certainly was not on the same bus as him, since he lived with his aunt far, far away on the other side of town. District Transportation Manager Gregory Collins was far too smart to schedule single bus routes crisscrossing the entire town like that — it would be a logistical nightmare! Gregory Collins had a Master of Science in Transportation Management (MSTM). He knew much better than to schedule single drivers to cover such a large area. And while the ridership may be low across the district, and more routes meant more overhead to operate against a smaller budget, he prioritized routes based on carbon emissions and "Door-to-Door Time" (D2D). It would be untenable for a single line to handle the entire town. Barnibus had thoughts on this, but he had yet to take the time to schedule a meeting with Mr. Collins (he felt ill-at-ease calling an adult by their first name, especially one with an MSTM) to discuss his ideas for improving, or at least slightly altering the fleet routing. Maybe in the spring, when he was past his mid-terms, he could—

Oh no. It's happening again. Barnibus felt his thoughts getting away from him. Write it down. *Out of the ether, onto the page.* He swung his bag around from his back, hanging it below his armpit as he grabbed the readily available journal from the front pocket. He scribbled intently as Nathaniel watched on, waiting for his opportunity to jump in with Barnibus' full attention.

"Hey man... how has your day been going?" Nathaniel asked.

Barnibus glanced up from his journal, hoping to see, somehow, if he had heard the question correctly.

"It's been... a little weird, I'd say..." Barnibus answered skeptically. "Why do you ask?"

Nathaniel shifted uneasily in his sneakers, glancing around the front of the school, searching to see if any of the other kids could hear their conversation.

"Have you noticed anything weird going on..." he hesitated, "with your parents?"

Barnibus inhaled sharply as his heart skipped a beat. *So it isn't just us!* He turned to find Saga, hoping he had heard this revelation as well, but he had long-since disappeared into the school.

"I thought it was just us," Barnibus hissed back in a hushed tone. "We've been trying to figure it out all morning!"

"Figures," Nathaniel sighed deeply. "I don't know what happened. One moment everything is normal, and the next—"

"Yeah!" Barnibus cut in.

"They're just being so uncool."

"Wait, what?" Barnibus inquired, the winds stolen hastily from his sails.

"Yeah, man. They're just being really weird about this weekend. It's like," he hesitated, "kind of a lot of pressure, you know?"

The trip this weekend! Amidst all the goings-on in the morning, Barnibus had completely forgotten about the school trip coming up in just a few days. *It doesn't really matter now*, he thought. *I think the school will understand not making the Eastern Mid-Sized Middle School Science Conference and Jamboree. At a time like this, there's frightful little else a young boy should concern himself with than the well-being of his parents.*

"I thought you meant something else," Barnibus finally blurted out. "It's been a kind of weird morning."

"They just need to get over it," Nathaniel postured in his best high-schooler-impression. "It's just a science jamboree. It's not like this one jamboree is our entire future. There will be other jamborees," he mused flatly.

"Jamboree?" someone called out from the crowd of passing students. Barnibus and Nathaniel both turned, excited that someone else wanted to talk about what the two of them considered to be *the big show.* It was Zachary, an eighth-grader from the water polo team. As excited as they had been a moment ago, they were now equally dreadful to realize this would not be a pleasant conversation.

"Science losers going to your little science party?" Zachary and his friends laughed, high-fiving each other. This was handily the highlight of their morning.

"Why don't you buncha losers just sit this one out, okay? Stay home in your basements and play with your little double helix models, make some of that *genetic material,* yougnomesayin'?" More high-fives. Nathaniel did not know what he was saying, but Barnibus, as much as he would rather not, did. Mercifully, Zachary and his teammates kept walking into the school, and the moment passed with relative ease.

"Don't worry about them," Barnibus assured Nathaniel.

"Why 'losers'?" Nathaniel wondered. " How could we have lost already? We haven't even gotten to the jamboree."

Barnibus admired not only Nathaniel's optimism but also how effortlessly he shrugged off Zachary's barbs.

"We can't have lost if we haven't even played the game," Nathaniel said flatly, shaking his head with mild bemusement.

Now that the unpleasantness had passed, Barnibus was eager to press Nathaniel for more information.

"You talked to your parents this morning, though? Er, about the jamboree."

"Heh, I wish I hadn't," Nathaniel lamented. "I tried to change the subject, but they're just fixated." He shrugged.

"Huh." Barnibus did not know what to make of this. Nathaniel's parents are fine. Maybe his parents are fine as well, and they just needed to run off somewhere. Maybe they had a morning errand. Those come up sometimes, right? Probably. He could not be sure, as, given his age, he did not have errands of his own to worry about. Barnibus considered this new information intently.

"You okay?" Nathaniel regarded Barnibus' deeply furrowed brow.

"Maybe it's nothing..." Barnibus said quietly under his breath as his gaze shifted lazily towards the ground. Nathaniel stared at him for a moment, expecting more to come out, but that was all Barnibus had to contribute to the conversation.

Nathaniel opened and shut his mouth a couple of times, hoping thoughts would come out to move onto another topic, but being unable to read Barnibus, he could not be sure where to go. After a moment, he stepped to the left and slowly walked past Barnibus and into the school, leaving Barnibus alone at the front of the school, quietly examining the ground at his feet. Whether he realized it at that moment or not (he did not), he once again found himself alone, and while he did not mind being alone, he found he was not a fan of it as an emerging trend.

* * *

"Page 94 this morning! If you don't have your book — I'm looking at you, Margaret — you can share with a neighbor. Just ask politely."

Barnibus knew scarcely that he was even in class. He had very little memory of navigating from the front of the school, through the halls and stopping at his locker on his way to class. But evidently he did, because here he was. *But how?*

"Page 94, Mr. Jones. That means you too."

Barnibus looked up to see Mr. Calhoun staring at him from only a couple of desks away. Mr. Calhoun was his science teacher, and while he always liked him as an instructor, he could tell that Mr. Calhoun's patience with him was wearing thin as the year went on. Barnibus knew he had a tendency to zone out during class. Probably not more than any other kid, but Mr. Calhoun always noticed, and always seemed to take a measure of offense. Barnibus had once tried to reassure him during a particularly awkward parent-teacher conference that it had nothing to do with him and was in fact just how

Barnibus absorbed the material, but Mr. Calhoun did not buy that excuse.

"I've been teaching a long time, Mr. Jones," Mr. Calhoun had told him during the meeting, more as a show for Carol than it was for Barnibus' benefit. "I can tell the difference between a student 'absorbing the material' and a student just daydreaming on my time." With that, he held Barnibus' gaze, smug, immensely proud of his perceived ability to call out a child in front of their parents. But as sure as Mr. Calhoun had been, Barnibus knew it was nonsense. Barnibus did not dream, and that, by definition, included daydreaming, a pastime that Barnibus did not enjoy, on his time or anyone else's.

"Sorry, Mr. Calhoun," Barnibus croaked as he rammed both hands nervously into his book bag and pulled out his Science book (*Custer K, & Wright M. (1963). Today's Basic Science.*) The peeling, dogeared corner of the front cover caught on the edge of one of his three binders and peeled back even farther. *At this rate, how is the school planning on getting another sixty years out of this thing?*

"Maybe if you spent a little less time in your head and a bit more time in my classroom, Mr. Jones," Mr. Calhoun broke in.

It sounded rhetorical, but Barnibus knew that Mr. Calhoun expected an answer. Right? He must, otherwise why would he phrase it that way? Mr. Calhoun continued staring at Barnibus, and Barnibus' eyes and palms felt hot. He did not like this kind of attention generally, and especially not in front of other people. *Why was he still staring? What is this?* Mr. Calhoun lifted the toe of his left loafer and pivoted on his heel, just as Barnibus offered, "I'm here, sir."

Mr. Calhoun stopped on a dime and slowly turned his head back to Barnibus, incredulous that the boy would speak in the middle of his signature dynamic heel-spin. That was his move. Everybody who had ever studied in his Science department (in the last six and a half years, at least) knew that move. They respected that move. But Barnibus just smiled a half smile, genuinely doing what he could to defuse the situation. After what felt like ten full minutes — but was actually about four seconds — Mr. Calhoun turned back towards the chalkboard, having said nothing further to Barnibus, and continued on with his lecture. Barnibus slid down in his chair, happy to have the brief conflict over with, and hoping not to be seen again. By Mr. Calhoun or, hopefully, by anyone else for the rest of the day.

Before long (about ten seconds) his mind wandered again. As he gripped his pencil tightly, trying to figure out if he could covertly remove his journal once again from his bag without anyone noticing, his mind quickly reached a logical, non-fantastical, hardly-a-dream conclusion: *Just go home.* It was so simple; so clean. *You don't want to be here, so you shouldn't be here, and you don't need to be here. So... just go home.* That's it. It really is that simple. Something much larger than middle school is happening right now. Larger than Barnibus and larger than Saga — *oh, no, Saga. I'll have to stop by his classroom and sign him out as well. Can I sign him out? Should I try to fake Mom's signature? No, I don't think that sort of thing works in person.*

"Medical terminology — both diagnostic and diagraphic — is paramount for triumph at this weekend's jamboree..." Mr. Calhoun droned on, as Barnibus weighed his options.

I'll just have to figure it out on the road, he thought as he sprang from his seat. His chair shifted back as he rose, causing the feet to shriek across the ground; a sharp, scathing shriek that brought the entire class — and probably the entire wing of the school — to a sudden, dead stop. Mr. Calhoun, eager to execute another heel-turn to redeem the tragically forfeited previous attempt, spun giddily on his left heel, more excited to nail the move than he was angry at the disruption. His scowl, however, did not betray such joy. While his heart sang, his face was — unfortunately for Barnibus — all business. And that business was that of a stern rebuke.

"I have to go!" Barnibus stammered by way of minimal explanation, announcing it for the benefit of the entire class.

"Is that so, *Mr. Jones?*" Mr. Calhoun hissed.

"My parents. Th-they're... they're not okay." He surveyed his classmates to find any signs of recognition. "They're not well." Or any sign that someone else was maybe — he hated to think it, but *hopefully* — dealing with the same thing. "It's just that I've never seen them... like this..." He was met only by a sea of blank stares from mildly annoyed students.

"You will return to your seat at once, and you will finish this lesson. Do I make myself clear?"

After one final sweep of his classmates, looking for anything close to a lifeline, Barnibus reluctantly slumped back down into his chair, defeated. Barnibus was not telling a lie. This was not an elaborate scheme to get out of science class. And he wished that Mr. Calhoun had known that, given how well Barnibus excelled in his class. He was earnestly looking forward to the jamboree this coming weekend until this morning. Now things had changed; his priorities had shifted. *But it's no use,* Barnibus thought to himself, resigned. *If I can't even make my way out of this room, what good would I be out there trying to solve... whatever this is?* Barnibus did not like feeling this way. Defeated. Resigned. All the other basic words that could describe someone who had hardly made an effort, let alone enough of an effort to make a difference.

"No," Barnibus muttered to himself.

Nathaniel, two seats over to the right, kept his head low as he turned to look. Barnibus counted himself lucky that Nathaniel was the only one who had heard his utterance, as Mr. Calhoun continued on rallying his troops ahead of the jamboree, undeterred by another opportunity to make an example out of him. Another opportunity to call him '*Mr. Jones*' in front of everybody.

Barnibus shook his head lightly to himself. *This isn't right. I can't have lost if I haven't even played the game.*

As Mr. Calhoun paced across the chalkboard, musing to himself about the inherent value of a firm command of technical health terms, Barnibus quietly returned his textbook and his journal to his book bag and gently looped the straps shut. He was going to need a distraction. He was simply too far into the room to slink out of the door without Mr. Calhoun noticing. And he had already drawn enough ire that the consequences would be substantial if he were to be caught ditching class — mid-lecture, no less! Mr. Calhoun would have him in front of the principal in no time, and he would wind up grounded for sure. That is, of course, if his parents ever came back.

A distraction. Something. He could be so lucky. Something loud, something disruptive. Something that would make enough noise and get enough people moving around that no one would notice one student disappearing in the shuffle. A fire alarm? No, that would be too dramatic and cause too much of a stir. At best, he would be able to get out of the room along with everyone else, but then he would be in a sea of students from the entire school, and the administration would keep an extra close eye on everyone. It would be loud, and people would be moving, but it's not the right—

Barnibus realized that not only was his mind beginning to race, but he had also just latched his bag shut with his journal inside. As he moved quietly to unlatch his bag once again and get his journal without causing too much of a fuss, he strained to divert his thoughts to something more reasonable. Anything at all, so long as it would not cause a panic. *Just think. No daydreams, no long, twisting tangents. Just think. Keep it grounded, keep it reasonable. Something simple. Something boring, even. Just keep it simple and boring. Like an announcement.* He was sweating, and his sweaty hands fumbled with the latches on his bag. *Yeah, something like that would be perfect. The principal could just pop onto the PA with something benign. Something inconsequential. Just something that could—*

"Attention, students," the Principal broke in on the PA. The class stopped on a dime and turned obediently towards the speaker on the wall opposite the door, their faces filled with an unmetered degree of gleeful anticipation. With that, Barnibus seized his opportunity, slipped out of his seat and made a silent dash out the door. Free and clear into the hallway. What luck!

CA-CHUNK CA-CHUNK CA-CHUNK CA-CHUNK CA-CHUNK.

Like a tidal wave of now terrible luck, each door to every classroom off the hallway swung open and students began pouring out. Barnibus did not know what to make of this, and his head was swimming indeed. *What luck,* he thought to himself. Behind him, his own classmates exited Mr. Calhoun's class, unaware that he had snuck out mere moments before.

"Hey man," Nathaniel said quietly behind him, "what was it you were saying earlier about your parents?"

"How's that now?"

"Earlier. You were acting all weird about your parents, about my parents acting weird about the jamboree... or something...?"

"Oh, yeah, just—" he drifted off as he scanned the hallway, perched up on the tips of his toes, trying to find Saga.

"Yeah...?" Nathaniel begged. Barnibus snapped back to it.

"Yeah, I just—" Barnibus was cut short as the water polo players clipped his shoulder hard as they walked past him in the hall. None of them stopped or gave much in the way of an acknowledgement, aside from Zachary looking back over his shoulder at Barnibus with a snide smile.

"C'mon, man," Nathaniel said, his voice trembling. "I'm starting to get kind of scared."

"What's going on?" Barnibus asked, his attention cracking like a whip as it landed squarely back on Nathaniel. "Why is everyone leaving class?"

"The Principal?" Nathaniel proffered as he pointed vaguely toward the PA system. "They're closing the school down. A bunch of the teachers didn't show up this morning. Bunch of kids, too. They're sending everyone home. No one knows what's going on."

Empirically, in no uncertain terms, Barnibus did not know what was happening. However, for the first time since he awoke, he felt as though he did. And for the time being, just feeling like he understood was of great comfort. Knowing that whatever was happening, whatever this was, was not just happening to his brother and him, meant that they would not be going through it alone. He wondered to himself if Saga had the same feeling; maybe they would be okay after all. *What luck.*

3

ALL THE LUCK IN THE WORLD

Saga felt no comfort. No solace in the fact that other adults were missing, and even less in the fact that now children were missing as well. The events of this morning already felt impossibly big, and while Saga has always known tragedy to reach well beyond the bounds of one home or another, seeing that theory put into action felt momentous; something he worried he was ill-equipped to handle on his own, or even alongside his brother. As he marched alongside his classmates, calmly filing out of the school, he wondered if Barnibus, wherever he was, was feeling the same way.

"What luck!" Barnibus exclaimed once again when he saw his brother emerge from the school. "You're okay!"

Around them, students crowded at the edge of the walkway outside the school, lining the curb against the parking lot. There was little order to be offered, as the school itself was dangerously understaffed, and those who had come to work were, in many cases, just as confused and scared as some of their pupils. Whatever was happening could still yet come for them as well.

"Why wouldn't I be okay?" Saga, ever skeptical of the intentions of others, rarely extended that skepticism in his brother's direction. But in light of today's new mystery, he knew not what he could trust, and every person who approached him needed to be assessed carefully, as Saga considered how they fit into the bigger puzzle.

"Kids are going missing, Saga. What wonder — what mystery!"

"You think that's good news?"

"Heavens, no," Barnibus gasped. He had a tendency to revert to a Southern debutante's exasperation when he was flustered. "I just mean that this is huge. Whatever this is, whatever happened—" he hushed his tone and surveyed the other students nearby, "—whatever happened with our parents... it's something. Something is happening, and it's not just happening to us."

"We need to go find them." Conversationally, Saga's attention was with Barnibus, but otherwise, he had shifted his focus to surveying the crowd outside of the school. He did not know what he was looking for, but he knew in a crowd this size, families coming and going, there would be enough of a sample size to get some good data; he could get clues to lead them to where they should look.

"What? No," Barnibus said. "The principal said everyone needs to head home. They've already called our families. It's like a curfew, or whatever."

"Which family do you think they called, exactly?"

Barnibus had not considered this, and the realization landed on him like a heavy weight, drawing his shoulders firmly toward the ground. *Which family could they have called for them?*

Barnibus and Saga were from a small clan. While their

family tree was broad and contained virtually every type of butcher and butcher-adjacent professional you could imagine, the branches of that tree that were still living had grown thinner and thinner with the passing years. The two brothers were young indeed, but in their short lives they had already come to know tremendous tragedy and profound loss. They had attended more funerals than they had hosted birthday parties of their own, a ratio that few people will be unfortunate enough to reach in their lives. To the Jones brothers, it was commonplace; simply part of their lives, and something they were never left to navigate on their own, thanks to the loving guidance of their parents.

Their parents.

First to go were their grandparents on their father's side. Natural causes of petty concern or note. They had passed within a few months of each other, which Saga had been emphatic in informing Barnibus was astonishingly common. Next up came a series of aunts and uncles of varying degrees of familiarity. Some Barnibus had known well since he was a baby, having been babysat or fed by any number of them on occasion. But others still Barnibus had not known at all; his introduction to these family members had been Carol informing him of their passing; an empty message that Barnibus always found considerably more tragic than the news of their passing. Not having known them means they had not known him either. And if they were unaware of each other, could they really be considered family? Is it family just because your parents knew each other when they were younger, but now do not speak to one another? At what degree of separation does one drop the 'family' moniker and call it something considerably more casual, like 'Friend' or 'Acquaintance'? The thought of the news carrying that term amused Barnibus, but only in a macabre way, attempting to protect him from the true hurt he was feeling.

"Honey," he imagined his mother calling as she entered his room, "My acquaintance Marge passed away this morning," she would say flatly, "you know, my sister."

But what family could the school have called on behalf of Barnibus and Saga? He had hoped to find a teacher to ask — the principal, a janitor, any adult at all — but the more he looked around, the fewer adults he found. Looking past the sea of jostling children, he could see some of the school staff climbing into their own cars and hastily exiting the parking lot. Though he had yet to voice any of this to Saga, his brother could see in his face that he had already put together this particular portion of the puzzle.

"Exactly," Saga muttered.

"Where do you think they're heading?"

"Somewhere they think they're safe. In their minds, nothing bad is going to happen at home, so they're going there for shelter."

This streak in Saga always made Barnibus uneasy. Looking at him, his brother was just a kid; a younger brother who should be looking to his older brother Barnibus for advice. Yet, time after time, Saga proved himself to be wiser, or more battle-worn than Barnibus. It was not a feeling of jealousy, nor that a younger child had somehow surpassed him or one-upped him in a given situation. It was purely a worry. Worry that his brother had seen in his young life something horrible or something that was simply too much for his brain to handle and that it had in fact broken him. Looking around the parking lot now, he could not help but worry that today was that day.

If his brother was not already broken in some way, losing his parents would definitely do the trick. And what then?

"It's starting to get thin out here," Saga said broadly towards the parking lot, remarking more for his own benefit than Barnibus'.

"Yeah…" Barnibus, lost in thought, had not noticed how many of his classmates had left. "Maybe not that many people are missing if this many kids are still getting rides."

"I don't think they're all getting rides," Saga added, as he pointed towards a group of eighth-graders scaling a fence at the side of the school and disappearing into the brush beyond. "I think plenty of them are making a run for it."

"They must be scared." Barnibus mused before he thought better of introducing fear into the issue. "Are y—are you scared, Saga?" he blurted out uneasily, shocking himself with the question almost as much as he shocked Saga. He winced as he caught the halting stutter he sometimes adopted when his nerves overtook him. It was a common trait between the Jones brothers, and while they never addressed it directly, they both believed it stemmed from the need to walk on eggshells around their mother, less they take a step she deems incorrect; her exacting tastes and standards acting as editor-in-chief to their own thoughts and words. As close as they were, this was getting close to uncharted waters now. Barnibus' job was not to worry about Saga. Neither boy liked it, and it felt deeply unnatural to both of them. He held his breath lightly, waiting to see how Saga handled this faux pas.

"No," Saga answered flatly, with a palpable measure of offense. "I don't get scared." He turned his attention back to the thinning crowd of students. "At least not by this. Not now." He threw up his guard quickly and thick. The images in his mind and the machinations of his processing of them would remain his secret to keep, Barnibus ventured, at least for now. '*Not now*' gave Barnibus hope his brother might be considering his counsel. He would be there for him when needed.

Barnibus knew there was no use responding, so he nodded gently and gave his brother a bit of space to process everything that was happening. He wanted to allow him to feel whatever it was he was feeling — fear or not — rather than prescribe his own thoughts onto it. Barnibus worried that whatever he said he was feeling — worry, fear, anger, jealousy — his brother would adopt on his own, knowingly or otherwise, and it would paint the two of them into a corner he was not sure he could navigate them out of if need be. He did not want to pull two people out of identical doom spirals if he could avoid it. One was enough for Barnibus. At least for now.

"Should we just head home? If they're just out somewhere, they'll come home, eventually. That's the easiest thing to do right now: just wait it out." Barnibus tried to play it cool to avoid urging too strongly.

"We need to go see my guy. We can wait around the house all day, but if they're dead, we'll be waiting a long time."

"Saga!" Barnibus scolded. "That's enough! No one said dead, we're not saying dead, stop saying dead."

"If they're on the other side somewhere, I think it would be really neat for us to know that now. At least then we could act accordingly."

"Absolutely not." Barnibus crossed his arms tightly across his chest.

"I can go there alone. It's just a couple towns over, and I bet in all this chaos I can probably get a ride over there. At least part of the way."

"You're not going two towns over by yourself! Especially when half of our family is already missing. That's dangerous and irresponsible, and I won't have it," Barnibus raised his voice, as if stamping his feet into the ground as he spoke was not enough to telegraph his displeasure at Saga's idea.

"Right. So you agree you should come with me?"

"Saga."

Silence. It was not unusual for the brothers to disagree. They were brothers after all. But the stakes this time felt somehow higher. Barnibus did not like to deal in definites, as he liked to believe that the world, for better or worse, functioned in a system of grey zones which kept each other balanced in a form of global and societal stasis. That being said, he felt reasonably confident in assuming that the stakes were higher this time because their parents were missing and possibly dead. That was a definite that he felt confident in putting money against.

What now? Barnibus needed to think of something that would bring both him and Saga comfort, and also have a degree of safety to it. Whatever was happening right now, no matter what, he knew that the two of them needed to stay together. Full stop. Splitting up simply was not an option. More than anything, he just wanted to be home. Home, in his room, with his lamp on and his fan running at a low speed, the gentle hum drowning out the din of the house. But the more he thought about it, the more he missed that din. That din was a house full of people. Full of his family. And the further he went down that path, the more it reminded him he might not see his parents again. Or, maybe worse, his parents might not see their children again. Resigned, Barnibus slipped his book bag from atop his shoulder, reached in and produced one of his journals. He pulled the ribbon that marked his current page and jotted down a couple of notes. Barnibus had his own shorthand at this point — something that he could read and refer to, but would be nonsense to the casual reader. He wrote quickly about fearing that his parents would never see their children, and what he worried that would look like for them. The heartache, the confusion, the deep-rooted depression that would set in. Above all, he did not see how anyone could recover from a loss so profound, and that filled him with fear. Fear for his parents more than for himself and his brother. With those couple of thoughts, he slapped the book shut and returned it to his bag. It was an action so rote with practiced routine that Saga had hardly even noticed, or had chosen politely to ignore it.

"If they're out there, they are just as scared as we are," Barnibus said finally.

"We'd be helping them," Saga nodded.

"We'd be helping them," Barnibus said simply, as if to further convince himself. "But I want to stop at home first. Just to grab a couple of things."

"We can't be too long; we've got a lot of ground to cover, and I—"

"It'll be quick, I promise."

"Okay," Saga said as a grin spread wide across his face.

"Wherever we go from here on, it's going to be you and I, okay? It's the Jones brothers in this one together. I'm the older one here, so that makes me, sort of, in charge by default. You got it? We can't get separated; we can't split up." Barnibus — or Saga for that matter — had not heard this confidence come from his mouth before. He could hear himself saying the words, and while he knew he felt them, he could not be sure that he was the one saying them. For a moment, it was as if he was out of his own body, watching himself act in a way that he had always wanted to act, but had not the bravery to do so. At first, this feeling made him uneasy, made him itch for his journal, worried that an out-of-body experience bordered a little too closely on a lucid dream and thus was off-limits for him. But the longer he let the sensation play out, the easier it felt. The more right. The more safe. "We can't take anyone else along with us. We can't let anyone distract us. It's just you and I from here on."

"Hey, that sounds great!" a bouncy, graveled voice called from the school entrance a stone's throw away. "Where are we headed?"

Barnibus and Saga both spun on their heels to see who had called out to them. There stood a man dressed all in varying shades of purple. Pants, vest, jacket, tie — all deeply purple, all carefully appointed, and all entirely out of place outside their suburban middle school. This was a person dressed more for Wall Street or a grape-themed high-power meet-and-greet than the halls of low-level public academia. Their vaguely neo-Gothic appointments stood out in a way that signaled an anachronistic confidence that gave the boys pause. They did not know this person, and at first glance they did not want to know them. They had not the slightest idea how to respond.

"Okay. Don't all answer at once," the Purple Man shouted, just a hair louder than his first question.

"We didn't realize anyone else was here," Barnibus opened. "We were having a private conversation. I'm sorry if—I'm sorry if you got the impression that we were talking to you."

"Aw, man!" Bigger than life. As if his suit was not enough to sell how entirely out of place he was, this exclamation sealed the deal, hardly in line with the rules of decorum in the hallowed halls of Anna Tuthill Harrison Junior High. This person did not belong here, and everything about them put Barnibus immediately on edge.

"Hey, why don't you worry about yourself?" Saga called.

Barnibus, eager not to make waves among the day's turbulent waters, reached out and squeezed Saga's arm. Easy, but certainly enough to make his feelings known.

"I think I'll do just that, thank you," the Purple Man squealed with a grin. They made no movement beyond that, holding their smile and Barnibus' eyes with equal fervor.

Saga turned, regarding his brother's visible discomfort. He watched for a moment, willing him to shift, or to move, or to break eyes with this strange person, but no matter how much he willed it to be so, he just could not get his brother to budge. "Barnibus," he whispered, "you okay?" These uncharted waters between them were becoming well-trafficked this morning.

"We both have the same gift, do we not?" the Purple Man proffered. Barnibus' knees locked and his mouth dried. "No one is available, so I have to use this door. Entering here with my own poison apple — do you have any idea how this makes me look?"

Saga reached out to grab his brother's hand, and he was surprised to discover instead a cold, limp appendage of little comfort. Barnibus was frozen in place and was unable to offer the safety that his brother was looking for; the safety that he himself had just promised in so many words.

"Tsk. See, now, that's a shame," the Purple Man said as he pulled a pocket watch from his vest and checked the time. "I'm afraid I have somewhere to be." He clicked the watch closed with a surprisingly heavy THUNK, enough to make the Jones brother recoil; enough to bounce off the surrounding hills and buildings, clapping back against their ears in a punishing register. "My train is due to arrive any minute, and if you don't have what I'm looking for... well, I'm afraid I must be going." He paused expectantly for a moment, a grin plastered unflinching and hollow on his face, his hand outstretched as if willing Barnibus to produce... something. Something he could not be sure of.

"I don't—uh, I don't know that I—" Barnibus stammered.

"Now that's unfortunate," he snapped brusquely at Barnibus. He punctuated his dissatisfaction by continuing to hold his gaze a moment longer. Until now, he had been laser-focused on Barnibus, hardly paying mind to the youngest Jones. But after a moment, he turned his head rather mechanically to lock eyes with Saga. "You can trust that you'll be seeing me again, Mr. and Mr. Jones. And soon."

DONG. DONG. DONG, the church bells called from across town.

DONG. DONG. DONG, the bells from the school joined in the chorus.

The brothers spun around, trying to discern the noise suddenly filling the surrounding air: DING. DING. RING. RING. The front of the school filled with noise and tones and the sharp screech of passing rail cars, the wind sending leaves swirling all around them, the cacophonous parade confounding the boys as their minds raced. There was enough confusion this morning, but they were supremely confident that there were no railways around the school, and certainly none that ran directly through this parking lot. Still, they hunched their heads down and sought shelter as the noise swelled violently. Deafening. They spun now faster than their minds were racing, looking for any sign of what was going on around them and where the incoming danger was going to approach.

It died as quickly as it began, and their school was silent once again. Like the flip of a switch, the sound died immediately. They turned once again to face the Purple Man, but found themselves face-to-face with an entirely unremarkable midwestern junior high school, not a person or shade of purple in sight.

4

SAGA

Saga was born only a few short years after Barnibus, and while the events that happened between those two events were largely unknown to him, Saga never much concerned himself with that lore. The story, as far as he was concerned, began on the day of his birth. Anything before that point was little more than mythology, world building and place-setting. As he got older and could understand the context of the family photos he would see around the house, or when he would hear the telling and retelling of holidays and outings best described as "pre-Saga", he would accept their existence as a piece of conversation, or a well-rendered piece of supporting fiction, but he could not bring himself to go much farther than that. Indeed, the idea of a "pre-Saga" time itself implied the coming of a "post-Saga" era, which was an idea he did not relish in. He would not lend these chronicles a sense of legitimacy, instead noting them as another passing moment, the official memory of which was the stories being told to him, rather than the event or goings-on which precipitated the tale. It was an act of self-preservation of which Saga was not proud, but had no intention of working through.

He would not confess these feelings; these blinders to his brother and to his relationship with his parents. Those relationships were not ones that would allow him to share that kind of open vulnerability. There was no genuine risk of retribution, and Saga knew as much. But he knew that this revelation might be viewed as jealousy, and that was not a color that looked good on him. By keeping it to himself, he cultivated an aloofness which he surmised every parent would enjoy in a child of his age. This Saga — this hidden Saga for Saga's sake — could not be considered the real Saga. Not to the world. The real Saga of record would be distant, with high walls constructed against the people around him. Perhaps in time he would let people in, but for now he was just a kid, so there would be time for that in the future.

The future was not something that Saga liked to spend much mental energy on either. In his worldview, the way his mind worked, the future was only darkness. Not in the way that Barnibus' mind showed him only darkness, an absence of light and information, but in cold, jagged facts. The world was a dark place. Saga did not need to stretch his imagination in order to see that. He needed only to look around — out the window at school, in the papers, on the news, from the backseat of his father's 1993 Ford Escort — everything he saw told him everything he needed to know about the world, and everything that he needed to know about what was in store for them. There was not a thing that could happen, Saga figured, that could catch him off guard, or that he had not worked through idly in his mind a dozen or more times before. His mind was absolute, his imagination more stark and factual than the best-run newspapers in the world, and through that mechanism he could game and extend through each thread of a given scenario and see exactly how history would be written about it. It was his burden, but he would hazard going as far as calling it a curse. *It's pragmatic*, he liked to tell himself. *I'm just being reasonable.*

As if his own walls were not constructed well enough, this only distanced him further from his family and friends. Classmates, really, as he could allow no one to get close enough to rise to the definition of '*friend*'. He simply could not stomach it. Any time he would get close to someone, he could not help himself from seeing exactly where that friendship, burgeoning as it may be, would lead, and after witnessing enough theoretical sad endings, enough tragedy and loss, he found it best for everyone involved if he stopped venturing some exercises in vanity as '*friendship*' and '*companionship*'. If he stopped himself from attempting to navigate those roads, no one would get hurt; the ending that he foretold could not happen if it did not begin, and in that, Saga felt immense power and a deep-rooted comfort. He would spend his life alone, in safe solitude.

When he entered elementary school, Saga made a friend. One friend, at the age of five, long before he made the quiet pledge to himself to abstain from such extravagance. His name was Walter, and his birthday was exactly twenty-three days after Saga's. The opportunity to take a young man under his wing thrilled Saga; to mentor someone his junior and help them come up in the world made him feel bigger than himself. Walter liked marbles. They would meet everyday outside of the school and head into class together, having been lucky enough to be placed in Ms. Jessica's class together, the place of their first introduction and now the place of their blooming young friendship. They would trade lunches and snacks on most days, and found themselves undeterred when Walter had a violent allergic reaction to the peanut butter pretzels Saga had traded him for his fruit leather. Ms. Jessica, in all the wisdom of her twenty-six years of age and two years of teaching, cautioned them strongly against sharing further for exactly that reason, but made little effort beyond that to prevent it. But now they had learned a lesson, and Saga, mouth rimmed with gelatinous fruit concentrate, excitedly declared to Walter that they could take that lesson and govern themselves. Quietly to himself, Saga vowed to be more vigilant, as he viewed the fact that he did not foresee Walter's histamine response as a personal failure, and one that he could not allow to happen again. Another lesson. More tools for self-governance.

Walter had always been a sensitive kid, medically speaking. His allergies were bad, his vision was blurred when unaided, and on the rare occasion he would move at a pace more brisk than a hurried walk, his breath would shorten and catch, rendering him a wheezing lug taking frequent breaks before finally switching to a more docile activity, much to Saga's disappointment. But friends are friends, he reasoned, so where Walter went, so did Saga. They would build blocks for hours, stopping occasionally to favor a toy car circuit, or a set of different, more enticing blocks (these had stud-and-tube infrastructure both vertically and horizontally, and the boys simply could not pass that up). Throughout the year, Walter's family grew more protective of their only son, his snacks and lunches becoming more focused, bordering on prescribed, in protection against his innumerable allergies and intolerances. Saga was no stranger to exacting diets, having seen both his mother and father undergo annual — and sometimes bi-annual — programs they declared to be for the sake of weight loss or better gut health. He was hardly fazed as Walter's diet grew more restrictive and exacting, assuming that his gut would not be impeccably healthy. Good for Walter.

After school and on the weekends, they would go on their own adventures, far into the forests and marshland surrounding their suburban community, far from the prying eyes of the townhomes and condos bordering the unexplored wilderness. They would venture into the unknown to chart the lands and make untold discoveries of new species, new landmarks, and previously unharvested resources. Their time outside of school was limitless, allowing them to mold the world around them into the reality they could not find elsewhere. Here they were kings. Here they were invincible, and the restrictions of their parents and teachers were a distant memory, having been applied to their ancestors of generations past, surely never to these young explorers. The air was heavy and thick here. Just muggy and damp enough to alight Walter in a way that breathed new hope and excitement into Saga as well. They fed off each other, and their adventures grew larger, unrestricted by things like 'safety' and 'reasonable restraint'. Their only limit here, in their kingdom, was their imagination, which, at this age, was boundless.

"There's something out there!" Walter would caution loudly to their army, gathered at their altar awaiting their command.

"Gentlemen," Saga would begin, pacing back and forth with an air of quiet dignity and restrained force. "Some of you may not make it back. We're venturing into the unknown, and while we hope for the best... We must prepare for the worst."

"This is a sacrifice we're willing to make," Walter would add as he searched through the fallen leaves and debris for a discarded stick of appropriate length and girth. "You knew what you signed up for when you enlisted."

And thus their battle began. Bloody, shattering. Families torn apart. Brother versus brother, the tragedy of warfare and sacrifice playing out in relative silence among evergreens and brambles a parking lot away from Mr. Middleton's General Store.

When school resumed following winter break, Walter was absent. A few students were absent, as their families trickled back into town in a stagger as vacations ended and delayed flights routed and rerouted back into town. But when Walter was absent for the rest of the week, Saga grew concerned. He tried to game out what he knew: Walter and his family had gone to visit family in the south, but he knew that his father had opted to drive, considering the flights to be an expense best left spared in favor of a thirteen hour drive in their mid-size sedan with its broken tape deck and CD changer which skips when playing disc numbers two, three, and five. But he could not make sense of what he saw. Absence. He could see nothing. No matter which thread he grasped, there was simply nothing there, and Saga did not know how to unpack that. When the weekend finally arrived, he took his bike and rode the four blocks over to Walter's parent's house, sure that he would see Walter's bike leaning on the side of their porch, or better yet, Walter playing outside in the yard, having just returned from vacation and now stretching his legs, waiting for his friend to come by to hear stories about life in the south. But as Saga rode by, he saw only the family car in the driveway, the curtains in the front window still drawn, as were the windows upstairs. He continued riding down the block, doubling back for two more passes before finally deciding to ride him, finding himself unable, for whatever reason he could not define, to bring himself to dismount his bike and ring the doorbell.

Walter passed away on January 4th. Returning from family vacation, Walter suffered a severe asthma attack in the back seat of the car, his father focusing on the last leg of the drive, and his mother sleeping in the passenger seat. They did not notice his breathing growing more shallow and weak, and Walter passed, unnoticed, in his sleep, mere miles away from his kingdom and awaiting army.

Saga's mother and father sat him down in the family room to break the news to him that Sunday night. Saga gave no response, betraying nothing of what was going through his head, or if he was even processing the news. But Saga knew, and had known for a few days now, finding himself unable — or unwilling — to accept what he was seeing in his mind. Absence. Even now, knowing the truth of what his mind had been striving to show him, he did not know what to make of this information or how he was meant to go on. He began trying to game that out for himself, but only came up with the same images and the same story he had seen before: absence. When he tried to read ahead, he saw nothing, no insight from which he could draw conclusions or likelihoods, and for the first time in his young life, he felt lost at a foundational level. Without his foresight, he found himself rudderless, without a moral compass to guide him. Empty and alone.

It would be his responsibility to inform their troops; a burden befitting a General, the weight and honor of his rank demonstrated in the starkest, heart-rending form. But as he passed Mr. Middleton's General Store and trekked out to their fort deep in the woods, he found nothing. No assembled troops, no kingdom. No freedom. No childhood. Just dirt and litter. Old magazines, sun-bleached and forgotten, lay on top of mulched leaves and silt. Their kingdom had fallen with a whimper, without its kings to defend it and without so much as a spat, let alone the battle they had so many times rehearsed and prepared for. Dark and empty, he felt little motivation to rebuild. How could he? Single-handedly, he knew nothing of assembling a great army or ruling over a caste system.

5

NOODLES AND DECK SCREWS

aga had hardly set foot inside their front door before he threw his bag across the entryway. He did not break his stride as he stormed into his room, slamming the door behind him before Barnibus was even into the house. He had rushed ahead of Barnibus from the moment they started their trek home, and did not break that pace the entire way home. Barnibus had cautioned to break their tense silence a couple of times, but Saga either could not hear him from so far ahead, or ignored him. It would not be unlike Saga to ignore his brother, but at a time like this, Barnibus wished that they could be in this together. Partners. But Barnibus knew that was asking too much of their relationship, at least as much of a relationship as Saga would allow, it would seem. They kept on walking, Barnibus concentrating on his breath to keep his thoughts from racing, Saga thinking god- knows-what. Barnibus hoped his brother was keeping himself from going to too dark a place, but he knew his brother well enough to know that would be the only place he would go.

Barnibus understood his brother. He did not agree with his

outlook on life, or some of the more dramatic flourishes Saga could be prone to when the mood struck. A few years before, when Saga had just begun primary school, he ran away for three days. Just walked right out the front door on Tuesday, with no gear or a change of clothes, and did not return until Friday. Their parents tried for weeks to get answers out of him about what he had done, where he had gone, and with whom. But Saga, unfazed, did not care to share more details. To him, this was a normal way to spend a few days. And in defense of Barnibus Sr. and Carol, they were pretty understanding about the whole thing. While they had been asking questions of Saga, those questions were not coming from a place of anger or disappointment. They were genuinely curious about how Saga had spent his time. They were young parents and remembered well their own youthful escapades, having themselves run away several times in their not-too-distant youth. Wandering and occasionally disappearing into the world bordered on a Jones family tradition, one that Barnibus himself was unknown to take part in, as he chose always to abscond at night and was sure to be back in his bed by morning. But even as commonplace as these excursions were, in this case, Saga was unwilling to share details or scraps of interesting anecdotes even with his brother. He tried not to let it get to him too much, but even at this young age, the distance that Saga created between them hurt Barnibus deeply.

Barnibus sat now on the family's couch, a musty number that had been in their family since the late 1970s. He sank into the cushions while he contemplated what the Purple Man had said. What did they mean when they said they would see each other again soon? What did they mean when they said any of it? Try as he might, Barnibus could not find a common thread among most of that character's monologuing, but '*the same gift*' rang out in his brain, echoing every other thought like its own punctuation. What were they talking about, and why did they seem to target Barnibus and his brother? Of course, the thought crossed his mind that perhaps, much like the rest of his rambling, it could have just been nonsense. As comforting as this thought was, Barnibus did not want to let himself off the hook that easily. This person — or whatever they were — had appeared from wherever, knew the brothers' names, and specifically referenced Barnibus' gift. He toed around the idea of a gift, stubbornly avoiding acknowledging what that could have been regarding, but the more the words bounced around in his head, the icier he felt. The more seen. The more in danger.

"We need to go," he called out to Saga. He waited for a moment, hearing only the brief reverberation of his words echoing back down the hallway, followed by the silence of an empty home. "He said he'd be back, and I don't think we should be somewhere he can find us." Still nothing. "Saga," he called again, this time louder, but he knew his brother was skilled at blocking the world out and was by now well inside his own mind and unlikely to be roused.

Think. *What can we do?* For a moment, in the swirl of activity outside of the school and in their trek back to their house, Barnibus had forgotten all about his parents' unexplained absence. It was not as if his parents were regularly at school with them, so not having them around in the afternoon was so commonplace in the moment as to be vaguely comforting. But now here in their empty house, unsure of what to do now, their current situation came screaming back into his consciousness. *Are these things related?* Yes. He gave no pause in answering that question, as his life, while it had its quirks, was not dramatic enough to have two disparate plots racing along concurrently without touching. Life was not a system of parallel paths, but a series of intersecting and cascading events. 'Tragedies beget tragedies,' he imagined his brother saying (although he had never heard him say that directly).

"We're staying here," Saga said flatly, startling Barnibus to find that he was no longer alone in the family room. "Whatever is going to happen, it's going to happen. There's no use in trying to run from it."

"He said he's going to come back. We can hide. If he doesn't know where we are, he won't be able to find us, and we'll be able to buy some time."

"Barnibus..."

"We can leave a note here, or something. Something to signal to Mom and Dad that we're okay and that we'll be back. This will work; this will be fine," Barnibus reasoned more for his own sake than that of his brother.

"He had a train, Barnibus." On its own, that was one hell of a non sequitur, but in this very specific case, it was demonstrably true, and the effects of that were broad and, if Barnibus was honest with himself, deeply unsettling. "His weird ghost train probably has other stations, don't you think?"

For a moment he could not help but admire his brother for attributing the appearance of the train to its having a station. In his mind, the train stood on its own as *the thing.* The train appeared, and that was bizarre enough to stand on its own legs; it did not need a support infrastructure. It was imaginative in a way that Barnibus could not allow himself to be, so he loved when he got to see it in others, especially in Saga.

"Right..." Barnibus said absently, trying to think through,

as logically as possible, what would happen if they stayed put. But try as he might, he could not.

"If we stay here, we at least have the advantage of being at home. Call it home-field advantage, but at least we won't be on our back foot, whatever happens." Saga's mixed metaphor notwithstanding, he had a good point. If they ran, they would give themselves another problem to solve on top of their already very full plates.

"We could be safe here," Barnibus offered, "but we should board up the doors and windows. Something to slow him down."

Saga, considering it briefly, shook his head. "He doesn't use doors."

"What? How do you know that?"

"Did you see him come or go? Where do you think he came from to begin with?"

"People need to come from somewhere. Unless he's already in the house, we should do what we can to slow him down when he tries to get in. Worst that could happen, I'm wrong, and he just appears in the house. That will be its own problem, but we'd be in the same place." He paused until his thoughts caught up with his words. Seizing the opportunity to agree with his brother, he snapped his fingers and exclaimed excitedly, "Whatever is going to happen, it's going to happen! Right?"

Saga nodded softly. "Whatever is going to happen, will happen."

Lumber, scrap metal, nails, screws — both deck and drywall — hammers, drivers. Everything that they could grab from the garage, they grabbed. They knew they would not want to have to re-up supplies once they got going, so they overstocked while they could. Better to have too much. As their pile grew and the garage became more threadbare, Barnibus checked his watch: it had been seventy-two minutes since they had seen the Purple Man. And while he had not given them anything of a deadline, Barnibus did not want them to be caught with their proverbial pants down. Brace the doors with scrap metal. Drive deck screws into the door jamb to make sure you anchor into the framing. The windows would be blocked with plywood. Not perfect, but it will buy them a bit of time. Prop the couch and the accent chairs up against the windows to protect against any broken glass. The family had an entertainment center which nearly reached the ceiling and held books and some ceramic pieces. Barnibus carefully pulled everything down and lined it up against the adjoining wall, then, with the help of his brother, leaned the entire unit diagonally against the front door, jamming it between the door itself and the doorway into the family room. If the scrap metal is not enough, the house's framing should create a hefty enough doorstop. The dining table came next, turned onto its side and stood against the back door. They then took the books that Barnibus had moved earlier and stacked them up against the table for added weight. He knew the weight was not enough to stop someone who wanted to get in, but if the books were to tumble down, it would make an awful racket, enough to alert them to someone coming and give them time to make a move toward another exit.

And now they will wait. Waiting for what, they did not know, but they did not know of anything else they could do, or how much time they would even have to do it in. Barnibus boiled a pot of noodles for dinner, tossing it with a knob of butter and some salt, just the way he knew Saga liked it. Without a dining table or a couch, they ate on the floor of the family room, sitting back-to-back. Barnibus told his brother that it was the best way for them to keep their eyes out for anything that might happen so no one could sneak up on them, but the truth he told himself was that he was quite tired and needed somewhere to lean, and the truth that he refused to tell himself was that he needed his brother now, and the closeness helped him to feel safe. Hopefully for Saga, it did the same. They felt safe here, regardless of the barricaded windows and doors, and despite the fact that they were — aside from each other — alone. They were unprotected in the classical sense, but as long as they had each other, at least to Barnibus, they were home, no matter where they were, or how reinforced the doors may be.

The noodles were okay.

* * *

It started as a scratching. Lightly at first, but then malice set in. Scratching became clawing, and that's when the Jones brothers stirred, ripped from sleep by the sound of incoming intrusion. They only now realized they had even fallen asleep, slumped against each other in a pile in the family room. Barnibus looked blearily about the room, trying to find the source of the sound, while Saga kept his eyes trained squarely on the doorway into the kitchen.

"Back door," Saga said blankly as he climbed to his feet. "He's trying to come in through the back."

Barnibus scrambled to catch up with his brother, who was already hurrying into the kitchen, determined.

"Wait," he called impotently to his brother, "that could just be a raccoon or something."

Saga stopped and turned to his brother, annoyed. "It's not

a raccoon. You know that." He turned and charged into the kitchen, Barnibus following closely behind. The clawing was getting louder, but Barnibus was confident it was still on the outside of the house, so they still had time. They stared at the overturned dining table, looking for any sign of disturbance, but inside the house, things looked still and secure, and after a moment, the clawing stopped. The brothers kept their eyes locked on the back door, sure that whatever was trying to get in was still out there, and possibly regrouping.

A light, shy tapping on the door broke the silence of their brief respite. As one might tap with one finger, like you would on someone's bedroom door to see if they were sleeping or available for a late-night chat. There was something honestly quaint and vaguely familiar about it, Barnibus thought, before the tapping became a pounding. This time Barnibus was the first on the move, his brother charging determinedly behind him, into the entryway. The wall unit was rattling violently, but still holding. The noise was cacophonous: the unit rattling against itself, chipping away at the doorway, driving into a deep divot of its own making.

"He's strong," Saga mused.

"We're going to be okay. We locked everything down. We're…" he searched for his words, "he can't get in. We'll be okay." Barnibus felt himself trailing off.

The rattling kept rising. Stronger now, more violent. Impossibly violent. The clawing at the back door returned now as well. They were surrounded.

"He didn't come alone," Barnibus warned. He wondered for a moment if the house itself was going to come down. The clawing and thrashing were so cacophonously loud, so terrifying encompassing, the walls shaking from the foundation to the rafters, there was no way the 1950s bungalow-style structure could withstand much more. But somehow, even with all this force, their barricades held. While the house trembled and shook around them, their measly self-made defenses held firm.

"Why hasn't he gotten in yet?" Saga wondered aloud. "We didn't build everything *that* well."

"I don't know," Barnibus answered in a worried, absent trance, his eyes remaining fixed on the barricades. If he watched them, they would hold. "I don't know," he mumbled. If the barricades held, the brothers would be safe. "We're going to be okay," he said to Saga. Just stay put, just keep watch. "We're going to be okay," he repeated once again.

"Why are they trying the doors?"

"What?" Barnibus could not follow his brother's logic. He turned to see Saga watching the barricades with the same unflinching conviction as he was, but with a noted skeptical glint, as if he were wondering why they even bothered to build them in the first place, almost doubting their very existence.

"He doesn't need doors," Saga answered finally, seemingly more for himself than for Barnibus.

"I've been here for a little while," the Purple Man said through a mouthful of buttered noodles.

The banging, the clawing, the violent shaking, every noise around them ceased immediately. The boys turned with a jump to see the Purple Man standing at the opening to the hallway, holding the pot of buttered noodles in one hand, a fork held daintily in the other. The boys froze.

"The noodles are okay," the Purple Man declared enthusiastically.

6

THE PURPLE MAN

arnibus and his brother had been Scouts for four years when they were younger. Barnibus Sr. was raised by first-generation immigrant parents, who themselves had been raised in a country with mandatory military service minimums, thought that the practice would be good character-building for the boys. Before they had even been born, Barnibus Sr. was concerned that their comparatively gentle upbringing would lead to — what his own mother would consider to be — weak children. Barnibus Sr.'s mother's definition of a weak child would fit most everyone else's definition of a child, but that comparison fell short of breaking through to either Barnibus Sr. or Carol. The boys cared little for the Scouts, but could not bring themselves to care enough to push back against their parents either. It was not their forte, to be sure, but they enjoyed that the whole program boiled down to two things: structured outdoor camping and knot-tying. Both boys had earned badges in knot tying, and both, despite their general indifference towards the Scouts, prided themselves on the depth of their knot knowledge. They competed against each other, against their troop, and against other local chapters. Knot drills, even blindfolded knot-tying races. That is how, by feel alone, they knew now that the Purple Man had used a constrictor knot to bind their wrists behind their backs, and two half hitches — an overhand knot followed by a half hitch — for their legs.

Back to back in the middle of the kitchen, tied to the family's dining-set chairs — Barnibus facing the well-barricaded backdoor, and Saga facing the archway into the family room — the boys wavered between fear and confusion. Scared, of course, about what was happening — or what was about to happen — to them; confused about how they found themselves here: how the Purple Man had gotten in, and how — at such unfathomable speed — he had subdued them and lashed them down prisoners. Saga searched his mind for any forethought of what was coming, but no matter the speed at which his mind raced, he simply could not keep up with whatever reality the Purple Man was creating. If their world is the trunk of a great tree, and each possibility is an arm from that trunk, and from those arms grew branches, and further branches still, and twigs, and twiglets, and from there, leaves and buds — he found himself high in the canopy, unable to discern how they got there or which trunk or arm or branch or twig or twiglet had carried them there. When he attempted to search further, he could only see blue sky, save for the impending grey storm clouds.

Barnibus's mind raced just the same, but he strained to keep himself in the observable, minding only what he could see in front of him, and what he could count on having happened. The facts were simple, he hoped: The Purple Man had appeared — somehow — in their hallway, and had — somehow —

restrained them with little fight. *But why hadn't they fought? They must have, right? Did they?* He shook his head gently, shaking loose the train of thought at once. All he knew was that they must not have put up much of a fight, because it happened so quickly and, taking inventory of his own body, did not feel as if he had recently fought. *But why not?* He could not stop himself from thinking. He pushed against the limits of his memory, like a prize fighter trying to recall the specifics of a title fight that had found him beaten and bruised, the memories knocked away with time, piecing together the story from the scraps he held onto. But all he could come up with was a grey blur. *'The noodles are okay,'* followed by nondescript commotion, and then, with little time having passed, here they were.

"Saga," Barnibus whispered over his shoulder. He could hear his brother breathing and occasionally pulling against his binds, so he knew he was alive. But he could not tell what shape he was in, or if he was even awake. "Saga," he repeated in a louder, forced whisper, "you need to wake up now."

"I'm not asleep," Saga said, defeated. "I'm just thinking."

"What do you see?"

"Nothing."

"Tell me. It's okay."

"I just did. I see nothing."

Barnibus thought for a moment.

"That's not possible," Barnibus protested, his voice now rising above a whisper.

"Keep your voice down. I'm just telling you what I see, and it's nothing. Grey. Nothing."

"That happens?"

"Sometimes, I guess."

Barnibus tightened his grip on his own mind tighter than the binds on his wrists; he needed to keep himself grounded in this moment. With his brother blind behind the eye, he could not allow himself to spin out now and leave them both rudderless. Not now. Not with whatever this is.

"Okay," Barnibus offered, "we're going to be okay; we can get out of this. We just need to—we just need to stay calm, and we'll be okay."

Saga snickered. He knew this advice was for Barnibus' own benefit and less for his.

"What do you remember?" Barnibus asked.

"*The noodles are okay,*" Saga said mockingly.

"Yeah," Barnibus sighed, "me too."

"I thought the noodles were good," Saga told his brother.

"I did too," Barnibus whispered through a breaking smile. "Beyond that, it's just a blur for me. Anything for you?"

"Nothing. The noodles, then grey, and now we're here."

"I was afraid of that."

Barnibus perked up.

"What do you—why were you afraid of that?"

"If we can't see the past, and I can't see the future, we're kind of just stuck here... now."

Barnibus was struck by the silence in the house now. He had been focused on signs of life from his brother — his breathing, hearing him shift in his chair — and was acutely aware of his own pounding heartbeat. He had not noticed the lack of any other impeding noise. Beyond the incredible noise of the onslaught against their house some moments ago, he also made note that no sounds from the outside seemed to make their way in. No passing cars, animals in their garden, nothing.

"You know what would help here...?" Saga whispered,

leaning hard over his shoulder to get as close as possible to keep quiet.

"I will not do that. Stop."

"If ever there was a time to use your... whatever it is... wouldn't it be now? Just think of a way out of here! That's all you have to do. It doesn't need to be anything extravagant, even, just something that will get us out of these chairs. Out of the house." His voice raised with excitement, but as he glanced around the room, it did not appear that anyone — or anything — had taken notice of their conversation.

"It's not that easy. I can't just—I can't do that. It's not safe for us."

"I don't think being tied to chairs in our kitchen is particularly safe for us either," he proffered, annoyed. "Comparatively, I'd vote we take our chances with your mind games versus whatever he has planned for us." He waited for a moment, but Barnibus made not a sound of acknowledgement or response. "He tied us up, Barnibus. That means he plans to do something with us, or *to us*. I can't see what it's going to be, and I'm scared, okay? I'm scared."

"I am too," Barnibus said in a low rasp.

"Then get us out of here," pleaded Saga, "please."

"I can't, I'm sorry."

"Barnibus!" Saga shouted.

"Keep your voice down — I just can't do it—"

"No, Barnibus, not that!" Saga said, seeing him first behind Barnibus' back.

"Yeah, Barnibus. It's not that. I'm afraid it's this," the Purple Man said briskly as he strode confidently into the kitchen. Barnibus could not see him as he entered, but he entered his field of view as he crossed the room. "I bet your little brother was talking about me." He grabbed another dining-set chair and, spinning it around backwards directly in front of Barnibus, sat close, his face practically touching Barnibus', the Purple Man's hot foul breath inescapably filling his nostrils. "I think you and I need to have a little talk. Just the two of us."

"Anything you need to say to me, you can say to Saga, too."

"Him?" he gestured over Barnibus' shoulder. "Oh, he's asleep."

Barnibus now heard his brother's small, gentle snoring. He tried to turn his head around far enough to see Saga's face, but could only barely draw into his periphery the back of his head, now drooped limply against his chest, rising and falling imperceptibly with each breath.

"What did you do?" he sneered as he spun back to the Purple Man.

"Don't be so dramatic," he scoffed. "I did nothing. He was tired from all the commotion, and he wanted to take a little nap. I just helped him find his way there." He paused for a moment, miming exaggerated thought. "So then, yeah, now that I hear myself say it out loud? I guess I did do something." A cartoonish, insincere deep frown spread across his face. "I hope you can forgive me," he pouted.

"Wake him up!" Barnibus barked.

"I can't. Or — I'm sorry — I *could*, but I won't. At least not now. He's not germane to this part of the play, so I'm afraid he'll need to wait in the wings while we run our scenes. He'll be back, though — probably — so don't worry too much about him. Look at him." He reached past Barnibus' shoulder and gave the back of Saga's head a firm shove. Saga did not stir at all. Barnibus pulled violently, impotently against the ropes, but the Purple Man paid him no mind. "He's fine. Just a little sleepy, that's all. It's cute, if you think about it," the Purple Man mused.

Barnibus, unable to move from his restraints, with sweat pooling against the ropes on his wrists and along his brow, felt his grip on his mind loosening. The Purple Man watched as the energy of his prisoner switched abruptly from outward to inward, as he ceased to struggle to get free and instead struggled within. The Purple Man sat back now, a proud smile emerging from the wrinkles and cracks adorning his rubbery face.

"When we get out of here..." Barnibus growled.

"Oh yeah?" the Purple Man taunted. "Then what happens?"

Barnibus shifted in his chair now, thrashing against the ropes, trying, it would seem, to pull the chair itself apart to get free, his eyes narrowed on the Purple Man. Present in the moment once again, back in the physical world. The Purple Man's accomplished smile now deflated to an annoyed grimace.

"Oh, come on, don't do that. You were so close; don't give up now."

Barnibus thrashed and pulled, and for a moment he felt the ropes on his wrists shift and slip, but they quickly caught on themselves as his sweat absorbed into the fibers and dried. Whatever ground he was gaining from his wrists being slick with sweat was quickly conceded as his struggling wicked the sweat away, chafing and cutting against his skin now. He stopped now, defeated in his fight, and drawn back into trying to understand the Purple Man.

"How do you mean?" Barnibus asked.

"You disappoint me. Do you have any idea how far I came,

just for you? Just to come see you—well, and I guess to see your little brother," he gestured limply towards Saga once again, "but he's, I don't know, I guess a bonus," he thought for a moment. "We'll get back to him later. But the main reason I traveled so far was for you! And then when I get here, and we meet — I meet my *hero!* — and it's nothing but questions and faux confusion." He shot up from his chair, sliding it hard out to the side, slamming it against the wall. He's bigger now, bigger than Barnibus had realized before. He danced about in front of him. *"How do you mean! How do you mean!* It's pathetic. You know. You know exactly why I'm here." He closed in on Barnibus now, grabbing his head between his massive hands. "This. All of this right here." The jester's tone and dancing theatrics had ceased now, replaced with a reptilian hiss and imposing stature. Barnibus' eyes swelled with tears, widening and trembling, but unable to break the gaze of the Purple Man.

"Please..." Barnibus asked meekly.

"You have a gift, my young Barnibus. Something that many people in this world — or others — would move mountains to get their hands on. Whether you realize that... Well, that's disappointingly inconsequential now. But it's something beautiful. Something unique." His dark, fiery eyes searched Barnibus' now. "And if that's what it takes, well, then I aim to kill you for it."

Barnibus searched the Purple Man now, desperately, for any clue, any insight, any hint into what he should do — what he *could* do — to free himself and his brother. The harder he looked, the farther away the Purple Man seemed. The deeper he tried to search into his eyes, the less he felt he saw. It was like staring into a painting, or worse, a print of a painting, a replica of a replica of a replica; all he saw was something pretending to be something it was not. This person — this thing — portending to be a man, to be a human as all guesses would venture, inside lacked anything resembling humanity. As he searched, he struggled to find the words within to buy himself more time.

"I can't—" he finally stammered, managing in just two syllables to draw further ire from behind the Purple Man's vacant, hateful eyes.

"Let me stop you right there. Because I'm tired of hearing all of this '*I can't*' nonsense." His eyes narrowed, looking through Barnibus now, beyond his face, beyond his eyes. Barnibus felt exposed, like he had not before. "I want you to think about this carefully, because the next thing you do decides the version of yourself that your family gets to see again."

Barnibus' vision started to go white. *No, no, no*, he thought. *Stay awake; you can't do this. Stay awake, you idiot!* He shivered, and as he felt himself trembling weakly, he struggled to keep himself upright, to keep himself here, present, here with his brother. Here, protecting his brother. The harder he fought, the more violently he shook.

"Stay awake..." he mumbled to himself.

"Barnibus...?" Saga's head perked up as he once again tried to twist around to see his brother. "Hey, are you okay?" he asked more urgently now.

Barnibus was fading now, his head beginning to droop as he lost consciousness. Saga sighed heavily as he turned back to face forward, alone now without his brother. He slinked down in his binds, feeling the weight of impending defeat holding him down.

"This is depressing. Just really disappointing," the Purple Man hissed.

Snow. At first, it was a light dust. Easy to miss, fluttering lightly down from the ceiling. The first flakes melted before they even made landfall, while some of their later cohort was lucky enough to make contact with the shoulders of the Jones brothers and the Purple Man before quickly evaporating. Before long, the flakes stuck, as Barnibus, his head hanging limply at his chest, saw his breath. His vision widened, the cold drawing him back out of the darkness and into the real world again. The temperature in their kitchen was dropping fast, which would be, in itself, quite remarkable if the rapidly increasing dropping of snow did not immediately overshadow it. Barnibus had known only one meteorologist in his life, a charismatic weatherman (as the boys' parents called them) by the name of Randy Jets on Channel 5. Barnibus was pretty sure that was not Randy's real name, but in his mind it did not cost the man any credibility, as he had always been deft in his reading of the weather, his predictions and cautions always proving to be spot-on and well worth heeding. Barnibus Sr. had taken the boys to the news station once when his butcher shop was to be featured on a public interest block on the Saturday news, and both boys had been lucky enough to meet Randy in person. They shook hands, and Randy, ever cordial throughout their visit, let them host their own mock weather segment in front of the chroma screen. They left with Channel 5 stickers and a great story to tell. That would be, until this point, the extent of Barnibus' exposure to the machinations of high and low pressure and how to predict precipitation. Even with his limited knowledge, he knew snow originating in a suburban kitchen was not a common weather system.

It caught the Purple Man's attention now. For the first time in what felt like hours, he broke his gaze with Barnibus and looked up, bemused, toward the ceiling. He sat back in his chair as he looked around further, now noting that snow was falling throughout the room, but seemingly not in the hallway and not, from what he could see, in the family room.

"Remarkable," he smirked to himself, his focus on the boys momentarily broken.

Saga's head erupted upward as his eyes were suddenly ablaze with activity. He looked about the room absently, looking beyond the room as he searched his mind. He could see it now. Whatever *it* was, he could not be sure, not yet, but he saw it. The snow falling, falling harder, before it melted as quickly as it came, their ropes loosening from their wrists, pouring with sweat, stunningly hot, stumbling, confusion now, crashing, lightness before the dark, cold now, blinding light, flashes before they sustain, loud, voices, more people here now? Not now, not yet. Couldn't be. Screaming. Chaos. He laughed now, as his focus whipped back into the now, back into the kitchen where they were, still with a light dusting of snow, the boys still bound to their chairs. He had seen it all now. For the first time since the Purple Man arrived, he had seen what was in store for them, and this realization had him brimming with joy. As his laughter grew louder, it shook the Purple Man from his investigation and brought his attention back to his hostages.

"See that?" the Purple Man laughed, leaning back towards Barnibus. "Your brother really likes the snow. That's great, because it's going to be the last thing he sees."

"Barnibus," Saga called over his shoulder. "It feels like it's getting kind of hot in here, doesn't it?"

"Too bad he's not very bright," the Purple Man snickered.

Barnibus, weak as he struggled to keep himself awake and upright, turned toward his brother, confused.

"It's snowing..." he slurred absently.

"In this heat?" Saga panted, his heart racing, "I don't think so..."

Water dripped from the ceiling. Heavy, thick drops slammed against the floor, against their heads, faces, along the counters of the kitchen, hard as rain now. The floor sloshed with water as the snow, long since melted, accumulated faster than it could evaporate now. Barnibus ducked his head now from the water, as he felt the mixture of sweat and melting snow dripping down his forehead and cascading off of his brow. It was hot now. Oppressively hot, even. His wrists slipped and slid around within their binds as he felt his brother struggling against his own.

The Purple Man arose from his chair and stepped back, trying to keep up with the changes in weather in their little microclimate. He stepped back, stumbling now.

"Remarkable..." the Purple Man whispered as he took it in. Where he had once been so confident, moving through the world as if it bent to his every step, his footing was now unsure. His purple suit, dark and heavy from rain and sweat, looked as if it was made of lead, weighing him down, keeping him bound to the earth with a weight that seemed to crush his previously airy, unfathomably light aura. His eyes, once blackened and fiery, now swelled with panic. He was no longer in control.

The lights cut. Perfect darkness. No moonlight penetrated the windows; the boys' barricades were thorough enough to afford them such lunar privacy. The only sounds were heavy panting and the creaking from the dining set chairs as the boys twisted and pulled against their binds, which were growing increasingly limp as they became saturated in sweat. Barnibus could hear the stumbling, shuffling steps of the Purple Man, but could not place where in the room he was. He felt far, but not far enough for them to feel safe. Not yet. Not while he was still here. A flash illuminated the room, like the blaze of a fire alarm — momentary, just enough to burn their environment into their retinas like a photograph. He saw him now; the Purple Man stumbling backward toward the doorway out of the kitchen, Barnibus regarding what he thought to be a measure of terror on his face. Darkness now as his hands freed from their binds. He swung his torso forward and made quick work of freeing his ankles. Another flash, gone as quickly as it came, as they crashed back into a void of darkness, this time accompanied by a chorus of laughter. Screaming, maniacal laughter from outside, from the family room, from right there within the kitchen, there with them. But as this photo was burned into his eyes, he saw the kitchen was empty aside from his brother and the Purple Man, caught in mid-fall as he tripped, stumbling backwards into the rolling wet bar left sitting near the far wall. In darkness once again, a loud crack rang through the room as the Purple Man landed heavily on a sheet of ice on the floor. Hearing the crackle of the ice splitting under his own feet, Barnibus realized how impossibly cold it was in the kitchen once again. *Move. Move quickly; you're losing time.* Barnibus ripped the icy ties free from his brother's legs just as Saga freed his own wrists and rose swiftly from his seat, slipping momentarily before he regained his balance. Another crash now, incredibly loud, as the room flooded with moonlight. Barnibus threw his arm up over his face, shielding himself from the light as the kitchen wall came crumbling down, a locomotive rumbling by outside, within feet of his mother's bay window plant collection, pots jumbling and cracking from the force. The boys ducked, each clawing and jockeying to protect one another. The rumbling of the screaming train seemed to go on forever as the house shook violently, shards of ice breaking free from the ceiling and crashing down all around them. Chaos begetting chaos, feeding on itself as the sensory overload snowballed and grew.

Abrupt silence. It was over. The kitchen light clicked back on, showing the damage all around them. Water sloshed along the floor as the boys shifted uneasily, each trying to look around to assess what had happened. Whatever that was.

"Are we…" Saga stuttered as he searched both the room and his mind, unable to focus himself on just one.

"It's over… I think he's gone…" Barnibus said, trembling. The boys separated, each weak and trembling from the strain. "Saga…" he panted, "what was that?"

"I don't know…" Saga offered. "I thought you knew."

The boys chuckled. Barnibus stepped forward to look out into the backyard through the demolished wall. It was still outside, and remarkably clear. He could not see or hear any sign of disturbance beyond their house. The neighborhood was still; undisturbed by the commotion. He did not know what to make of this. *Who was the Purple Man, what did he want,* and *most pressingly — what the hell just happened?*

Saga picked up the wet bar, which had fallen when the Purple Man stumbled backward over it in the commotion. The spirits that were stored on top had come crashing out when it tumbled and now mixed into the water on the floor all around them. The wet bar sat upright with a loud thud, and as Barnibus turned and saw the mess it had made, he wondered how they would explain the mess — all of this horrendous mess to their parents. It seemed like something he would need to work out eventually, but he noted it as something that was not urgent for the time being. He reached out to touch the jagged edges of the crumbled wall, trying to confirm to himself that whatever he was seeing had actually happened. The insulation, sticky and damp, broke apart easily in his hand, as more around it dislodged and fell lightly to the ground.

"He's gone now," Barnibus said, "but he'll be back."

"What makes you say that?"

"I don't know," he said flatly, "shouldn't you?"

"Yeah, I should. That's what worries me."

Barnibus crossed the kitchen and into the family room, stepping over fallen furniture and debris. The family room was torn apart, but mercifully was not full of water or runoff. Just normal, run-of-the-mill hazards and earthquake damage. He sifted through a pile near the door and pulled out his bag, throwing it onto his shoulder as he surveyed the front door, still firmly barricaded and secure. He turned and crossed back towards the kitchen, striding with purpose as he passed Saga in the narrow doorway.

"Alright, let's go," he called back to Saga as he climbed out of the hole in the kitchen and into the backyard. "We need to go see Uncle Ted."

7

UNCLE TED'S HOUSE ON THE HILL

Things look righter
When the sun shines brighter.

~Or~

B E
P R E S E N T

Or if you wanted to look a little closer at the fine print, *This too shall pass (just don't ask me when).*

From floor to ceiling, on every wall and every surface that could hold them, Uncle Ted's house was a monument to tchotchkes. Slogans, mementos, curios, doodads, trinkets, industrial swag, whatever you wanted to call them. He always maintained on the rare occasions that the family came to visit him that there was order to the chaos. But Barnibus could never see it. To him, it just felt like a mess, like someone was collecting things just for the sake of having them nearby, despite having nowhere to put them. It was all

70

noise in the broadest sense, bombarding the eyes with colors and patterns, slogans and puns, arresting the mind with more information than it could possibly take in, even if one wanted to. They rarely visited Uncle Ted, Barnibus mused, because the clutter was simply too much for his father, who liked things orderly and minimal. His mother was the same way, but she never batted an eye at her brother Ted's decor, having grown used to it long ago in their youth. His house was as close to the opposite of their house as you could get, and Barnibus found that equal parts confusing and comforting. Uncle Ted's space was *lived-in*, as his mother had put it before. It showed life, in whatever form that was, because it said something. It said a lot, Barnibus thought, possibly too much, but he understood what his mother was trying to say.

Uncle Ted lived on a quiet road, high on a hill above a busy street. There were no other houses along his stretch of road (Esquire Blvd) so cars had no reason to venture past his door, and the bends in the road created the illusion of a dead-end when viewed from the turnoff below. When combined with the steep incline, pedestrians never ventured their way to the top of the hill. Ted enjoyed this municipal privacy, having elected to purchase this house decades ago specifically because of the improbability of other houses being built around his, creating a by-default private neighborhood of his own. The hillside surrounding his house was too steep a grade to support new construction, and as time passed and opportunities presented themselves, he would purchase the vacant lots down the road in either direction for pennies to ensure privacy.

As the Jones brothers climbed the hill and felt the noisy traffic below grow quieter, Saga watched Uncle Ted's house bob into view over the horizon. His Victorian-style house stood stately and unique among the terrain and surrounding neighborhoods. This house was unlike anything else in town. He always found the house's exterior comforting, the walls being overtaken by ivy and bramble; the earth reclaiming the wooden siding and frame, drawing the structure back down into the ground, counting the decades until the house with its timber was assimilated back where it belongs in the cosmic cycle. The inevitability struck a chord with Saga, who appreciated the opportunity to see the future approaching in real time, so predictable and measurable for anyone who cared to notice. He felt like it opened up his mind and the life and death he saw for the rest of the world to see, giving everyone a chance to see, all at once, both the past and future, leaf-by-leaf. But tonight, as the house drew closer, the absence of, well, everything struck Saga. No ivy, no bramble, hardly any landscaping left aside from some succulents and decorative boulders. The house on the hill that Saga was expecting and hoping would bring him some familiar comfort looked foreign and uninviting. He tried not to let his disappointment register, for Barnibus' sake, but he could not help but expel a small sigh as Barnibus reached, stretching from the tips of his toes up through an outstretched arm, and struck the door-knocker.

Uncle Ted was a smoothly appointed man. While his friends down at the hill may be dressed for comfort, resigned to be casual in their advanced age, Ted was not. Everything pressed, every corner sharp, every color coordinated with another. Out and about in the real world, incongruous to the house he kept, Ted was the definition of *put-together*. The person who answered the door, however, was anything but. His bathrobe hung slack, dragging along the floor behind him, draped lazily off his shoulder, and his hair scattered across his forehead in the front and stood straight up in the back. It took the Jones brothers nearly ten full seconds to recognize their uncle at the door in front of them, stuttering and stammering with their mouths agape as they searched for anything familiar they could grasp onto.

"Boys," Uncle Ted commanded flatly. "What's the call at this hour? Is everything alright?"

"Oh," Barnibus stumbled, "Uncle Ted, I'm sorry, did we—did we wake you?"

"No," he offered, along with zero explanation.

"What happened here?" Saga asked, more to the house than of Uncle Ted himself.

"What happened here—living happened here, my dear boy. The free market happened here, that's what happened." He stuck his head out of his front door and into the night, quickly assessing the front side of his house in case there was some-thing that he was as-of-yet unaware of. Satisfied that every-thing looked prim and proper, he leaned back into his foyer with a heavy grunt, which betrayed his age. "I'm fixing to sell the place, and I can't very well do that if it's being driven back into the earth by Mother Nature herself, now can I."

"*This* house?" Saga gasped. *Why didn't I see that coming?*

"I only have the one, I'm afraid, and God willing, within the next month or so, that won't be the case. Come. Come inside out of this dreadful chill." He ushered the boys quickly into the house, letting the heavy solid-core door swing shut behind them, the weatherstripping around it whispering a *hiss* as it sealed. "Boys," he dusted their shoulders as if they had come in from a blizzard and not a mild 62-degree evening, "I'm afraid I must ask — where are your parents? Do they know you're out in the middle of the night? I can't imagine they would be okay with it. No, no, something must have happened. Of course, something must have brought you here at this house — *parentless!* — in the middle of the night. Oh bother. Oh mercy. Please tell me, boys. Deliver the news that brings you to my door."

Barnibus could never quite grasp his uncle and his many idiosyncrasies, but Uncle Ted's uncanny ability to have a complete conversation entirely on his own always charmed him. Once he got rolling, he did not need a scene partner to bounce ideas off of or to answer his many questions. His inquisitive mind was natural — indeed, something that Barnibus could recognize in himself as well — but quickly his innumerable questions were revealed to be rhetorical when he would, in the very same breath, pry the answer from himself.

"We don't know where our parents are," Barnibus began slowly, "and we were kinda hoping that you did."

"My lord... that can't be good."

"That's what we were thinking too."

"How long have they been missing?"

"Don't know, but they were gone when we got up this morning, so at least that long." Saga nudged Barnibus on the shoulder, and as his brother turned, he nodded towards the large nautical clock hanging on the wall just outside of the entryway. Four A.M. "Well, yesterday morning now, I guess."

"That's not like them. But I'm confident that I don't need to tell you boys that." He perched his hands on his hips now, head down, searching the floor for answers. After a moment, he swung his hand up and back through his hair, suddenly aware of his shoddy appearance. He scrambled now. "Barnibus, Saga, I beg your pardon. I'll be just a moment." He disappeared swiftly out of the entryway and up the stairs, uncomfortably quiet for a man and a house of this age.

The boys were alone now, which they were growing accustomed to. They stood in the entry stiffly and distant from each other. Neither of them had anything new to offer, no need to check in or comment on what had happened. They both knew precisely as much as the other, and that fact brought them no ease. Saga was the first to make himself comfortable at Uncle Ted's house, finally coming in from the entryway and flopping onto the sofa in the parlor. Barnibus pried his shoes from his feet before he trudged in behind his brother, dropping into the easy chair next to him. Saga perked up for a moment, only now remembering that Uncle Ted preferred a shoe-free house. He leaned forward to remove his shoes as well, but finding himself devoid of energy, quickly resigned to disrespecting the house. Just this once.

Staring blankly into the cluttered, dimly lit parlor, Barnibus heard infomercials droning quietly in the other room as the light from the old CRT TV flickered across the wall in the main hallway which connected the rooms on the lower floor. Uncle Ted must have been up watching ads on the television. Barnibus' mind walked the path of how he himself could one day turn into an Uncle Ted, awake at all hours, rambling about his house in a bathrobe, startled and skittish about unannounced visitors. A few strands of his hair fell in a wisp across his forehead.

"Now," Uncle Ted announced as he reemerged, perfectly appointed, hair neatly slicked, three-piece suit pressed and pocket square peaked; the Uncle Ted they knew was now awake and ready to jump in. "We haven't a second to waste. We must get to work." He stood before them confidently, shoulders drawn back, head held high, a man of action. "Where do we begin?"

"W—what?" Saga chuckled.

"We were—we were kind of hoping you knew what we should do. You're—you know, you're the adult, so we were hoping you could—maybe you'd help us." Barnibus struggled to find the words, mindful not to sound ungrateful.

"Darling, we're in uncharted waters here. They're your parents; you hold all the clues, relatively speaking. The investigation simply must start with you. I'll do what I can to assist, but in the grand scheme, I am but a cosmic bystander," Ted addressed Barnibus.

"Unbelievable," Saga muttered, sinking further into the sofa and shutting his eyes as Uncle Ted watched him out of the corner of his eye. Confident now that the boy had shut himself off from the conversation, he motioned Barnibus towards the door into the hallway. Confused, Barnibus reflexively checked his brother, but Uncle Ted shook his head and once again motioned, this time more emphatically, for Barnibus to follow him from the room. Uncle Ted rose, exiting with Barnibus following wearily behind him.

"Did you do this?" Uncle Ted inquired in a whisper.

"What? No!" Barnibus protested, louder than he expected, quickly bringing his voice back down to a whisper, "obviously no."

"You didn't think about what it would be like to be without your parents?" He hunched over, leaning closer to Barnibus now. "Maybe they gave you a hard time about your homework or something — normal kid stuff — and maybe you mused about a simpler life without them?"

"I—no. I wouldn't do that. I couldn't—I wouldn't just *disappear* our parents like that."

"No one is saying you did it on purpose. But the sooner we find that strand, the better chance we have of drawing it back. This is fixable. Everyone makes mistakes. It's okay."

"What are you implying?"

"I'm not implying anything. I'm just asking." They locked eyes for a moment, both knowing perfectly well the line they were toeing, but neither wanting to be the first one to say it directly. "It's okay." He peered back into the parlor, confirming that Saga was all but asleep, likely lost in his own thoughts by this point. "I know how things can get when you get a little lost in your thoughts. There are certain... costs... that the rest of us have to pay for that, whether we realize it or not. It's okay; it's hard to control, I know. But we can fix it if we just act fast."

"This wasn't me," Barnibus scowled.

"Son, there are only two people I know of that can do what you do. One of them is you, and you're standing here telling me we can dismiss that particular suspect, notwithstanding motive and clear opportunity." He hesitated. "And the other person is me."

Barnibus' brow furrowed as he searched Uncle Ted's face for a sign that this was some sort of joke; a trick to ease Barnibus' conscience and compel a confession to something he knew was not true. But try as he might, he saw only sincerity on his uncle's face.

"I'm sure that's not a surprise to you," Uncle Ted said easily. But as he registered the shock on the boy's face, he leaned back, standing upright now. "Your mother didn't tell you? I thought that's why you came here."

"My mom doesn't know about me... She doesn't know what I can do."

"Oh, right," Uncle Ted chuckled. "Barnibus."

"I've worked very hard to keep that all under control. She doesn't know. She's never seen it, I'm sure of it."

"Your mother knows, Barnibus. Trust me. We've talked about it before. Why she hasn't told you that, I do not know. That's not my place to guess, but she knows, and more relevant right now, I know. I know better than anyone, I'm afraid." He sighed heavily now, taking a moment to collect himself before he reentered the parlor and jostled Saga, who awoke with a start as Uncle Ted shoved his legs off the sofa and took a seat next to him. "What do you see?" he asked of a bleary-eyed Saga.

"I finally got to sleep."

"We haven't the time for that now, I'm afraid. Now, what do you see?"

Saga turned to Barnibus, looking for information or approval or any guidance at all. Barnibus nodded with a slight shrug.

"I think this is our only move now," Barnibus said. "I don't know how or why, but yeah. Tell him." Saga turned back to his uncle, eagerly awaiting his answer.

"Nothing."

"Nothing!" Uncle Ted declared. "Well!" He took a moment to look at both boys. "That can't be good."

Saga chuckled and let his eyes close as he tried to get settled again to go back to sleep. Uncle Ted did not bother trying to rouse him. He turned instead back to Barnibus, who kept his eyes fixed on his brother until he knew he had drifted off back to sleep. He hesitated to turn back to Uncle Ted, as he had a hard time coming to terms with this new information. *Uncle Ted is like me? And he knows about Saga? What else does he know, and why didn't anybody tell us?*

"You look worried," Uncle Ted's voice rattled Barnibus.

"Wouldn't you be worried?"

"Not necessarily," he mused.

"Right," Barnibus scoffed, "you'd be just fine having lost your parents."

"My dear boy, I have lost my parents. Maybe not in the same way that you did, but I lost them. Quite young, in fact, your mother and I were alone. Cast adrift."

Barnibus did not know how to respond. He regarded Uncle Ted for a moment before nodding, trying not to betray the guilt he felt for being so callous.

"My hope is — more than anything — that doesn't happen to you two. We can get your parents back. I can feel it. We just need to look at the problem and use the not-insignificant strengths we have between the three of us. I think you'll find that there isn't much that these gifts can't accomplish once you know how to use them."

"I'm not going to do that."

"I'm sorry?"

"I'm not going to do that. I can't."

"That's simply not an option."

* * *

Barnibus could think of every single thing that his mother had ever told him and Saga about his Uncle Ted. It was simple to recall because they had in fact been told fleetingly little. He knew that Uncle Ted was his mother's older brother, five years her senior, and that they had not been particularly close when they were younger. He was a student athlete, having spent much of his youth committed to the track and field team at

William Berkeley High School, receiving an exception when he entered the eighth grade, allowing him to compete at the high school level in exchange for assurances he would continue with the program once he entered the school the following year. He would leave their house in the morning for school, same as Carol, but would not return from practice or various after-school programs until well after dinner was finished and she was getting ready for bed. As far as Barnibus and Saga were aware, the two of them had spent virtually no time together in their youth, and neither seemed bothered by this. Barnibus was not aware, until this point, that his grandparents had passed at a young age, having given very little thought to him not knowing much of his grandparents growing up. They were simply not a known quantity in his life, and their absence was unremarkable to the young Jones brothers.

They had found each other again later in life, reconnecting when they both settled into homes relatively nearby. When Barnibus was born, they had spent a couple of days at Uncle Ted's house helping organize some family keepsakes he had moved from storage into his new home. Carol and Ted spent a couple of long days stashed away in Ted's study, Carol emerging from time to time to feed Barnibus, who otherwise spent the days in the backyard with his father (so he's told, having no memory of this long weekend when he was only a few weeks old). Time at Uncle Ted's house became more frequent when Saga had been born and grown older, with the family going over for dinners or afternoons every couple of weeks. On these occasions — the ones that Barnibus was old enough to remember — Carol and Ted would often spend their time locked in hushed conversation about this or that, the content of which Barnibus was not privy to. Now he could not help but wonder if the topic of such conversation was in fact him and his brother. Uncle Ted knew a lot more about him and his brother than they knew about him, and that idea — as abstract and unattainable as it may be — made him uneasy. Though they never discussed it directly, the Jones brothers both felt more comfortable in situations where they could wrap their minds around the people involved; understanding the players helped them to understand the play.

Barnibus Sr. offered little in the way of insight into his wife's family, either in fleeting conversation or in anecdotes or stories from their courtship years prior. Barnibus' father was known to make a sly aside or two when it came to Uncle Ted, but nothing that Barnibus or Saga clocked as being enlightening or off-base. They took their mother's mild admonishment to be more typical of her lack-of-sense-of-humor than a comment on the material of Barnibus Sr.'s ribbing, and her reaction was as immaterial to them as it appeared to be to their father, who would chuckle mildly to himself and then carry back on with whatever periodical or paperback novel he was reading at the time.

"*Eccentric* isn't thrown around too lightly," he once said in the car heading over to Uncle Ted's house, in response to Saga talking about the knick-knacks he was hoping to find around the den and along the hallway when they arrived. From the passenger seat, Carol gave him a firm pat on the forearm, and that was the end. Barnibus Sr. exhaled sharply from his nose, satisfied with his little comment. The boys would (incorrectly) use 'eccentric' to describe most things in Uncle Ted's house from that point forward, but would rarely — if ever — apply it to the man himself. Uncle Ted was so jarringly different from Barnibus' mother that it was, at times, hard to believe they even knew each other, let alone had grown up together — as separate as that may have been. The differences between them, stark as they were, comforted Barnibus when he saw pieces of that dynamic cropping up between him and Saga. If these two could be related and continue their bond into their later life, then the Jones brothers should be able to manage similarly.

It occurred to Barnibus that they knew immeasurably more about his father's side of the family than they knew about their mother's. Carol had always been so particular about everything having to do with her children and how they interact with the world around them that she had grown, to Barnibus, to be a woman of singular origin. There was nothing that went into *creating* Carol; she simply was. So much of who she was, regardless of how that came to be, was now in Barnibus and his brother, and not knowing the origin of those qualities — the genesis of what he often heard people call her '*quirks*' — made him feel somehow empty. If he did not understand where his mother came from, how well could he really understand where he came from himself? And how much of that entire equation was built upon or stemmed originally from his Uncle Ted? And why, he could not help but wonder, was that kept from him? There was something about the idea that his parents did not want him and his brother to know their uncle that made him afraid. Not scared directly of the man himself, but as an idea it gave him pause. They wanted him kept from them. There must be something there.

"There are only two people in the world who can do what you do." That must be it. They did not want the boys to grow up knowing what their uncle was capable of. It was beyond reason. It stretched the bounds of what was believable. It would be a lot for two young kids to take in, especially if it became an issue

of keeping it secret from other people around them. This idea that the information was kept from them in order to protect them felt comfortable to Barnibus for all of thirty seconds, because he gamed the idea out to its logical conclusion: if they knew what Uncle Ted was capable of, while also knowing that Barnibus shared the same gift, and Saga was not dissimilar, why would they keep them in the dark? Barnibus thought how much knowing there were more people like him in the world would have helped him feel some sense of normalcy. If he knew his Uncle Ted — really knew who he was and how much they had in common — maybe Barnibus would not have tried to bury his gift, not have tried to distance himself from his own power.

Maybe then his parents would still be here.

* * *

The sun crept in through the lace curtains along the picture window at the front of Uncle Ted's house. They had been awake all night — aside from Saga — and had not said a single word further. Barnibus and Uncle Ted sat in silence, both trying to think their way out of a problem that neither of them fully understood. Now it was morning, and they had no better idea of their next steps. As Barnibus stared in the window's direction, his eyes drawn to the daylight while he himself was unaware of the rising sun, Saga stirred, looking about the room, confused why his brother and his Uncle were both sitting nearly upright, dazed and beaten, around him.

"Morning," Saga croaked as he looked around. "Uncle Ted, could I have some water?"

"Oh," he blinked, "yeah, yes. Yes, of course." He got up and stumbled out of the room on sleeping legs and feet.

Saga turned to Barnibus, who remained staring absently at the window, unaware of any other movement in the room.

"Hey," Saga waved his hand in front of Barnibus' eyeline, "you there?" Barnibus' head dropped forward just as he caught himself, having just narrowly nodded off. He took a moment to figure out exactly where he was, the lines between reality and the empty, dreamless vacuum of sleep having momentarily blurred.

"Yeah. Yeah, good morning," he finally whispered weakly as he rubbed his eyes and adjusted in his seat. "Did you get some sleep?"

"I think so. Depends on how long we've been here, I guess." He tried to crane his neck enough to see the clock, but could not quite make it out. Barnibus looked over, barely able to make out the time.

"Oh, wow," he muttered to himself. "It's 7am. I think you were asleep for a couple of hours."

"Feels like a couple of days," Saga said as he stretched and settled himself back in. "Did you sleep at all?"

Barnibus did not answer, looking sheepishly down at his feet.

"I didn't think so."

Uncle Ted shuffled back into the room carrying two pristine glasses of ice water. He handed one to each of the boys, who eagerly drank them down as he once again left the room. His suit was sagging, and his hair had fallen a bit, and when he returned hardly a moment later, he once again appeared prim and proper, his suit crisp and his hair good as new. His energy had not yet returned, but the clean appearance lent itself to someone in control of the moment, something that none of them felt on this particular morning.

"Let's talk through what we know," Barnibus offered. Saga sighed as he nodded. As much as he did not want to relive the previous day's events, he knew that they all needed to gain an understanding of their collective stories, something that he was sure did not happen between the other two while he was asleep.

"Capital idea," Uncle Ted exclaimed. He quickly shuffled a couple of stray boxes near the fireplace out of the way and, making a few other slight adjustments, made a clear stage-like area in front of the mantel. He hurried out of the room once again, this time returning with a rolling whiteboard like the ones the boys had seen when guest teachers came into the school to teach them about things like drugs and biomedical sciences. "We can use this," he mused as he scribbled '*What We Know*' along the top of the board. Barnibus could not help but smirk at the academic absurdity of this approach as he gathered his thoughts.

"Where should we start?" Saga asked.

"Step one!" Uncle Ted declared as he wrote his words on the board, "missing parents. And you're sure they weren't missing prior to yesterday morning?"

"Yeah..." Barnibus tried not to let the question annoy him. "We're pretty sure."

"Great!" Uncle Ted added a '2.' to the board and turned back to the boys with great excitement.

"We went to school," Saga offered.

"School, great, okay, and what happened there?" Uncle Ted wrote *School* on the whiteboard for step two, trying to mask his boredom at the monotony of this detail.

"It didn't seem like anyone else was... affected. . ? Nobody else had any problems in the morning, I mean. They didn't know what we were talking about when we started asking about it."

"You were asking about it," he scribbled some notes in shorthand on the whiteboard. "Did that draw attention?"

"It's middle school," Saga rolled his eyes.

"Not really any attention, no, just kind of, like, conversationally, I guess."

"Okay, got it," more notes, "just two boys chatting with their school chums." Saga scoffed and nestled himself further into the couch. "It's good to keep a finger on the pulse of the world around you, but we really don't want to draw attention to ourselves. Sounds like we're fine there." He added a '3.' onto the board and, without prompting, once again turned eagerly to the boys.

"Well, and then step three, I guess, was that school got dismissed early."

'*Went home from school early,*' Uncle Ted scribbled onto the board as he read it aloud to himself, barely above a murmur.

"We didn't go home from school early. They closed the school down early. Everybody went home," Barnibus corrected.

"Interesting!" he slashed through his previous note. "Now, why would they do a thing like that?"

"Other, uh," Barnibus began sheepishly, having found himself backed into a corner of his own making, "some of the other parents, you know, it turned out that, while *at the time* we didn't know—"

"Some of the other parents and teachers had disappeared, apparently," Saga cut in, with a shrug. Uncle Ted, who had turned reflexively back to the whiteboard to write when the boys talked, kept his head turned away from them now, eyes locked onto the whiteboard. Neither Barnibus nor Saga could discern his mood from the back of his head, but they both were confident in their guess of the general tone this conversation was about to take.

"Why wouldn't you begin the story with that?" He turned now to face the boys. "Last night — this morning — as soon as you walked in the door, why wouldn't that be the first thing out of your little mouths? '*Hey Uncle Ted,*' you could begin, '*love what you've done with the place. A funny thing happened at school this morning*'." His eyes, lightly glinting now with fear, darted between the two of them, sharing the blame for their delay with both of them equally.

"It was hard for—a lot happened yesterday, and honestly that's barely more than a footnote at this point," Barnibus said, nearly pleading. "We came here for help, but I guess we don't really know what kind of help it is we need." He looked toward Saga now, searching for help.

"A mass disappearance event is the top story on any news broadcast," Uncle Ted said, shaking his head incredulously. "That's your lede. That's the opener. There's frighteningly little else we could do at this point, short of understanding what happened there. Your parents — my sister! — that's one thing, and yes, it's tragic and it's very dear to us personally. But think of the other families that are hurting this morning — hurting the same way we're hurting now — and we have a chance to help. We have an *obligation* to help these people." The room was quiet now, the gravity of the previous day now landing on each of them in their own way. The responsibility, the admonishment, the fear and uncertainty hung heavy in the air at Uncle Ted's house. Just outside the door, in the hallway, a vintage promotional *Wally Weasel*™ wall clock began to chime for 8 AM. The time was currently 7:52 AM.

"Parents disappearing is one thing," Saga mused, "but once you get to a guy in a dumb old purple suit bringing a whole train outta nowhere, you kind of move onto other things." This addition hung heavy in the room for a moment, Saga and Barnibus unsure what to make of Uncle Ted's initial lack of reaction, as if bereft of oxygen, like the information had knocked the wind from his chest.

"What did you just say?" Uncle Ted hissed, astonished.

"Yeah," Saga nodded with quiet confidence. He pointed at the whiteboard, "Step four." Uncle Ted once again searched Barnibus for confirmation, but Barnibus could not help but avoid his eyes, first watching Saga before he turned his attention to the front window, now illuminated brightly by the morning sun. For a moment Barnibus felt transported from the tension and only concerned himself with what the coming day would bring, something that he did not often pay much mind, but with the events of the previous day ringing back and forth in his head, he did not know what to make of the sunrise, or if he and his brother would witness the sunset. He was rocked back into the moment as the dry-erase marker squeaked feebly across the board as Uncle Ted etched a light, sloppy '4.' onto the board.

"You must tell me what you know about this person, boys. And you mustn't spare a single detail," Uncle Ted cautioned, "do you understand?"

The boys nodded as they both sheepishly avoided directly addressing Uncle Ted. Between them was a mixture of fear — not wanting to relive everything that had happened, particularly their night in the kitchen — and shame for having not brought this to Uncle Ted sooner. After exchanging a few glances, they walked Uncle Ted through what they could piece together from the school: watching students leave with the parents, while others just wandered off on their own (they figured those were the ones who were similarly missing their parents, but they were unsure, as they were not intimately familiar with their particular family unit). Saga recalled more details about the Purple Man, although neither of the boys knew exactly what to call him, alternating instead between the basic '*he*' and the occasional '*purple guy*'. He told Uncle Ted now about how he seemed to appear out of nowhere, as Barnibus cut in, adding that very little of what he said made any sense to them, neither grammatically nor in substance. '*Scattered*' was the best they could muster to describe how he approached them, while Barnibus conceded that he appeared to have a purpose, a reason to be approaching them and not any of the other students.

"Did he approach anyone else? Did any of your school friends take notice of his arrival, or mention him to you since then?" Uncle Ted cut in as he scribbled notes on the back of the whiteboard.

It was only now that the boys realized their encounter seemed to be entirely unique to them. No one around them appeared to notice the Purple Man talking with them, and while they had not interacted with anyone but Uncle Ted and the Purple Man in the last twenty-or-so hours, they had no reason to believe that his arrival — or indeed his theatrical exit — had made any impression on anyone who may have been at the front of the school with them. They continued to describe the details they could pull, Saga going as far as describing the material of the Purple Man's suit, and Barnibus recalling, to the best of his ability, the cautions he left them, and the slithery, weaving way he moved and spoke. Uncle Ted's notes were thorough and feverish. It was not until the boys reached the train that he broke focus on his notes, the pen drooping in his hand as he turned, uneasily, back to the boys.

"The train," he stated matter-of-factly.

"That's right," Barnibus said cautiously, "like Saga said earlier, a train. Just appeared, I guess... out of nowhere."

"Were there any markings or anything on the sides? Did you see any people — any passengers — or anything that would... I don't know... that would establish this train at all?"

"What do you mean?" Barnibus asked while looking to Saga to see if he understood.

"Was there anything to indicate to you that this was an *actual* train? Anything to establish to you — in your mind — that this train came from a specific time, or a specific place?"

"Seemed pretty real to me," Saga scoffed. He was curled back into the couch now, and as brave as he wanted to appear, he wanted just to be comforted. He guarded himself against his scene partners here by curling into himself; part of the conversation, but apart from the group.

"I don't remember seeing anything that looked familiar," Barnibus answered.

"Okay..." Uncle Ted picked his pen back up and left a final note before he put the cap back onto the pen and placed it on the tray below the board. He looked towards his notes now, although did not appear to be reading them. He sighed heavily and wiped his brow, not realizing that his hair had once again fallen across his forehead, and his suit jacket — which he had been tugging at nervously at sporadic intervals — was stretched now and hung oblong on his shoulders. This realization solicited another sigh, albeit a smaller one. "Okay," he said again as he rose from his hunched stance and stretched his aching bones. "We have missing parents across town, a man in a purple suit, and a ghost train," he ran down the list, "and at this point it's... 10 AM yesterday?"

"We haven't even gotten to the good part yet," Saga said.

"Saga," Barnibus lightly scolded his brother, but Saga paid him no mind.

"I think I'm going to put on some coffee. Do you boys want anything?" Saga closed his eyes now, trying to sneak in a few more minutes of sleep before his uncle returned. Barnibus shook his head imperceptibly from side to side, and Uncle Ted once again exited the room with a dash.

Barnibus had noted earlier in the morning Uncle Ted's habit of leaving a room and coming back prim and proper, and wondered how exhausting that kind of care must be. He felt a little bad when faced with the notion that his uncle was putting in extra work on his appearance for their sake. He wished his uncle did not feel compelled to such vanity on their behalf, but he knew from experience with his parents on their mornings that grown-ups had a different approach to getting ready for the day, and many cared deeply about how others in the world experienced them. It reminded him of how much time his mother would spend on her hair in the mornings, draining what seemed like a full gallon of hairspray into her hair each morning before the brothers woke up, and never leaving the house on the weekends without a similar regimen. It made sense, he supposed, that Uncle Ted, being his mother's brother, would have similar quirks. Something in their upbringing, he figured. He wondered if Uncle Ted spent that kind of time in the morning as well, and how much money and overall time he must spend on those suits.

Uncle Ted returned now, and as Barnibus turned back from the window expecting to see him now refreshed and possibly in a new even-crisper suit, he was taken aback to see his Uncle was arguably less put-together than he was when he left. He had clearly been tugging at his suit while he brewed his coffee (which he carried now in a large thermos, with a single mug balanced on top), and his pocket square hung sloppily out of his breast pocket, having fulfilled its unspoken role as an ad hoc hanky. Barnibus made specific note of the bags under his uncle's eyes, having not seen him look this tired and stressed before. This was a side of his uncle that he had not seen before, and he wondered now if that was in fact by his uncle's design. As Uncle Ted put his coffee onto a conspicuous gap on his mantel, Barnibus turned quickly to Saga to see if his brother was seeing what he saw, but Saga was already on the verge of drifting off to sleep. Barnibus hesitated for a moment, knowing how badly his brother needed sleep — avoiding the thought of how badly he himself needed sleep — but something compelled him to give the leg of the couch a swift, but quiet, kick. Just enough to jostle him from his twilight and open his eyes. Saga looked to Barnibus now, immediately annoyed, but without Barnibus' prompt, as he clocked Uncle Ted by the mantel, now studying his own notes on the whiteboard once again, Saga's brow furrowed as he worked to understand what he was seeing. Barnibus could see that it took his brother a moment to even calculate who it was that he was seeing. He looked back to Barnibus again as Uncle Ted poured coffee from the thermos into the mug and turned from the whiteboard back to the boys, his voice raspy and drawn, eyes and frown drooping warily.

"I hate to say it, boys," he began. He hesitated for a moment as he noted the boys' strange, vaguely cautious looks as they regarded him. His hands drifted up and began absentmindedly tugging at his lapel before he caught himself and stopped, embarrassed. He sighed and cleared his throat, shifting uneasily now. "Right," he muttered to himself before inhaling sharply. His eyes locked with Barnibus now, but Barnibus, feeling a degree of secondhand embarrassment now, could not shake the quizzical look from his face. Uncle Ted reached up confidently and shifted the knot in his tie. As he tightened his tie precisely, with great care and practice, his suit jacket shifted itself upward, shrinking the slightest bit to resolve itself to a crisp fresh press, his pocket square receding into its cocoon of Uncle Ted's breast pocket before reemerging perfectly angled and, well, square. His hair pulled back up his forehead, reacquainting itself with its brothers and sisters, and each strand pulled comfortably back into its place as if guided by an invisible comb, aided by an invisible hairdryer. Uncle Ted drew his hands back over his face as one might splash their face with cold water, and when he emerged his eyes were refreshed and bright, full of life and clear. His smile was broad now, while his shoelaces tugged and lay themselves true, the closing step.

The boys both stared, wide-eyed now, unsure how to interpret what they saw. While Barnibus felt a sense of familiarity in what he was seeing, he could not himself put a name to it. He also could not draw reasons for why, exactly, this looked familiar to him in a way that he knew it did not to Saga. Within him was both a deep sense of recognition and the biting sting of shame he felt in watching it. Like seeing a private moment of a loved one, to which you know you are not meant to witness.

"I hate to say it, boys," Uncle Ted repeated, now in the clear, commanding voice of a practiced orator, "but I think I have some idea of who it is we've found ourselves entangled with." He let the words sink in with his young wards. "And this is going to get a lot worse before it gets better, I'm afraid."

8

MEAT FROM JONES

There are three entrances and exits at Uncle Ted's house. Barnibus was careful to note them as soon as they walked into the building, a habit that he had never noticed before. For a moment he wondered how long he had been doing that, before concluding that this was in fact a new behavior, and he knew what precipitated it. He wanted to know every way that the Purple Man could get in and, more importantly, how they could get out. Three doors, eight windows on the ground floor and another six on the second. Two of the windows off the den stuck about midway up. He remembered this from previous visits, and while he had not tested them since they arrived, he knew better than to try them in an emergency. He kept them in his back pocket, but knew that their place in the order of ideal egress was minor, close to null. As he did his math, he knew, to some degree, that it was pointless. They had seen not but a few hours before that the Purple Man found his own way in or out, no matter what they did to prevent it — to prevent *him*.

Then why isn't he here now? Barnibus wondered to himself

as he listened to Saga recall to Uncle Ted the final — what he considered to be final — events of their night last night: their apparent hostage situation in their kitchen, their destroyed kitchen, or whatever happened with the ice and snowstorm that appeared and receded with unseasonal power. As Saga recounted that particular portion of their evening, Barnibus knew acutely that Uncle Ted kept his eyes fixed on him and not on his brother. Barnibus knew, whether he braved saying it aloud, how that storm had transpired. So did Uncle Ted. Barnibus heard Saga's series of events winding to a close, going as far as describing their uneventful walk to arrive here.

"I guess the obvious question then is, why isn't he here now?" Uncle Ted proffered, much to Barnibus' surprise. "I'm not seeing a link between when he arrives versus what is driving him away. It's clear that he wants something — although he doesn't hazard saying directly what that *something* is," he continued, as Barnibus' throat caught. He realized Saga was not privy to the details of his discussion with the Purple Man, and thus had not known to include the fact that he had made specific reference to Barnibus' "gift," as he had called it. "Then why not take whatever it is? He can come and go as he pleases, so why not simply arrive at the time and space necessary and then retrieve it? Why the game of cat and mouse? What allows him to come and go?"

"None of it seems reasonable to me," Barnibus croaked, realizing how much his throat had seized up the more he replayed everything in his mind. "I don't think he — or whatever this is — is something we can apply rules to."

"I don't think you're too off-base with that assessment, my dear boy."

"But how do we stop him if we don't know... I guess... if we don't know how?" Saga added.

"How do we play the game if we don't know the rules?" Uncle Ted put it bluntly as he doodled a question mark — another in a series of errant punctuations littering the board. The three of them tried to work as a single mind, but with each only generating questions and no one having answers, Barnibus found the conversation to be an exhausting loop and did not seem to take them anywhere. He was up now, pacing about the room, back and forth behind Uncle Ted, looping around the couch behind Saga, back around, dipping into the hallway occasionally before returning to the den.

"I think we need a change of scenery," Uncle Ted suggested now, breaking the silence and shaking Saga from his impending slumber.

"No," Barnibus said with more force than he intended, "I think it's best that we stay here for a bit. I mean, until we know what we're doing, we at least know that we're—"

"We're not safe here," Saga interrupted. "We're not safe anywhere, and it's silly to think otherwise."

"That's not what I was going to say," Barnibus protested.

"Okay. Then what *were* you going to say?"

"I was—okay, I was going to say that we were safe here. But come on, if we're not safe '*anywhere*', then what good does it do for us to move? Even just traveling from one place to another could be a mistake." An idea struck Barnibus like a bolt of lightning. "What if he shows up again, like, in the car with us? We're driving along and suddenly he's right there, right in the seat next to you, then what do we do?"

"Next to me?" Saga says. "I'm going to be sitting shotgun, so... So, is he driving?"

"I'm not kidding, Saga. What do we do in that situation? We

can't get away, and it might not be safe to stop the car for all we know. So we're trapped, or worse, we're in active danger with the car moving while we try to defend ourselves or listen to his little sing-songy questions."

Saga tittered with laughter as Barnibus' pacing grew faster.

"For all we know, his train could come out of nowhere and just," he thought for a moment, "he could crush the car." He paused, waiting for the other two to catch up, but felt they were not finding this theoretical as damning as he was. "That's right, he could just crush the car. A train comes by and — BAM — that's it. Shows over."

"I think we're getting a little ahead of ourselves," Uncle Ted cut in as he placed a hand on Barnibus' shoulder. "We don't know what he can or can't do. But — and I hate to take sides on this — I think Saga has a point that since we don't know, there is equal danger staying here as there would be if we go out."

Barnibus, having momentarily stopped pacing, is deflated. In the back of his mind, he knew that his protest was an impotent one. But he had equal hope his companions did not realize that themselves.

"What we need to do is get out, and specifically aim for somewhere that we think he might go. We've been at this for a while now and he hasn't shown up yet," Uncle Ted shrugged. "I don't know why — maybe he doesn't like my house; I'm not sure."

"Maybe he didn't expect us to come here," Saga said, clearing his throat. "He knew we'd be at school, obviously, and our going home when we're dismissed early was a pretty safe bet. But our coming here? I don't know; maybe he didn't see that coming. Now he can't find us." Barnibus pointed enthusiastically at his brother now, hearing in his words that he would come around to his stance that they should stay put.

"Exactly!" Barnibus exclaimed. "He can't find us here, so we should *stay here*, where he can't find us."

"Yet," Saga added. "He can't find us *yet*. At least he hasn't yet."

"He's right, I'm afraid," Uncle Ted piled on.

"But he will, Barnibus. He's going to find us. And when he does, it doesn't matter where we are, or how hard we try to keep him out. He's going to come for us eventually, and if we're able to make that happen sooner rather than later — make it happen on *our terms?* I think that's the best thing for us to do."

Barnibus considered this for a moment, his eyes shifting between his brother and his uncle, both now watching him closely.

"What do you see, Saga?" Barnibus finally asked.

"Nothing. At least nothing yet. I'm too tired, I think."

"You should get some rest," Barnibus said, more for his sake than his brother's.

"I would like that a lot, but I don't know that I can fall asleep now. I keep trying to, but when I close my eyes, all I see is black, and I think it's keeping me awake. So," he shrugged, "maybe later."

Uncle Ted crossed to the built-in bookshelf on the opposite side of the room and, shuffling through a couple of stacks of books placed in front of the properly organized books on the shelves, produced a travel guide book for the town, complete with a highly detailed map of the city and surrounding county.

"Alright boys! Lead the way. Where to?" he asked excitedly as he thumbed the pages of the fold-out map.

* * *

The journey to the family's butcher shop was mercifully short and uneventful, Barnibus passing the time by counting the steps down Uncle Ted's hill and across town — 7,935 in total. Saga was in and out on the walk over, periodically trying to peer into the unknown to make any sense of what they had seen, or, better yet, make plans on how to stop it from happening again. Unfortunately, he could not make much progress in this regard, finding himself facing dead end after dead end. With a couple of blocks yet to go before they arrived, he gave up for the time being, shutting the proverbial blinds to his little personal window into the future — or whatever you could call a boulevard of infinite possibilities.

Barnibus had a key, the only person besides his mother and father who could boast about that fact. Saga was too young, and Barnibus Sr., while a generous and jovial man otherwise, trusted very few people, even close friends and business associates he had known nearly his entire life. The door swung open, a deep screech peeping from the oil-starved hinges. He made a mental note of this ailment to be sure to address it the next weekend he worked in the shop. Barnibus and his brother were too young to work the counter, the Butchers' Code being an ironclad tome which was exacting in the requirements of who could and could not sling meat, but they were to earn their keep by contributing to the shop in other ways. On the weekends they would clean, make minor repairs, restock items from dry storage under the shop and into the main working storage room just off of the kitchen. He had already clocked the location of the silicon-based lubricant he would use; he hoped this coming weekend to make quick work of that stubborn hinge. He knew it was not worth his time at the moment as they crossed through the front of house and into the kitchen in the back, punching in the code to disable the alarm.

Barnibus would hazard calling the prep space a '*kitchen*' as it had very few of the features — the culinary bells and whistles — that one would expect from a professional food prep area. However, the space fit the legal requirements to be considered a commercial kitchen for permitting and from the perspective of the Health Inspector. The sinks featured instantaneous water heaters which were properly sized to deliver hot water at a 60° F rise, and a minimum flow rate of 2 gallons per minute, the ventilation system was sized for efficient vacating of smoke, steam and other hazards, and hung proudly on the wall one would find Foot Managers Certificates for both Barnibus Sr. and Carol framed for anyone who card to inspect them (exceeding the requirement that only one person carry the certificate by 100%).

"Why would you do a thing like that?" Saga asked Barnibus privately as he came in just a few steps behind his brother. Uncle Ted had splintered off from the boys and made his way to check the back door to the shop, down the hallway near the back office. They heard the heavy register of the door as he gave it a good tug. It did not budge, as designed.

"The alarm is super loud. I don't think we want to be attracting that kind of attention."

"Maybe we should turn it back on," Saga hinted uneasily.

"Do you not remember how ungodly loud this thing is?" he said, gesturing to the keypad on the wall. "It's deafening, and my head is already killing me."

"If something gets in here, I think '*ungodly loud*' is exactly what we should have, don't you think?" Saga looked up at his brother, trying to keep their conversation quiet so as not to let Uncle Ted hear him worry. Barnibus thought for a moment, acutely embarrassed by the fact that he had not thought about the alarm providing them a tactical advantage over the Purple Man. He shrugged meekly at Saga as he quietly punched in the code for the alarm, which then beeped and began its countdown to arm.

"Brilliant idea, Barnibus," Uncle Ted cheered as he walked back into the kitchen area. "Best that we be alerted if anybody — *anything* — were to make their way into the restaurant with us."

"Thanks, Barnibus," Saga rolled his eyes as he walked over and pulled open the massive commercial refrigerator built into the far wall of the room.

"And better yet — if we were to leave, the ungodly noise that thing'll make will surely cause a nice distraction which would very much come in handy for us." Uncle Ted surveyed the items pinned to the cork board on the wall outside of the office. Mostly vendor bills that needed some redress, or yellowed notes of thanks left by customers long since forgotten. Saga reemerged from the walk-in carrying a couple of popsicles, one still wrapped and the other he had already made his way a third of the way through. He handed the unopened one to Barnibus, who took with cordial reflex, not so much as a nod shared between the two.

"You're running this play, Barnibus," Uncle Ted called. "What say you now?"

"Now we wait."

"Capital plan, my dear boy! If not maybe just a bit boring," he deadpanned. "But it sounds like just what you two boys need is a touch of boring. Am I right in that regard?"

"I could have done boring at home..." Saga grumbled.

"The last two times the Purple Man showed up, we were just on our own, just sort of... being there. I don't think we did anything to make him show up. I think we were just somewhere that he knew he could find us. At least eventually," Barnibus carried on. Saga's steady nodding betrayed the sour face which otherwise implied ardent disagreement.

"The Purple Man," Uncle Ted snickered to himself, before adding for the boys, "that's cute." Barnibus surveyed the kitchen area. In his head, he weighed the back office as another option before ultimately landing on the kitchen as the ideal option, given its larger size, brighter, more even lighting, and the multitude of weapons, were things to come to that point. For now, the Jones brothers, accompanied by Uncle Ted, would make camp there in the kitchen, choosing not to bother with additional fortifications, which had previously proven to be ineffective. At times he glanced over at Saga, hoping that his brother was running through a similar exercise in his mind and could confirm — or cast doubt on — his plan. But no matter how many times he looked, and how strongly he cleared his throat, it was apparent that Saga's mind was elsewhere. Before long, the waiting game and the long couple of days caught up with him. Saga fell asleep there on the floor of the kitchen, leaning against his father's prep table.

9

AND NOT THE BONES

Meat from Jones and Not the Bones stood at Columbus and 32nd Ave, occupying the space formerly operated as ***Giuseppi's Delicatessen***, where Barnibus Sr.'s father had worked as an apprentice decades prior. The building had been there for nearing ninety years, and of that time, seventy-six of those years it operated as a delicatessen and/or butcher. The shop was purpose-built as a deli counter from the beginning, with Robert Edmund Johansson having borrowed money from the bank — with his family's home as collateral — to finance both the purchase of the then-empty lot and the construction of the building to house his shop. Having previously worked as a printer, he wanted to get away from the arduous work of letter-setting and print-pressing, and into what he felt was a comparatively simple life as a delicatessen owner.

After four years of construction marred by setbacks from lack of material and a long string of inept superintendents and project supervisors, Robert Edmund ('*Eddy*' to his friends) opened the doors to ***Eddy's Deli Counter*** and enjoyed six long years of middling business, best described as "adequate". The deli generated just enough business to afford the family to keep both their home and the shop itself, but not enough business to generate a profit, or enough to pay a living wage enough to pull the Johansson family out of the self-imposed poverty of having leveraged their house for a business venture that was, unfortunately, not the payday they had hoped for. At the end of those six years, in November, just thirteen days shy of Thanksgiving Day, Eddy shuttered his shop and quickly sold the property back to the bank, breaking close enough to even to keep the roof over his family's head.

The bank, with equal quickness, turned around and sold the property to an enterprising hat maker, who was drawn to the kitchen space as a spacious workshop — certainly less cramped than the current workshop space in his house — with the deli counter and seating area serving as obvious facsimiles for a counter and showroom. Caprilio and Joyce Hamberg opened their shop the following February, having put in minimal work to redress the insides and spending little to retrofit the remaining kitchen equipment. **CapJoy Hattery** enjoyed a similar business to **Eddy's** in that it did very little business. Their margins were better. Relying on fewer orders with larger quantities, they could price aggressively to cover their overhead easily and stretch the remaining revenue to cover the next shipment. Caprilio and Joyce fell behind in payments on two occasions: the first was in September of that first year; the second was in June of the following year. When their business could not keep itself afloat, Caprilio resorted to selling off the remaining kitchen equipment, which had been gathering cobwebs in his workshop and was now long-since outclassed by newer models, to up-and-coming restaurateurs.

He used these small injections of cash to pay for the next order of materials and get back to work, now with a slightly less-cramped workshop. *CapJoy* followed a similar trajectory to its predecessor, closing its doors after five years in business.

Joyce secured a buyer on her own, Francis Heather Galbiati, who was interested, having not been in town during the less-than-stellar run of **Eddy's Deli Counter**, in starting a delicatessen of his own. There was something about this block of Columbus in particular that seemed to attract deli-men — those keenly interested in entering the deli and butchery business — but did not attract the average deli-goer. At least that was the case until **Guiseppi's Delicatessen** opened just three short months after the sale between the Hambergs and Mr. Galbaiti, who operated under the name 'Guiseppi' as he felt his given name of Francis instilled little confidence as a traditional Italian butchery. The shop was a quick success, riding the wave of interest in Italian-Americans in the media, and attracting a larger crowd of average consumers, and building a sturdy base of repeat customers. Barnibus Sr.'s father, Barntholomew, was hired as an apprentice butcher shortly after he graduated high school, having been referred by his own father, who had been known to glad-hand Francis down at the local vet's hall. He studied under Francis for twenty-three years, until his death at the age of 41 from complications stemming from his two-pack-a-day smoking habit.

Although his father never reached beyond the apprentice stage of butchery, as Francis felt he lacked the steady hand needed for world-class butchering — he always liked to joke that he *didn't make the cut* — Barnibus Sr. sought to purchase the deli when Francis retired eight years later. The sale was unremarkable and speedy, as Francis was at this point prepared to step down and move to sunnier pastures. Barnibus Sr. was eager to shake the hex he felt in the shop, as he could not help but shake the feeling that his father's smoking habit and eventual death both stemmed from the stress of *not making the cut.*

He registered the business anew as **Meat From Jones and Not the Bones,** and sunk significant capital into refreshing the decor and some of the shop's infrastructure. And there the shop has stood, in its current form, for going on twelve years. Sometimes staffed by his family, usually run solo by Barnibus Sr. himself, toiling away in solitude in between the breakfast and lunch rushes. Business was moderate, enough to support their lifestyle, and that was more than enough for the Joneses; Barnibus Sr. had no aspirations for a larger life, or a life lived in greater infamy in the butchery community. For a brief moment, he served on the Chamber of Commerce, representing the voice of the family-owned culinary concerns of local merchants. But before long he found this extracurricular to be too much of a time-suck and, after several long discussions with Carol, he stepped down with very little fanfare. This near-century-old brick and mortar deli, its storied past of very little import, returned to its place in the greater monotonous backdrop of the community; a staple, a mainstay, but never the star.

Saga saw all of this. Every sale, every slow day, every late payment, and every thumbed scale from the dozens of vendors that have exploited these businesses over the years. The owners, their families, their customers. Everything. The entire life of this place, from the very beginning, and now, regrettably, the very end. For Saga saw tonight this place being torn brick-by-brick, razed to the ground, the earth all-but salted by the uncontrollable, unfathomable evil now beset on them. Saga

saw, how only he could, what remained.
   And then he woke up.

10

BEFORE IT GETS BETTER

Outside was as near-silent as it could get in a suburban outskirt downtown corridor. The occasional howl from a neighborhood dog – or the scattering of the hard-working rats that the community ignored – would sound loudly unchallenged in the empty street, but otherwise there would be no foot traffic at this point. A few hours had passed since they had arrived, and Saga was relieved to find when he awoke that there had been no action in his absence. He surveyed the room to find Barnibus and Uncle Ted chatting quietly about nothing of much import — old stories from his time in school, questions about his house, small talk. He weighed the positives and negatives of telling them what he had seen, but thought better of creating a panic. What he saw, regardless of what they did to prevent it or slow it down, was inevitable. No amount of stress or panic could divert them from the road that they blindly navigated, so, he reasoned, the merciful thing to do would be to let them carry on.

Saga arose with a stretch, Barnibus and Uncle Ted both giving polite nods and smiles of acknowledgement, Barnibus quietly relieved that his brother had been able to get a little rest — something that he himself could not manage much of yet. As Barnibus and Uncle Ted continued their chat, Saga made his way around the kitchen, taking a final survey of everything around them: a small wash sink, a moderately sized commercial eight-burner stove, standard pots, pans, knives. Nothing jumped out at him as being an option for a classic, *capital W 'Weapon'*, but he found himself drawn to a single 6-inch copper sauté pan he found stored hap-dash in the lowboy to the right of the stove. He grabbed the pan and hefted it in his hand. It felt light but sturdy. Something about having this pan made him feel powerful. Not invincible, but someone to be taken seriously; someone who should be feared if one were to find themselves up against in an old-fashioned commercial kitchen showdown. He studied the pan both inside and out and, finding a small S-hook at the end of the handle, he slung it onto a belt loop on the right side of his jeans. The pan hung lightly just behind his hip, and as he likened this placement to the gun holsters he had seen in countless westerns, he felt like a cowboy. He dipped his head as he imagined crowning himself with a Stetson hat, brushing the horsehair from the rim as he tipped it low against the sun. Just for a second he felt like he was back with Walter, ready to begin another adventure, creating a scenario that would find them heroes of an old mining town, riding into town as two lone gunslingers and leaving just as mysterious after they saved the townsfolk in a proper dust-up. For a moment, he forgot all about the Purple Man and was, for once, just a kid.

Barnibus saw this from across the room. He could not see the Telenovela playing out in his brother's head, but he recognized the look of imagination and knew exactly what Saga was up to.

He could not help but smile, happy to see his kid brother not mired by his gift or buried under the tremendous loss of his best friend. Glimpses of a happy, innocent Saga are fleeting, and whenever Barnibus was lucky enough to see it, he considered it a wonderful gift. No matter what he had tried, he could not shake the constant awareness of their peril. But in this he found peace: seeing the innocence of his kid brother caught in a moment of imagination, he was happy knowing that they were not entirely lost. Everything in the last couple of days had not broken his brother. And maybe if that were the case, it would not break him either.

Tap.

Under the brim of his Stetson, Saga's eyes flicked upward to the single barred window on the sidewall of the kitchen.

Tap.

Barnibus and Uncle Ted turned now too. The noise unmistakably stood out against the hum of the refrigeration systems in the deli, ringing through the din as an unidentifiable stranger in the night.

Tap.

The Jones brothers looked to each other, Saga's Stetson now a footnote in his mind, no longer obscuring the look that Barnibus regrettably recognized in his brother's young eyes: terror. They both, in turn, looked to Uncle Ted, who kept his eyes affixed to the window, as if he could see through the frosted window — or indeed through the wall itself — if he could just stare a little harder. Barnibus noted, with quiet impress, that the tails of Uncle Ted's shirt, having bloomed from his waistband through the long evening spent roughing it in the kitchen, silently and almost imperceptibly, tucked themselves back in, smoothing back into a fine pleated press.

They stared, the rhythm of the tapping having created a pattern that they expected to be resolved. Tap, tap, tap, they knew when they could expect more — not too fast, not trying to break in, just to menace, to make itself known. And then it stopped. They hung in the air for a moment, the preceding tap having brought their anticipation up as nothing came to swing them back down. When the noise stopped, it created a floating feeling in each of them, subconsciously waiting for the next shoe to drop.

"That's him," Barnibus cautioned. The boys moved closer to their uncle now, huddling as they guarded the window. One on each side of him now, they tried to keep an eye out while putting themselves safely behind Uncle Ted's once again immaculately pressed slacks.

"I had a feeling," Uncle Ted whispered, his throat catching as he swallowed dry. Saga shifted his pan on his belt, the gentle *ping* as it caught a brad on his jeans giving Barnibus a small start. "I hate to be the one to ask this, being the adult in the room and as such feeling compelled to be in control," he said, metering the silence, "but any idea what comes next?" Saga chuckled, his amusement bringing Uncle Ted a trickle of self-consciousness.

"Whatever it is—" Barnibus paused, anticipating chaos in their near future.

"Nothing good," Saga interjected.

"—it's about to get very loud, very quickly."

"You can say that again," the Purple Man cut in, huddled with the boys behind the safety of Uncle Ted's suit, his eyes also wide and fixed on the barred window.

Saga jumped back from the huddle and reeled back with his trusty 6-inch sauté pan. As he lifted it high above his head and back as far as his little arms could reach, ready like a batter taking aim at a fastball screaming toward home plate, the Purple Man, having not risen from the huddle or even turned to watch Saga, lazily lifted his index finger in a universal *hold on* gesture to the young boy.

"Just a moment," the Purple Man said, his hand held with a finger aloft out to his side in Saga's direction, as Saga slid backwards, pushed from where he stood, his sneakers screeching across the floor. He stumbled as he lost his balance, falling backward as the pan crashed loudly to the ground. Barnibus jumped back now. Uncle Ted was the last to react, having taken a couple of beats longer than the boys to put together exactly what was happening now.

"Saga!" Barnibus yelled as he watched his brother hit the ground.

"Someone should put a muzzle on that kid," the Purple Man said of Saga as he absentmindedly dusted his clothes off and straightened his cuffs. He looked at Uncle Ted as he freshened himself up, Barnibus noticing a look of recognition in his eyes, a sense of familiarity between Uncle Ted and the Purple Man. Uncle Ted pulled himself backward now, putting space between the two men. Barnibus rushed over to Saga to help him up as the Purple Man remained in place, unreasonably relaxed and, subjectively, unthreatening in his demeanor.

"Are you okay?" Barnibus whispered to Saga as he grabbed his arm to help him up. Saga pulled away slightly, not wanting to seem like one who needs help.

"Okay. Alright," the Purple Man offered, as if he had been tasked with defusing the situation that he himself was solely responsible for creating. "That was a touch dramatic, and I think we should all take a moment, take a few deep breaths, and reflect on what's happening right now." He carefully looked them each in the eye, taking an extra moment to hold eye contact with Uncle Ted. "We're just four guys in the kitchen of a small-market suburban delicatessen," he continued.

"Butcher," Barnibus corrected defiantly.

"Right. Butcher. Where are my manners?" the Purple Man said, smirking lightly at Barnibus.

"Barnibus," Saga cautioned, squeezing onto his brother's arm.

"And you," the Purple Man said, turning to Saga. "A sauté pan? That's hurtful. I thought we had moved past that, you and I." He shook his head, disappointed. "We've been through so much these last couple of days, and I really thought we had grown closer," he continued, "developed a sense of trust between us." He paused. "Tsk. And after I let you both go back at your house. *This is how you repay me?*"

"That's not how I remember it," Saga hissed bravely from behind his older brother.

"Adorable."

"What do you want with these boys?" Uncle Ted cut in now, speaking in a firm diction that the brothers had never heard from their uncle. It was commanding and, were it pointed in their direction, quite intimidating.

"Theodore," the Purple Man said warmly. "Let's not be coy. There's no reason for us to put on airs here. You know perfectly well why I'm here, and you know exactly how this is going to go." He turned to Saga. "I get the feeling you do, too," he said, his eyes darkening. "Is that right?"

Saga nodded meekly, scared.

"Yeah, that's right," the Purple Man said, his eyes piercing into Saga. "Now," he exclaimed, his demeanor once again returning to that of a showman, a salesman presenting to a captive audience. "I don't think there's much use in our drawing this out, making it more of a thing than it needs to be. That's tired, it's cliché, and honestly, who has that kind of time?" he turned to Barnibus now. "Am I right?"

"Leave us alone," Barnibus croaked, his voice tired and shaky.

"Okay. I can tell that I'm not getting through to you. I get it — *who am I? Why would you trust some random, impeccably dressed person who shows up in the kitchen of your family's delicatessen?*" he held up a hand towards Barnibus, who flinched at the action, "Butcher. My apologies."

"I think it's best if you leave now," Uncle Ted said, trying to regain control of the conversation as he moved closer to the boys.

"Let's just run through what happens next. I think understanding the '*how*' of our situation here will be key to us jumping ahead of the *what* here," he said as he popped open the button of his purple suit jacket and tugged lightly at his purple suspenders. "That's just good business." He focused once again on Saga. "You. The small, weak one. You know what happens now."

Saga reached out to his uncle and pulled him the last couple of steps back into their huddle.

"I tear this place down, isn't that right?" the Purple Man began. "Brick by brick, this entire building is coming down. And," he grew more excited. "I'll tear *you three down* in the same fashion! It's not pretty, I'll admit that much. I don't want to sugarcoat that part, because I feel like that would be unfair here and would honestly be counterproductive to helping you understand the world of hurt you've found yourself in. That just wouldn't be helpful." He let his prediction hang in the air for a moment before pointing at Saga. "Am I on track so far?"

"He's right, " Saga croaked, barely above a whisper.

"I'm right," the Purple Man said proudly. "So, let's do what we can to just *avoid* that whole part of this story, shall we? Does that sound good?" he asked rhetorically. "Great!" He disappeared into the back office momentarily, and nearly as soon as he fell out of view, the desk chair from the office came careening out of the door, rolling roughly into the middle of the kitchen. The Purple Man came striding out behind it, for a moment betraying the anger in his heretofore jovial face. Before the boys could quite register this change in demeanor, which would confirm what they knew to be coming either way, the Purple Man quickly donned a veneer of showmanship. The chair eased to a stop a few feet shy of the middle of the room and, just as he caught up with it, the Purple Man gave it another firm kick, the violence of which was enough to make Saga jump. Barnibus pulled him closer to him.

"You," the Purple Man said, pointing at Barnibus. "I'm going to ask you to take a seat there," as the desk chair came to a stop across the room, just below the previously tapping barred window. Barnibus did not move. "And *you,*" now pointing to Saga, "I want you to take your little pan and your little uncle and go take a break in that office back there." Neither of them moved either. The Purple Man waited for a moment, sighing when his instructions were not followed.

"Anything you have to say to me, you can say to them too." Barnibus said, puffing his chest out, trying to appear bigger than his age.

"That's so painfully cliché, I honestly don't know how to answer it. I guess... Yeah, I guess I'll just say *no*. But I do—

really, I do appreciate the effort."

"They're not going anywhere," Barnibus repeated, this time raising his voice, Saga noting the full body and presence that he found unfamiliar in his brother. Barnibus stepped forward, urging his brother back towards their uncle as he spoke. Before the words could come out, the Purple Man cut in.

"You really need to relax," he said calmly.

Barnibus' mouth shut, his body becoming visibly slack, tranquilized. His tired, drooping eyes searched the room in a panic.

"Have a seat right over here, why don't you. You're looking a might tired." The Purple Man crossed to the chair. Grabbing the back of the chair, he jerked it violently, swinging it to a stop between him and Barnibus. "Are you sure you're getting enough sleep?"

"Barnibus, don't..." Saga pleaded, the sound barely audible beyond their huddle. But it made no difference, as Barnibus was now shuffling uneasily over to the chair.

"You two, I suggest you take that break now."

"I'm not leaving you alone with him," Uncle Ted said. "I'm not leaving." He turned to Saga now. "I don't think you're going to want to see this, kid." Across the room, Barnibus sat in the creaking desk chair, slumped so deeply that he almost appeared to be sleeping.

"I've already seen it," Saga said, defeated, as he watched his brother. "All of it."

Uncle Ted sighed deeply as he regarded Saga, painfully wise for his brief, inexperienced life.

"You know, Barnibus," the Purple Man said, "it would be a real shame for your brother to get involved in this. I told you before: he doesn't need to be." He turned to Saga and flashed a transparently fake look of pity, then turned back to Barnibus. "In fact, he doesn't need to be here at all. I think you could agree that this would all go much more smoothly if he were simply gone. Right?"

"Easy, kid," Uncle Ted called over to Barnibus. "Careful. Don't listen to him."

Barnibus shifted uncomfortably in his chair. He could feel something. He was not sure what it was, or where it was coming from, but it was something inside of him. An unnamed desire, or his body fighting off some sort of reflex response, but what reflex or why escaped him. It was a feeling he had not experienced before, and as such he could not assign it a name. It made him uncomfortable, made him uneasy. He did not like this feeling and did not like sitting with it. He wished so badly now for it to go away, and as suddenly as the urge had come on, now he found himself overtaken with the need to make it go away, to satisfy it — whatever it was — as quickly as he could. He could feel the sweat gathering on his brow now, and the sensation brought him immediately back to the last time he and his brother found themselves in this position with the Purple Man, and realizing that familiarity and how viscerally he could still remember the last time, he felt himself beginning to panic. Now *this* was a feeling that he knew well, and while he had been able to quell it in the past, he felt himself too tired to fight it now. His heart was racing, so was his mind, and he struggled to keep his grip on his thoughts as best he could. He needed to focus on something — anything — to ground himself. The floor. It's slick; it's shiny. Not shiny enough; he'll have to mop in here when he's back on the weekend. If he gets back. If he's still alive. *No. No, this is not helping. Focus on something else. Someone is talking now, so focus on that. What are they saying?*

"If your little brother could just go away now, just go somewhere else where he'll be safe, far, far away from here, that would be better, wouldn't it?" the Purple Man hissed quietly into his ear, a private whispered command, just for him.

No, Barnibus thought. *Not him. Don't focus on him, whatever you do.*

Saga and Uncle Ted tried to hear what the Purple Man was whispering to Barnibus, but could not hear, no matter how they strained. Saga, his eyes fixed squarely on his older brother, felt a twinge of pain as he watched Barnibus struggle, a measure of terror filling his tired eyes. He felt a deep fear now. Fear at the realization that he had seen their family's shop demolished tonight, and that he had seen the indescribable force that brought the shop and their lives crashing down. But this right now, this look in his brother's eyes: this was new. This was something that Saga had not seen, and that realization filled him with more fear and more dread than any vision could. He felt adrift.

"I bet you'd love to see your brother safe. I can assure you — and I need you to really hear this part — anywhere in the world will be safer than right here in this kitchen."

Barnibus shook his drooping head, trying to shake the Purple Man loose. But his focus on him now was too great, and the more closely he heard him, the more he could feel him in his mind, like the Purple Man was pulling strings and turning gears in his head. *Is that what I'm feeling? Is that what this is?*

"Saga needs to go now, Barnibus."

Saga squeezed tightly onto his uncle's arm, pulling himself in closely. Barnibus strained as he squeezed his eyes closed.

When they opened, his eyes widened as they swelled with tears. The Purple Man turned to survey the others, but saw only Uncle Ted, unmoving, alone. Saga was gone.

"Attaboy," the Purple Man snarled as a smarmy smile crept across his face. Uncle Ted turned his head with a start as he found his young companion — who had been there not but a moment ago, was now missing.

"Barnibus..." he turned back to his nephew, "what have you done?"

"No, I didn't—I didn't do—this wasn't me, I didn't—"

"Oh, don't be so modest!" The Purple Man bellowed proudly. "That was a big help! That's a good thing you just did, lad, kudos! Very brave indeed!" He stared at Uncle Ted. "Now, what should we do with our other guest here?"

"Don't," Uncle Ted cautioned.

The Purple Man shrugged in an exaggerated show of innocence.

"Don't... *what,* exactly?" he proffered coyly. "I didn't do anything. I'm afraid it was your darling nephew here who sent his brother off... somewhere?... to die. Or to live. I don't know. Hard to say, really, but what I do know is that this boy here has a remarkable gift."

"Stop..." Barnibus protested blearily.

"Quiet, you," the Purple Man said with the force and tenor of a weak grandmother.

"Where's my brother?"

"We don't need to get into all that now."

"Where's my family?"

"It's all questions with you." He shook his head at Uncle Ted. "Doesn't that bother you? Just nonstop questions with this kid. It's like he has an unquenchable thirst for knowledge," he scoffed.

"You'd better not touch him..." Uncle Ted cautioned as he stepped slowly, cautiously, towards the Purple Man.

"I'd thank you not to come any closer. I don't think either of us really knows what this thing is capable of," he said as he thumbed towards Barnibus.

"He's not a thing. That's my nephew. You get away from him!" he shouted as he lunged at the Purple Man, his hands outstretched like mangled claws ready to strike. Barnibus flinched at the sudden noise, turning his head away from the source and closing his eyes tightly.

And then: Nothing. Silence. Barnibus peeled his eyes open cautiously. The room was empty, save for him and the Purple Man, who stood next to him, dumbfounded, staring into the kitchen where his other hostages had stood mere moments before. After a moment, the Purple Man clapped, skipping and dancing about the room in a tasteless show of celebration.

"That's how it's done!" the Purple Man shouted. "I knew you could do it! I knew you could do it, but *hot damn!* I didn't know you'd be able to do it so... so... Well, I guess so *well!* Wow!" He turned to Barnibus, who was anything but excited. "You just made two whole people disappear! Just *poof!* Gone! Can you even imagine? Well, I guess you can imagine, right? Because that's—well, that's exactly what you did," he laughed.

"Saga?"

"Don't get caught up in the logistics, Barnibus."

"What have you done?"

"Why does everyone keep blaming me for this? *Oh, it must have been him. It was the person with the train. He disappeared, that young boy and his fancy uncle.* No, this wasn't me." He leaned down, now face to face with Barnibus, the familiar sting of his breath invading Barnibus' nostrils once again. "I can't do what you do. Not yet, at least."

Barnibus tried to stand now, his legs wobbling, fatigued. As he took one step forward towards the doorway out of the main shop, he wavered and nearly lost his balance. The Purple Man snickered at the sight, but made no attempt either to stop or to assist him. He just watched, bemused, as the boy struggled.

"What do we do now?" the Purple Man mused. "I suppose the options are limitless, apparently."

Barnibus reached the doorway and fell against the doorjamb, bracing himself. He felt tired, more than the weight of the last couple of days catching up to him, and more than the weight of having lost his brother. His world was collapsing, and he felt as though he was holding it all together on his own, and that was not something he was strong enough to do. Not now. Not ever. He felt dizzy, his head spinning as he tried to comprehend what was happening.

"Your parents were right about you. You're a remarkable young lad. Not that I ever doubted them, but you know how parents always say some nonsense like that about their kids. That's just kind of part of parenthood, I guess."

Barnibus felt a jolt of energy fire through him. *My parents?* he thought. *What does he mean, they were right about me?*

"I want to see my family." Barnibus lifted his head and turned towards the Purple Man, feeling more awake now than he had in quite some time. "Can you take me to them?"

"In due time," the Purple Man cooed. "But right now we have other things we need to attend to, and they could really impede that, so it's just you and me for now."

"If you won't bring me to them," Barnibus' mind raced as he tried to calculate his next move, and he could feel the words spilling out more quickly than he could think and plan for them. "Then what good are you to me?"

"Aw, that's cute. *What good am I to you?* That's really cute — and brave!" the Purple Man said, genuinely impressed. "But I hate to break it to you, kid, as if this wasn't abundantly clear from the outset: you're not in charge here."

Barnibus wavered now, the momentary jolt of energy quickly wearing off. The Purple Man saw this and pulled the chair in front of him.

"It's probably best that you take a seat for this next part. Things are going to get a little hairy, and I don't want you to hurt yourself."

Barnibus struggled to shake his head.

"Okay," the Purple Man said, "have it your way. But don't say I didn't warn you." He shoved the chair off to the side, sending it screeching and skipping across the kitchen before it slammed against the lowboy under one of the prep counters. Barnibus kept his eyes fixed on the Purple Man despite the noise as he tried to compute his next move. Everything seemed to be happening *to* him, he thought, and he felt like he could not keep ahead of *anything*, but especially the Purple Man. If he could just get some distance between them, he thought, he could think, to put together some sort of plan, or anything, to get ahead of him — maybe even find his family. If the Purple Man knew where they were, then that means they are somewhere he could find them. He just needed a little space. Space means time, and with time, he could work his way out of this.

"Stop that," the Purple Man cautioned. "I know that look, and I don't like that look."

Barnibus regarded the Purple Man, unsure of what he was

talking about.

"Now, you and I are going to work together like good partners on this one. I like what I see, I get what I want, and you'll be back with your parents in no time. But if you try anything — you try to burn me — then I'll burn them, and you'll never see your family again." The burners on the stove flickered to life as flames rose quickly from each burner. "Sit down, Barnibus, and let's get to work."

Barnibus turned to the stove, trying to make sense of what he was seeing. He wanted to bolt for the stove and shut it off, but found himself unable to move his feet from where they were planted. He heard the pilot light of the ovens click and clack before he heard the familiar *flume* of the oven kicking on.

"Sit. Down. Barnibus," the Purple Man growled as the kitchen filled with an unbearable, remarkable heat.

Barnibus sat down with a heavy thud, compelled into the chair against his own best judgement. His eyelids flickered as he worked to wick away the tears and sweat pooling in his eyes. He did not like this feeling; the loss of control made it difficult for him to read the situation and to judge how to react, what to do next. One thing he knew now, though, was how he felt, and he paid no mind to how naturally his worries revolved around his brother and his safety. Whatever happened to Barnibus, so be it. The Purple Man was clearly concerned primarily with him, and for whatever reason that may be, fine. He will accept his part in that, as unfair as it may be. But Saga — his role in this lacked definition, and as far as Barnibus could tell, he was collateral damage. He felt as much to blame for Saga's current predicament — wherever he was now — as the Purple Man was. Unless Barnibus acted immediately, he would be doomed, and his brother would be lost to time. The Purple Man joined him with a familiar closeness that filled Barnibus with disgust, crouched low directly in front of his face. He worked to avoid his eyes, but they loomed so large in his field of vision that he could hardly avoid the morbid draw of curiosity.

"I really want this to go smoothly, Barnibus," the Purple Man said. "You understand that, right?"

Barnibus nodded reluctantly.

"So the sooner that you give me what I need — what *belongs* to me — the sooner I'll leave, and you'll never hear word one from me or my ilk again. You can go back to..." he looked around the kitchen, the walls already beginning to darken with soot. "...whatever it is you call this insignificant life that your parents have built here for you."

Barnibus bucked at the mention of his parents, but even in the face of his sudden violent outburst, the Purple Man did not flinch.

"I know, I know. You need to stop being so sensitive about them. It's unbecoming of a boy as powerful as you. What you have — what *you and I have?* You're bound to lose some people that you love. That's just a fact, and I'm sorry to be the one to tell you that. You ask me, they must not be exemplary parents to have never taught you something so basic. That's just my two cents."

Barnibus jolted in his seat, throwing his hands up to wrap his small hands around the Purple Man's neck, bent on choking the life from him, ending this whole putrid dilemma for once and for all, summoning however much strength he had left in his tiny, exhausted body. But though he tried, and felt all the force he could muster into his pounce, his arms did not move from his sides. His hands stayed grasped to the underside of the chair in defiance of his commands, despite his brain —

and his heart — screaming to attack the Purple Man. Nothing happened.

"I want you to look me in the eye now, Barnibus."

His eyes snapped with laser focus into the Purple Man's.

"Good. That's good. Now I want you to picture something simple. Let's start small. I want you to picture what it would look like if everything outside of this kitchen — the little deli, the storage room, that sad little office — came crumbling down."

Barnibus snarled as he concentrated as hard as he could at silencing his mind, finding it more of a struggle than normal to shut out the noise.

"Come on now. I said I want this to be easy. Do you remember when I said that?"

Barnibus, once again against his own wishes and without thinking, nodded his head in agreement.

"I want you to think about that — the nodding of the head, your hands gripped onto your chair — and I want you to think real hard before you try again to fight me on this. Because I'm losing patience with you. Do you understand?"

Barnibus nodded again, this time with intention.

"Good. Now, I want you to imagine the world that I describe to you, and I'm going to look into your eyes while you build it in your mind. I want to see the machinations of how you do what you do. And if I sense that you're holding anything back from me, or that you're going off-script, you will not see your family again."

Barnibus breathed heavily now, trying to keep his heart from racing, and more importantly, keeping his mind as clear as he could muster. The Purple Man regarded the sweat pouring down Barnibus' forehead and gave a heavy sigh.

"Look at you. You're going to pass out, how hard you're exerting yourself." He stood up for a moment, looking around the kitchen once again, as if he were looking for ideas. "Alright. Okay, I can see we're going to need a bit of a palette cleanser. Something to wipe this entire slate clean between you and me, let you unburden yourself of what ails that little brain of yours, kind of — I don't know — reestablish the stakes here." He crouched back down in front of Barnibus, his pungent breath once again stinging his eyes.

"I'm not doing what you say," Barnibus insisted between shallow breaths. "You might as well just give up now."

"Fair enough. I want you to raise your left hand and kinda hold it flat about right here," he demonstrated, "about chest height right here in front of you."

Barnibus thoughtlessly raised his left hand, holding it in front of his chest in a perfect imitation of the Purple Man's demonstration.

"Good. Good. Very good, Barnibus, I'm proud of you." He patted Barnibus on the knee, as Barnibus' left hand shook while he struggled against his body having revolted against him. "Next, I want you to raise your right hand to kind of about the same general level," he showed again, "like this, so your two hands are about right here."

Barnibus' right hand raised laboriously, as both hands trembled in front of his chest.

"You're doing so well. Really great work on this one, Barnibus." The Purple Man watched Barnibus tremble for a moment before he cleared his throat. "You're going to take your right hand and pinch your left index finger between your right thumb and index finger. Do you understand?" He demonstrated the simple grasp to Barnibus, who shakily mimicked it with his own hands. "Now, I'm going to ask you to take that left index finger and bend it sideways towards your thumb as hard and as swiftly you can."

Barnibus whimpered, his hands shaking more than ever, his bottom lip trembling as he fought back tears. His breath was growing increasingly shallow and fast now. In his head he was screaming – pleading – with himself, *Please don't do it. Please don't do this. Just let go. Fight back.*

"You're going to hold your breath when it happens, but you really want to be careful not to do that, okay? Just breathe. It's only a transverse fracture. It'll probably heal eventually." The Purple Man held up his own mangled hand closer to Barnibus, who now noticed the odd angle at which his index finger emerged from his hand.

You need to do this, he found himself thinking. *It's okay, everything will be fine. People break their own fingers all the time. Now it's your turn.* He shook his head, his better angels now turning against him. *He knows what's best for you*, he whined. *The Purple Man wants what's best for you.* He knew he was wrong – this voice was wrong and with equal fervor he hated what he was saying just as much as he believed it to be true. But persuasive as it was, he simply could not shake it. He studied the Purple Man's hand for a moment while it hung, mangled, directly in front of him. "Now be a good boy, Barnibus. Snap," the Purple Man whispered.

Barnibus wrenched down hard on his index finger and heard a loud pop like a broken stick as his field of vision filled with white, his ears ringing. He struggled in his chair, wanting to run, to do something — anything — to get away from the pain, but there was nothing he could do. He held onto his finger, unable to let go of it even if he wanted to.

Breathe, Barnibus, he told himself. *You need to breathe.* He sucked in air as deep as he could, but his body was shaking so much that he found it difficult to get anything better than a couple of small puffs at a time. He looked back up to see the Purple Man sat fixated on watching him, a smirk of disapproval showing across his face. Barnibus' hands broke free and fell to his lap, his head dropping along with them. He wanted so badly to stay strong, to not let the Purple Man know he was broken, but before he could stifle himself, his emotions overcame him.

Barnibus's eyes welled and overflowed with tears as he stifled his wincing and the heavy, chugging why he was breathing. The Purple Man perked up at hearing this and let out a mighty bellow that soon transitioned into loud, delighted laughter.

"Relax," the Purple Man said between chuckles. "It's just a hand. You've got two of them for a reason!" He laughed as he crouched back down in front of Barnibus. "Now," he began as he took a moment to find his balance on his haunches, "we're going to do that again. But this time I want to feel like you really understand what we're doing here, okay?"

Barnibus's focus on the Purple Man narrowed as despair and pain turned into hatred and rage, and that rage overflowed from his belly as quickly as it came on, and poured outward from his eyes.

"When we're done here, I want you to remember how I made you do this." He leaned in closer to Barnibus. "Do you understand?"

Barnibus' hands, now pale and drenched in a sweat that was both hot and cold, mindlessly entangled one another as he unwillingly grasped onto another finger.

"Once more with feeling, Barney."

His hands trembled, fighting against themselves as he felt

the venom boiling up from his stomach, drying the back of his throat as it colored his words, filling his voice with a presence and volatility that surprised even him.

"You need to leave," Barnibus stated emphatically and with stark finality.

The kitchen was filled with smoke; the stove smoldering in flames that grew and worked at the ceiling, catching combustibles on the nearby prep table. The kitchen was rapidly catching alight, and it would only be another couple of moments before those flames reached Barnibus. He felt his legs relax, and a massive weight moved from his shoulders. The Purple Man was gone now. Barnibus had not seen him go and had only realized his departure when he felt his influence exit from around him. Barnibus was alone now.

* * *

It only took five minutes for the kitchen to become engulfed in flames. Barnibus watched from across the street as the fire took the rest of the building, feeding on the nearly century-old timber that made up most of the framing. First, the roof crumbled, which fed the flames below. The building took on a new identity as the brick pilings at the corners and the back wall remained standing among the rubble. The Fire Department showed up as quickly as they could, but as Barnibus had not called them, their arrival was destined to be too late to save the deli. There was no loss of life. Of that, Barnibus was certain. But he could not help but feel like a part of him had perished alongside his father's shop, as he watched the firefighters raining gallons of water down on the flames and smoldering embers. Without realizing it, he had taken a seat on a park bench now and sat watching long after the scene had died down, with only a single engine and the fire inspector remaining. He found two decently sturdy sticks in the brush just off the road and fashioned a splint around his index finger. It was far from perfect, but with no medical training or, for that matter, sleep, it did the job. At least for now. The thought had not crossed his mind to ask for help from the Fire Department, which was within shouting distance. Similarly, no one paid him much mind, which was all the better for Barnibus, as he knew not what he could say to anyone about what had happened tonight, how the fire started, or any of the natural questions that would come from such an interaction. *What happened here? Were you alone? Where's your family, son?*

Later that night Barnibus returned home, alone. He could not be sure where his brother or his uncle were, only that he felt singularly responsible for their disappearance. Uncle Ted would be fine on his own, Barnibus had to imagine. But he found it hard to stomach the idea that Saga was out there on his own. He wondered what Saga saw, and if he could use that information to get himself to safety or, better, home. As he walked, he searched for ideas on what he could do to find them, but he came up empty. Without a lead to begin, he could not know which direction to head. For now, he would just have to wait. Either for them to return, or for the Purple Man to come back. He swallowed hard at the thought, not wanting to experience that helplessness again. He felt his mind race, but for the time being, he would concentrate on walking. *Just get home, Barnibus.*

Get home safe.

11

IN THE MIND OF SAGA

It had been days since Saga had last slept. Real, restorative sleep. The sleep that cleanses the mind and allows you to process the world around you without succumbing to overwhelm. Saga was past that point now. But this was a speed at which Saga was used to functioning. His life existed, he felt, on the margins of reality and surreality. He needed little energy to process the world around him, because the world *around* him was only a small fraction of *his* world. Within him lived myriad other worlds, infinite in their possibilities, a web of chance and consequence that took nearly every ounce of energy he had to keep in check. He was careful to not devote much thought to what could become, and had, despite his young age, become quite deft at navigating the seas of his mind, venturing out only when he had a specific question in mind, or needed to peer into a specific depth as best he could at a given moment. So when Saga tried now to keep his bleary, wandering eye focused, he did not have the strength to keep to one strand, instead finding himself venturing down narrow halls hung with vignettes and tapestries that he hardly recognized.

The school was lost now. Not destroyed, but vacant. Empty. No students here, and without students there was hardly a need for teachers, and without teachers there was hardly a need for administration, and without any of them, hardly a need for the facilities staff. Saga could not find a clue where the students had gone — a tragedy or not — but could see that whatever happened at Anna Tuthill Harrison Junior High happened quickly and with great violence. Along the walls of Hall B hung the school's *'achievements'*, plaques and awards that the principal, along with the district superintendent, believed best exemplified the capable middle school minds they professionally molded. The polished brass nameplates, sun-damaged wooden bases, and letters of dedication and praise were gone now, tattered and smashed along the front of the display case they used to call home. Whatever had pulled the front of the display case off had done so easily, as the front doors and their assembly lay across the hall in one mostly solid piece, with the glass doors themselves only showing minor superficial damage. Saga found himself strangely relieved by the idea that the doors could be used again in the future, but he paid that feeling no mind as he continued down the hall, past the administration and nurses offices, and into the principal's office two doors down on the right. Principal Cahill had been with the school for eighteen years and enjoyed a fair amount of latitude from the superintendent in how they ran the school. They left much of the day-to-day governance of the school to Vice Principal Adcock, and instead focused on the big-picture achievements and initiatives that would drive better funding and notoriety for the school into the future. Principal Cahill's forward-thinking vision of education as a byproduct of institutional advancement was far from unique in the neighboring public schools, which regularly made painful cuts to vital systems in order to keep their doors open. Principals, Saga reasoned, based on his passing familiarity with his own middle school principal, were more immediately focused on hustle and promotion than they were on the betterment of their students. However, in this case, Principal Cahill could not be faulted, as their efforts — no matter how outlandish — routinely paid off respectably for the Anna Tuthill Harrison Junior High students — *Go Toadfish!* Unfortunately, what had been a stellar eighteen-year run in education was seemingly yet to come to an end in the surreality that Saga now explored. Principal Cahill's office, though unmolested, was empty. Prior to what happened throughout the school's halls, the principal must have boxed up their desk, as any personal effects are now gone, leaving only administrative binders and boxes upon boxes of reports and policies. If Saga did not know any better, this would look like just another admin storage room; hardly the hallowed den of authority he and his classmates knew it as.

The cafeteria fared little better. Tables were overturned and, strangely, chairs were lined along each of the exterior walls. Lined single file along each wall facing inward, posed as an audience, having watched something — some wretched show — in the center of the room. Once again, Saga could not see what happened here, only the aftermath, but could feel the presence of evil and the lingering stench of terror and suffering. This was an afterglow that Saga unfortunately knew improbably well; well beyond what any child of his age — roughly the same age as the dozens of students made to watch here — should be made to experience. The lingering toll in this room especially was almost too heavy for Saga to bear, as he did his best to wade through the heavy air and residual heartbreak that filled the dark, echoey chamber. The farther into the cafeteria he pushed (he neared just left of center now), his head filled with screams. Distant at first, they quickly became overwhelmingly harsh and shrill. Saga threw his hands up over his ears to block the sound, but it was no use. He squeezed his eyes shut tightly; anything to limit the sensory input. This too was feeble against such a staggering degree of brutal, broadly dispensed violence and terror. Saga moved quickly now, pushing as hard as he could to get past the makeshift stage He had built in the center of the room. He. '*He*'? Saga realized he had picked out a single presence among the chaos and could discern that a single person, or single *thing, was responsible.* His mind struggled to wrap around the idea that such hate and rage could emanate from one point — from one heart and one brain — but that was not something that Saga hoped to understand at this point. He had finally found a clue, and as horrifying a clue as it was, it still shed a light on a thread that could lead them to answers. And with answers comes hope that they may stop whatever death was dealt here; to get in front of whatever freight train of terror made Anna Tuthill Harrison Junior High its terminus. Saga felt confident in the '*who*' of this scenario: the Purple Man. But he had no proof and had not seen it himself. Not yet. But who else could wield this type of power?

The ice came, the same as before. A common theme, Saga thought. Snow, then ice, then more ice. It overwhelmed Saga — the sheer scale and magnitude, endless sheets of ice and show, the sky blindingly clear above him, weighty from the lack of interruption, like a heavy blanket keeping him contained. He tried to run, but as his legs moved and his chest burned from the numbing cold, he seemed unable to move, as sheer flat ice continued outward infinitely in all directions. The feeling of infinity, of endlessness, terrified him.

Saga is back outside the school now, running through the forest that bisects the town, the school on one side — among other things — and most of the neighborhoods spread neatly about the other. He is gliding over the sticks, stones, and discarded cigarettes and soda bottles that make up the forest floor, moving much too quickly for his feet to catch anything or for obstacles to cause him much delay. He cannot think of a time he moved as swiftly as this, and thought for a moment, fleetingly in the back of his mind, that this must be what flying feels like. He wished he had the type of childhood that allowed him to daydream about flying, but alas, here he was instead: daydreaming about fleeing. Fleeing what, he could not be sure of at the moment, but he knew he needed to put as much distance between himself and the former middle school as possible. Past this forest, past their home, beyond the edge of town and past the next. He wondered how Barnibus had managed to make his way to the edge of the world and mused that this might be the same path he had taken on that journey. He missed his brother and felt like he needed him now more than ever. As quickly as that thought flashed across his mind, he pushed it back and replaced it with another: a flash of Saga himself, living a happy life. He was older now, but he recognized himself instantly. He was happy. A family man. He had left town with his partner, gotten married, and started a new life far from here. A smile spread broadly across his face as he watched his two kids run and play in the backyard of what must be their home. After a moment, his partner places a coffee mug in front of him as they drape their arm across Saga's aged, knotty shoulder and pull him close. This is comfort. This is home. And Saga felt the wash of relief to know that this was a possibility for him. Not a fantasy, or a hope, but a true possibility, somewhere in the tangled mess of threads that one could pull, he had found himself content, sailing through the world with a partner and with children; a happy family unit that he could throw himself in to, and through which he could focus his world. He longed to stay here, to move past all the struggling tragedy that he would need to cross to arrive here, to earn this life. If this was inevitable in some combination of happenstance and coincidence, could he just skip the unpleasant eras? He concentrated hard, feeling that if he put all of his strength into it, he could stay a moment longer, possibly longer still, and drink in every detail: the silverware laid neatly on the placemats before him, the plates awaiting breakfast — *mom and dad's plates! A hand-me-down!* — the cup of fresh, hot coffee — a cozy medium roast — all atop a beautiful hand-carved dining table in their warm ranch home. Idyllic and comfortable, this felt like his forever home, and he had not known this kind of warmth before, and prayed he would feel it again soon as the silverware rattled. He saw the coffee in his mug begin to ripple and sputter, the plates jostling with enough force to chip and crack with each jump, some sliding clean off the table and shattering on the ground at his feet. The sounds of his children playing and chattering birds in the mature evergreen trees that adorned the yard became crowded and muffled against the familiar approaching sound of an arriving train. Impossibly loud now, as Saga watched the children, he knew in his heart to be his run from their playground towards the shed between them and the house, desperately seeking shelter from a monstrous presence they could not possibly understand but would soon have no choice but to know with heart-wrenching familiarity.

Saga opened his eyes.

12

WELCOME HOME.

O*h, right,* Barnibus thought. *The kitchen wall. Dang.*

In all the commotion of the last couple of nights, Barnibus had completely forgotten about the giant hole ripped into the kitchen wall.   Or, more accurately described: the complete lack of a kitchen wall where there had once, mere days earlier, been a complete wall. He sighed as he dropped his bag onto the chair he had spent the previous night tied to and tried to work through the conversation he would have to have with his parents to explain everything that happened and why their now-three-walled kitchen had decreased drastically in property value. *Oh, also the butcher shop was destroyed, so that kitchen is gone entirely.* He wondered if maybe this whole thing resulted from the Purple Man simply not liking kitchens, and he was surprised to hear himself chuckle lightly. It was strangely comforting to hear, as if it proved he was still alive.

"What's so funny, lad?"

Barnibus jumped with a start as he turned to see Uncle Ted pushing his way through the backdoor into the kitchen.

Barnibus could not help but feel charmed by the fact that Uncle Ted chose to enter respectfully through the door, rather than climbing through the missing wall only a few paces away.

"This is a doozy," Uncle Ted whistled as he looked around at the crudely built, mostly furniture-based barricades and battlements knocked about throughout the house. "Your mom will *not* be happy about this one. Hope your folks have good insurance."

"Their policy is actually pretty expensive. They let it lapse a couple of years ago, but Mom made Dad get coverage again a few months later." Barnibus was unsure why that felt important or even relevant at the moment, but seeing his uncle again — in the flesh! — filled him with a strange, duty-bound sense of honesty. Losing so many loved ones so quickly and in ways that he did not fully understand made him feel compelled to open his heart if the opportunity were to present itself again. And in this instance, that meant sharing the details of their homeowners' insurance policy(s).

"So," Uncle Ted began as he leisurely dusted off his suit and shoulders, "that was some new trick, huh?"

"I don't know what that was. I've never done anything like that."

"Me neither, but it's one hell of a new page in our playbook."

"I don't see how it could be helpful if I don't know how — or why? — I did it."

"Do you know how to ride a bike?"

"Wha—" Barnibus guffawed awkwardly. "Yeah, of course I do."

"And have you always known how to ride a bike, or did your mom teach you?"

"My dad taught me. My mom doesn't think bikes are safe

for kids."

"Bikes..." Uncle Ted stared through Barnibus for a moment, lost in his thoughts. "Bikes are extremely safe for kids. Kids are basically the ideal audience for bikes." He shook free of his confusion and snapped back into their conversation. "And when I see my sister next, I will remind her of such."

Barnibus laughed, but still felt lost on what, if anything, Uncle Ted was getting at. Sometimes he spoke in such broad circles and loops that it made it difficult for Barnibus to follow, and when they were all together like they were last night, he would notice Saga zoning out, having long given up on keeping track of the thread.

"Someone taught you how to ride a bike. You weren't just born knowing how to do it, just like you don't know how to do... this... thing... now."

"Can you teach me?"

"Me? Oh, heavens, no. Er, probably not. I don't know, now that you mention it."

Barnibus could feel himself getting annoyed as he sensed Uncle Ted getting into another one of his loops, but was thankful when he saw him find land once again.

"I don't know what you did, or how you did it, Barnibus, I'm sorry," Uncle Ted offered. "But I imagine it's at least acutely related to some things that I *do* know how to do. Some thoughts of yours that maybe some of your school friends don't know about, or maybe they don't understand? And maybe you don't entirely understand on your own. Does that sound familiar?"

"That's not something that I do anymore. I don't—when my mind races and I see things around me start to—whatever... It makes me feel unsafe. I know that it's coming from me, and that I... I guess I control it? But I don't know how, and it makes me think it's going to get out of hand fast. It feels like my brain is working against me sometimes."

"It can! Definitely."

This did not fill Barnibus with confidence.

"But that's why you learn, my dear boy," Uncle Ted continued. "When you have a special talent — anything! Not just something like you or I have — it can be intimidating when your friends and family can't do the thing that you do. It can make you feel different, or make it hard to relate sometimes."

Barnibus did not like this type of conversation. There was something about someone else purporting to understand his thoughts or how he felt that made him feel seen in a way that felt too vulnerable. It felt to him like someone had opened a window into his mind and was watching him at his most exposed; the one place he should feel entirely free from spectacle, here he was observed. Studied.

"You're special, Barnibus. And not in any scary way that makes you..." he searched for the right word for a moment before continuing, "undeserving or different. It just makes you, *you, the* same as your personality or your sense of humor. It feels unsafe because you can't control it, but I bet you and I can figure out some good ways to make that brain of yours work *for* you."

"Why didn't my mother ever tell us about you?"

"You know me," Uncle Ted deadpanned.

"We know you, but I guess we don't really know that much *about* you. Why didn't my mother ever tell us about what you can do? Does she know? Or did you keep it a secret from her, too?"

"She knows. There are a handful of people in my life who understand — to one degree or another — what I've gone through in life and some struggles I have around the way my mind works."

"*The way your mind works,*" Barnibus mused under his breath.

"That's what it is. This is simply the way your mind works, Barnibus. Same as mine. We're just lucky enough to have minds that are stronger than others. Do you think everyone could handle what you and I can? Absolutely not. They'd crack. It would break them."

"I'm not sure it won't break me."

"It hasn't yet," Uncle Ted answered with a shrug. "Now, I'd imagine that's why your mother never told you kids about me. The full story, at least. It's not her secret to tell. Your mother is a stand-up person like that."

"She should have told me!" Barnibus exclaimed, startling even himself. He took a moment to recompose himself, breathing deeply and gently twisting his neck with a light *pop*. "I wouldn't have felt so alone. I would have had someone to talk to."

"We're talking now. That counts for something."

"Yeah..." Barnibus deflated. The events of the last couple of days had long since fully caught up with him, but now he felt the weight of the last few years resting on his shoulders. Where just a few moments ago he felt seen and exposed, now he felt a kindred touch; he felt like he had an ally in the world. In realizing that he did not need to go through all of this alone after all, he felt silly and somehow betrayed. But now that he had someone to talk to, he reasoned, maybe it would be best not to dwell on the past.

"It's best not to dwell on the past, Barnibus. I'm here now to help you."

"What happened? To you, I mean."

"You mean tonight?"

"No, we'll get to that. What didn't my mother tell me?"

"Okay, we'll get right into it, then," Uncle Ted heaved a heavy sigh. "It came up when I was a little older than you are now. I was probably just getting into my teenage years at that time, but a lot of the timeline here kind of blurs together." He crossed the room, lost in thought, pacing mindlessly in the same way that Barnibus recognized in himself. "Like the flip of a switch one day," he snapped, "suddenly this was my life. At first, I'd wake up every morning, mind racing a mile a minute, and I would just struggle to hold on — literally, holding on to whatever was near me to feel grounded and keep some semblance of reason or of reality. But before long I figured out I could avoid that awful feeling if I... if I just didn't wake up. So, then, that was my life for a while. I slept. I slept as often as I could. I stopped going to school for a while until your grandparents put an end to that. Then I'd drone through school everyday trying to keep myself willfully disengaged from everyone around me until it was time to come home. Then I'd get home and get right back to sleep. I wasn't eating, and I wasn't talking to anyone. But at least I could keep my thoughts quiet and didn't need to deal with all the noise."

"But the dreams..." Barnibus began.

"The dreams weren't the problem. A dream is like a movie; it's something that is shown to you, and you just lie there and watch with no active participation. Dreams only have power if you wake up and decide to give it to them. There is a world of difference between what your subconscious cooks up while you sleep versus what you think up yourself while you're up and walking around."

"Oh..." Barnibus tried to hide his embarrassment.

"What's the matter, my dear boy?"

"Well, I—a few months ago, I went out one night after everyone else had gone to sleep."

"Oh yeah," Uncle Ted chuckled, "I did that back when I was your age. Such a thrill. So freeing."

"Right. But, see, I went out and I found the farthest place I could... and I..." Barnibus trailed off, but he knew he did not want to disappoint Uncle Ted, who was sharing with him such a stark look into his internal life. "This is going to sound stupid."

"Don't worry about that. Please go ahead."

"I went out that night, and I found the farthest away I could get, and I buried my dreams."

"You buried your dreams," Uncle Ted repeated flatly.

"Right."

"So... Right now, you have no dreams."

"Precisely, yes."

"Oh, Barnibus," Uncle Ted sighed as he leaned against the countertop, taking a rest to process this revelation.

"All I knew was that my imagination was doing... whatever it does—"

"Changes the world," Uncle Ted interjected, frustrated.

"Right..." Barnibus did not know what to make of that, but he made note of it. "My imagination was the problem, and my imagination is most active with my dreams, so I figured..."

"Enough," Uncle Ted cut him off coldly. "I understand." And then silence. Barnibus believed them both to be on the same page now, but without knowing where to go next, he waited for Uncle Ted to make the next move. They sat for a couple of minutes, avoiding each other's gaze while each of them thought. "Well, you'll have to go get them back," Uncle

Ted cut back in.

"Get them back? How is that going to work?"

"You got rid of them, right? It stands to reason that you'll be able to get those things back again, doesn't it?"

"They're buried out there, and I'm not even sure that I know where..."

"You found your way there once before. I'm sure you'll be able to do it again." There was no longer a jovial tone in Uncle Ted's voice. Barnibus was struck by how flat and prescriptive his uncle had become. He could tell that what he had done was a mistake, and he knew that mistake was, for whatever reason, disappointing, but he did not understand why. And one of the few things that Barnibus detested more than feeling unsafe was the feeling of being misunderstood. It made him feel unintelligent, and he knew himself to be anything but that. And as he milled this all over in his head, he grew more frustrated, both at the situation at hand and more specifically with his uncle.

"It's not that simple," Barnibus heard his voice rising as he spoke. "You're saying that like I can just walk out there and undo what I did. I can't! And I don't want to!" Barnibus did not believe himself, and as such, he knew that his uncle more than likely did not believe him either. But he had already begun, and that made him feel like he needed to keep going. "And just because you ran away from your problems by sleeping the day away doesn't mean that's the only way through this. That's pathetic. Maybe your dreams were an escape for you, I don't know, but they're not that for me, okay? We're not the same person, and I'm not going to pretend like we are."

"Barnibus, I'm hardly saying we're the same pers—"

"Saga and I came to you asking for help! And what exactly

have you done to help us? My brother is *gone*; our house is *destroyed*. And we're no closer to finding our parents than we were when we first even found out they were missing. What a big help you've been!" Barnibus turned away from Uncle Ted, determined not to let him see the tears welling in his eyes, not to let him see how unsure he was about his impassioned speech. "I'm going to my room. You can head back out the way you came."

"Barnibus, you're a child. I can't just leave you at home by yourself," he turned to gesture at the mess all around them, "look at what happened when you were here fending for yourself."

"Then the couch should be comfortable enough for you to get some rest," he said as he crossed quickly to the hallway. "Goodnight."

* * *

In his bedroom, Barnibus wondered how much of his life he had spent pacing, either as a function of time, e.g., number of total hours, or as a percentage of the time he had spent thus far on earth. Percentage to him felt more impactful, as a number of hours would by itself be unimpressive until compared to the total hours overall. And by that point, you would stare down the barrel of a percentage anyway, so you might as well just finish the job.

He paced when he worried, and Barnibus often worried. Recently, he had taken to pacing when he wanted to keep his mind clear, having found quite by accident that the rhythmic stepping and the unchanging environment were quite thera-peutic and lent a certain Zen quality to any situation.

Who does he think he is? He spat to himself. *He's in my house acting like he's my father. He doesn't know what's best for me. He doesn't know how to raise children — how could he! He doesn't have any kids of his own, so he needs to stop trying to bully his way into our family. Or better yet—* he stopped himself. Uncle Ted was family. Why was Barnibus in his room trying to make the case to himself that he somehow is not? He needed to get to sleep. The problem was rest, or rather the severe lack thereof, and that was something that he could control, at least to a certain degree, and at least right now. But no matter how loudly he thought that to himself, he just kept on pacing. He had too much energy left to burn, and before he knew it, it was already nearing one o'clock in the morning. As he turned for what must have been his thousandth lap around the middle of his room, he heard footsteps coming from the hallway. At first, the footsteps were to be greeted with a sneer. But as he grabbed sternly onto the doorknob and ripped the door open, the anger melted from behind his eyes. Stopping in the middle of the hallway with a start, having not expected anyone to be awake at this hour, was Saga.

"You're back!" Barnibus declared in what could be described as 'hostile whispering'.

"I just need to get some rest, Barnibus," Saga said as he walked again. "I'm going to my room."

"Are you okay?"

"I just need some rest." Saga said flatly.

"What happened? " Where—where did you go?" Barnibus realized he had so many questions that teetered on the edge of embarrassing.

"We'll talk more in the morning, Barnibus," Saga said as he pulled his bedroom door shut behind him. With his exit seemed to exit the life from the hallway. Barnibus had scarcely noticed it before, but without his brother he felt somehow incomplete. It took his brother disappearing into the ether for him to notice how badly, at a fundamental level, he needed his brother in order to feel complete. He always knew that he loved him, naturally, as any boy would feel a deep connection with their brother. He wondered now if Saga felt the same way, and based on their brief, curt interaction, he felt a twinge of sadness as he imagined the answer to his question. He shook loose the idea, knowing he could follow up, unsubtly as he would, in the morning. 'The morning brings a clearer mind,' their mother always said. Better to leave this until the morning.

The morning, Barnibus thought. *It's practically morning already.* He closed the door to his bedroom and continued pacing for a moment before his bag caught his eye. He did not know what was going on — with his family, with the town, with that strange Purple Man — but he felt reasonably confident that both he and Saga would play pivotal roles. The Purple Man had singled out, targeted, and even hunted him and his brother for a reason. He felt his breath shorten for a moment before his mind moved backwards towards the conversation he had with his uncle. *Maybe Uncle Ted has a point,* he thought to himself. *Maybe in order to be the best version of myself, I need to be all of me.* Barnibus felt an icy chill echo through his chest at the thought of what this implied.

13

A SHORT REST

Barnibus once again packed his things. A boy of his age had very few things that he could call entirely his own, but given that scarcity, every single thing he owned or took possession of as a hand-me-down carried with it immense importance to the young man. Barnibus had not long referred to himself as a 'young man,' as he felt it was incongruously formal and conveyed a degree of learnedness that he was not confident he could mirror. But as he grew older, and he tried to distance himself from the vices of boyhood, he felt it vital to act the part he would like, not the part he was currently playing. "Fake it 'til you make it," Carol liked to muse, before thinking better of it and appending "But don't lie" to the end of her platitude.

Into his bag went a journal, along with a blank back-up journal for when the first one was full. He packed a flashlight, a water bottle, a fresh undershirt, a book of jokes that his father had bought for him and attempted to pass off as a gift from his then-two-year-old brother Saga, a small zip-lock baggie of low-sodium granola, three pens — two black, one blue — a military-issue folding entrenching tool that had belonged to his grandfather, and an old glass Gerber jar full of tacks. He was not immediately sure what his plan was with the tacks, or why he felt compelled to pack them into his makeshift bugout bag, but something somewhere in the back of his mind signaled to him that they were a necessity. He wrapped the jar tightly in his spare undershirt to help mute the jar's jingle and — hopefully, if he wrapped it properly — jangle. Once he was confident of having silenced the tacks at least for the time-being, he wedged them into his bag, and he was ready to go.

Tiptoeing down the hall, he worried he might wake his brother. They had been through enough, and the last two things that Saga needed were to be woken up in the middle of the night when he should be getting much-needed rest, and to awaken in the middle of the night to find his older brother abandoning him for what would amount to the second time in 24 hours. Barnibus tried as best as he could to shake his head free from that worry, and the returning worry about whether their bond had been irreparably damaged by his own... whatever that was. The word *banishment* entered his mind, but was quickly forced out. But this time, he reasoned, he was not abandoning his brother. He was simply absconding in the middle of the night to run a clandestine errand under the cover of darkness. That is fundamentally not the same thing; therefore, his brother could not possibly be offended or otherwise hurt by such a discovery. Nevertheless, Barnibus crept carefully and slowly past Saga's door. If he could avoid another confrontation, he would love to.

Once outside, he breathed a little easier and a little deeper. There was always something about fresh night air that Barnibus was careful not to take for granted. The crisp bite as it filled his lungs made him feel light and free, refreshed, baptized by the moon while the sun got some rest on the other side of the planet. His mind cleared, and while he could not be certain that it would not fill with noise once again — and soon — he could at least enjoy the quiet for now. It would be some time, he hoped, because his imagination caught up with him on their walk, and longer still, he hoped even more, before the Purple Man returned.

It was spring. Late enough in the season that the days were warm and the nights were temperate. Weeds and grass had grown and been removed, and grown, and removed once more. Plenty of their neighbors had resewn their gardens, and in any other year the Jones household would be no exception. As he trudged along, he surveyed the yards that he passed. Mint, tomato, blackberries — he could not help but feel envious of his neighbors and their green thumbs. He hoped for them a respectable bounty come harvest time. The ground creaked and crunched under his boots. It was remarkable, he mused quietly to himself, how similar the crunching sounded to dredging through the snow. Crunch, crunch, crunch. The more he thought about it, the more his chest burned from the near-freezing air. *It's simply too cold out here! I should have brought a jacket, or a sweater or two,* he thought as he crossed his arms to rub his shoulders. In less than a moment's time, he felt all but ridiculous. He knew it was not cold, and the ground he trekked on was not snowy at all. And just as soon as the crunching ceased, so too did his chills and the burning in his lungs. He had allowed himself to get reckless with his imagination, and even in moments like this where he was completely alone, he could get himself into real trouble if left unchecked. He counted his steps to quiet his mind. He knew acutely that his grasp on his mind was tenuous at best. He wondered for a few paces how he could quantify the strength of the grip he held on his mind, when by definition that meant the mind evaluating itself. And in that case, would not the mind choose to overstate or understate the conclusion of such an evaluation, depending on which put the mind in a more advantageous position? It was akin to self-sabotage, Barnibus reasoned, to trust the mind's evaluation of itself, similar to how you cannot truly trust an assessment of oneself as being truly objective. Of course, it stood to reason that his mind generating the doubt of whether it could be trusted was itself also indicative of its objectivity. This was not for Barnibus to decide, at least not now. He would circle back to this another time, when it was quiet again.

Quiet. Barnibus could scarcely remember the last time he had felt truly quiet. Quiet of the mind, quiet around him, quiet in his soul. Even before all of this, with his parents, with the Purple Man, everything going on with Saga — it had been some time since he felt himself quiet. If it was not one worry, it was another. His mind could not help but race, no matter what safeguards he put in place. Even so many nights ago, when he decided to rid himself of dreams entirely, he was a fool to believe that would be the solution. He knew that, though he did not want to admit it to himself.

He retraced his steps. From his home to the farthest edge of the world, determined to retrieve his dreams. Or return his dreams to himself, depending on how you viewed the directionality. Barnibus was not sure who belonged to whom, but he knew that in order to get out of this, he needed his dreams, and that meant he was the one to retrieve them. Just as he owned the decision to rid himself of his dreams, it was his decision, now, to undo that mess. It was for the best, he knew, to bury his dreams where they could hurt no one, where he could hurt no one. But as push has come classically to shove, someone needed to get hurt. Barnibus prayed — at least he thought this is what prayer was — that it would not need to come to that, but he knew reality meant that was very unlikely to be the case. Maybe that was just Saga rubbing off on him, skewing his world view to that of his brother's, seeing through the darkness of the world and seeing it for what it is: a world of violence, a world of putrid forgotten people powering through life at the expense of better souls.

Just over two hours later, he arrived at the spot. He hoped. He could not be sure until he started digging. He found himself rooted at his feet when he realized he had not the foggiest idea where he was meant to dig. He had tricked himself, and for that he could not help but give himself a pat on the back. So he slipped the folding entrenchment tool from his backpack and extended the handle softly, wrapping his hand around the deploying hinge to muffle its mechanical locking stage. He paid no mind to how loud the digging itself would be, but shuddered at the idea that someone — anyone! — could hear him preparing to dig. Something about being caught in preparation felt too intimate. Too exposed.

He began once again to move the earth. Piece by piece, shovel by shovel, he removed loads of dirt and clay, probing for the cache he had left here — somewhere around here — not too long ago. He'd know it when he felt it, when his spade struck the proverbial pay dirt, but for the first couple of hours, he felt nothing. Sweat dripped heavily from his brow, wetting the soil beneath him as he dug. He hoped that eventually, if he were to sweat enough, the newly loosened dirt would melt away a bit easier, and he could pull away a great amount of ground cover with a minimal amount of effort, but he found himself with no such luck.

Before long, he took himself a short rest. He found a small patch of undisturbed land wide enough to house both himself and a small fire. He gathered tinder from the nearby treeline and, striking a rock against the backside of his entrenching tool to send a spark into the dry timber, created a fire of modest size. Nothing flashy. He could not signal passing travelers with this setup, but it was enough to provide him with a reasonable degree of warmth. He plunged his hand into his baggie of low-sodium granola and waterfalled a hefty handful into his mouth, swallowing just about as quickly as his jaw could chew it. Before long, the baggie was emptied, his water bottle about to follow suit. Barnibus pushed his backpack out and, using it as a lumpy pillow, laid himself down for a quick nap. He could pull a lean thirty minutes without costing himself too much working nightfall. As he assured himself that he would wake up in adequate time, he fell fast asleep.

* * *

He awoke to find that a nearby tree had fallen. Not recently, he was sure that he would have been awakened by that. This tree had fallen some time ago. Long enough, in fact, that nearby plant life had grown around it. Barnibus shot up from his makeshift campsite. His fire was long extinguished. He surveyed his surroundings. It was still night out, but his fire had burned to ashes. He hovered his hand over the grey pile. No heat. He moved it still closer, but even within inches of the ash, he felt no heat. *How long have I been asleep?* He panicked as his eyes darted around for clues, but there was nothing around to show what time — or what day! — it was now.

"Fantastic. I was beginning to think you would never wake up! Do you have any idea how worried I've been?"

The Purple Man. Barnibus knew that voice, as did the hairs on the back of his neck, standing ready at attention now. But where? There are no tracks in the dirt around him, and though it's dark now, his silhouette would be certain to leave its mark on the horizon if he were somewhere in the treeline.

"You really need to take more magnesium. It's terrible for your digestive tract, but it does wonders to help your body regulate energy. I think it'll really help keep you from keeling over for these '*naps*' of yours."

He's not here to talk, Barnibus thought; *he's just here to taunt me. Don't let him in. If he were here to hurt me, he would have done it when I was asleep.*

"I'm here to hurt you," the Purple Man offered flatly. Barnibus froze. "Oh, not really. Could you imagine? How lazy would that be?" As Barnibus turned in circles trying to find his scene partner, the Purple Man stepped out from behind a tree directly in front of Barnibus, making no effort to obscure his location or sneak up.

Why does this seem so easy? What is he not telling me?

"I just thought, you know, enough is enough. This whole back-and-forth thing we have going on — it's getting to be a bit... pedestrian. It occurs to me that I may be more interested in the theatrics of this whole ordeal than I am in the final act. So I figured I would just cut out the nonsense and just do some good old-fashioned stalking. Okay?"

"Stay back," Barnibus cautioned.

"That's not a line that often works on stalkers, but boy, do I respect your willingness to try it. I do." He took a long stride towards Barnibus. "But I'm afraid I can't do that. You have something that I want, and I followed you out here for it and have been waiting behind that blessed tree for *hours* waiting for you to dig it up. I was really hoping you would do most of the work for me. But then you just sort of laid down. On the ground. Like a dog. And left me just standing there with nothing to do. Which is, frankly, pretty rude. No offense. Well, actually, offense. I mean that."

This is exhausting, Barnibus thought to himself. *He must get tired at some point, right?*

"I'll never tire of our back and forth, you know that? There's something magical about our patter. You lob one of your zingers at me, and then I lob another one right back. Maybe one of us follows the other one into the woods. It's like a beautiful fairy tale! Go ahead. Hit me with one of your classic zingers. Let's get this going!"

"What do you want?"

"That's the worst zinger I've ever heard. It's not even — frankly — good dialogue. People don't just ask each other pointed questions. You have needs; you have desires. You're here for something — just like me — so stop this whole bumbling kid act. It's an *act.* Stop *acting.* Your performance is terrible."

"Stop."

"Better, closer. But I don't feel you really *believe* it. Again! From your gut! Show me some emotion!"

"Just stop talking!" Barnibus erupted. He clenched his fists tightly, his arms rigid against his sides, his gaze fixed squarely on the Purple Man. He could feel like upper lip curling into a snarl, and the more aware of his physicality he was, the more he felt himself as a cornered dog, bubbling over with instinctual violence. He tried to focus his energy on interpreting what he was feeling, trying to figure out his next move, but no matter what he tried, he could only see the Purple Man. Inside himself was blank, not operating off logic or reason. "That's enough. I'm sick of this. You show up and you monologue these... these inane ramblings that don't make any sense. You try to act like you're, I don't know, like you're trying to help us or something, but everything you do just gets in the way, or just makes things worse. I don't know what you're after or why it involves my brother and me, but I'm sick of this."

The Purple Man stood up straight, with a height and air about him that Barnibus was unsure he had ever seen before. *Has he been hunched over this entire time? When did he get so tall?* An air of dignity surrounded him now, turning the Purple Man from a jester to a king with the flip of a switch. The immediacy and magnitude of the shift made Barnibus uneasy, but he did not have the time to process what was happening.

"There he is. That's the boy I knew was in there somewhere."

Barnibus shifted uncomfortably. He could feel the caged dog beginning to wince, and he tried what he could not to wither.

"Let's drop the stories," the Purple Man continued. "You know exactly what I want from you, and why that involves you and your brother. Don't pretend. Pretending is for babies, and you," he pointed accusingly at Barnibus, "you're much more than a baby. You're hardly even a kid." He chuckled lightly to himself. "You have no idea how much of a force you truly are."

He circled Barnibus in a broad arc. Barnibus turned slowly to make sure the Purple Man always stayed in front of him, eager not to give him an opportunity to catch him off guard.

"I know exactly who I am," Barnibus countered, "so don't make me show you."

"Oh! Oh, *don't make me show you,*" the Purple Man mocked. "I'd love to see what you think you mean by that. Really, I would. Tsk tsk tsk. But you know, if I'm being honest, I don't even think you know what you mean. And that's disappointing."

"Stay back…"

"I'll stay wherever I'm going to be, and you will not be the one to stop me. Do you understand?"

A branch snapped free from high atop an evergreen at the tree line to Barnibus' rear. A widow-maker. Barnibus spun around to see, taking a step away from the noise as the branch landed nearby with a heavy thud. He turned back around to find the Purple Man, but for a moment, he could not track him.

"Mr. Jones, I do believe I'll be taking that now, thank you," the Purple Man called from the other side of the clearing. Barnibus was surprised to see the Purple Man had put a significant amount of space between them. He had expected him to close the gap, to seize the opportunity to pounce while Barnibus was distracted. "Oh, I'm sorry; maybe that was a little unclear. It would probably be best for you to come here for a moment."

Barnibus felt his feet drag along the ground, as if he was sliding downhill on unsure footing. He shuffled and stomped to stop himself, but the more he struggled, the faster he seemed to move. The faster he moved straight toward the Purple Man and his smug smile of accomplishment. With one last thrust, he found himself standing mere feet away from the Purple Man, with only a medium-sized boulder between them. The Purple Man pointed downward.

"This is the place, by the way. You made a splendid effort with how many silly, pointless holes you dug all night, but what you're looking for — what *we're* looking for — can be found right here, below this medium-sized boulder."

Barnibus stared at the Purple Man, frozen. The muscles in his neck strained to keep from looking down. He wanted to look so badly. To reach down and snatch it up. If he made a run for it he could probably make it to the tree line before the Purple Man could catch up. Once he's in the woods, he will hide, or evade his pursuit, or something. Anything. There must be something he could do to get out of here. But without his dreams, he was just a kid of average height, who could run at average speed, and would be unlikely to make it back to his average home alive. Finally defeated, he looked down at the boulder, down past the rock and the dirt, down to where he had buried his dreams not so long ago.

"Now get back to work," the Purple Man snarled, venom practically firing out of his mouth with such violence and finality that Barnibus leapt backwards to safety.

And then Barnibus awoke, his lumpy bag under his head, and his modest campfire crackling away in front of him. Slowly he arose as he looked around the clearing with caution, but saw not a soul and heard nothing beyond the gentle breeze rustling the trees and the crackling sizzle of his fire. He was alone. Looking across the clearing, and among the smattering of started and aborted holes he had dug earlier in the night, he saw the same medium-sized boulder, hardly a stone's throw away.

Now it was time to dig once again. Because for the first time in a long time, Barnibus Jones had dreamed.

14

BEFORE, BUT NOT TOO LONG

"This place is a sty," Carol cut in through the din of the boys playing, a trail of toys and paper and garbage and clothes and various other child ephemera spilling out of both their rooms, down the hallway and into the living room. "Stop what you're doing and clean this up! This is too much." She had a way of grinding fun to a halt, but neither Barnibus nor Saga held it against her or viewed it as anything other than '*Mom*'. That is just how she has always been. That's Mom.

"We just need to get to the summit! Just a little farther," Saga called out to his brother, a means of pleading with their mother for just a little more time.

"Get to it," she said plainly, momly, as she made her way through the hallway furtively, onto the next task on her list. She was everywhere and nowhere, Carol, and as far as Barnibus could tell, always had something she needed to tend to. She ran this house; there was no question about that. Everything was under her exacting vision; all assignments and responsibilities ran through her, and if anything was done not to her standards, she would not shy away from letting you know. But again, that's just *Mom.* It is the only life the boys have ever known, and while it may be at times stressful — or as Saga had been so bold to venture a description: annoying — it was by no means bad or anything that would rise to the varied definitions of an unhappy home. But it was suffocating. And that suffocation kept the Jones brothers from feeling they had their own identities; their own thoughts. The boys, including Barnibus Sr., felt incredible love in their family and felt deeply cared for and protective. But at the same time felt the unmistakable feeling of being under thumb. Exacting detail. That is just how Carol expressed her love. And that exacting, prescriptive love enveloped Saga more than anyone else.

On paper, or to the casual outside observer, Carol and Barnibus Sr. were not ones to play favorites. Both boys were impeccably dressed, tended to, and fed. They were each enrolled in their respective enrichment programs, and each could lay claim to their own robust bedtime routine, full of plenty of affection and solo parent time. But there was a warmth that Barnibus keyed into shortly after Saga had arrived. He did not know what it was he was sensing at first. He was too young to put a name to it, and caught up in the hurricane of activity of a new sibling, suddenly finding himself no longer an only child, he was only acutely aware of it for the first few years. Around the time Saga turned four, Barnibus Sr. took the boys to the park. Two boys; both of his sons. When they returned from the park, Carol was surprised to see only one of her sons return. Barnibus Sr. had left Saga at the park, a minor detail to which he remained blind until Carol quite emphatically (and loudly) brought it to his attention a few steps inside the front door.

"Are you out of your mind!?" Carol hollered from the driver's seat as she raced back down to the park, as Barnibus Sr. had been relegated to the back seat.

Barnibus always recalled his mother weaving deftly in and out of traffic as she raced to rescue her youngest child, but the fact of the matter is that the park was merely two blocks from their family home, and the suburban streets lacked even parked cars, let alone traffic. They arrived back at the park within three minutes of the two Barnibuses — young and old — having left, Saga blissfully unaware that he had been playing solo at the park for less time than it would take to listen to *Saturday in the Park* by almost a full minute. Carol threw the car into the parking spot closest to the access ramp to the park, and as she tore out of the driver's seat (the only time Barnibus could recall his mother so boldly avoiding the seatbelt of which she was such a strong proponent) Barnibus noticed how quickly her demeanor changed. He had expected his mother to charge, hysterical, over to his little brother, swoop him up in her arms, make a scene of the whole thing — a family reunited, a child saved from the cusp of danger. Instead, Carol so effortlessly dropped any pretense of worry or stress, approaching Saga with the calm of a mother who had just returned from the restroom, or maybe having been talking to a former coworker at the grocer. She scooped Saga up from the sandbox, lightly dusted his donuts-and-croissants pajama bottoms, and strolled back over to the car to buckle him in, lightly cooing affirmations into his ear like everything was totally normal. Barnibus expected a show of protection, something performative in its explosiveness. He had seen that type of thing before from other parents. A big show to make up for whatever perceived misstep a father or mother is hoping to correct. What he found instead was something deeper, something more meaningful in the long-run, and something he grew to expect and admire about his mother: calming comfort. Looking back, he understood the change in her demeanor as having sought to protect Saga from the fear that she had felt at that moment. He did not need that stress, the narrative of danger that she had spun in her head, or need to grapple with the hypotheticals of what could happen to a child left unattended in public. Barnibus understood wanting to protect Saga from such darkness, because he found himself with the same instinct towards his brother as they grew up together. He recognized the beauty of this. But, in seeing that beauty, he also saw that the same all-encompassing, everything-is-okay blanket was not one that he often saw himself wrapped in. On that Saturday morning at the park, he had expected to see an explosion of emotions from his mother because that was what he had always gotten — and would continue to get — from his mother.

"Dinner is in fifteen minutes, and I swear if this place isn't spotless by then, you can eat cold pot pie over the sink." Carol loved to give these hollow consequences. Somewhere between a carrot and a stick, this type of consequence or punishment was dangled in front of them but was rarely, if ever, actually realized. Carol wanted to instill a sense of responsibility in them, considering nothing in life to be more valuable than a person's word, but did not have the heart to give them a cold dinner, or to take away that book that they are so engrossed in. She was aware of the irony as a parent of stressing the importance of doing what you say you will do, while herself not following through with the punishments she so emphatically declared imminent. The boys were aware of this too, as the household remained in balance so long as everyone understood how this system worked. She would make her declaration; the boys would interpret it more as it was meant, as a statement exemplifying how important a task or misstep was, and they would play their part and do what they had been asked. No reason to poke that teddy bear, Barnibus and Saga both figured.

Fifteen minutes later, nearly down to the second, the family gathered around the dining table, a golden-brown, perfectly filled pot pie displayed before them. Barnibus Sr. took the lead on dishing everyone's plates, the two young boys loading up on shockingly large portions given their own bodily proportions. Barnibus always liked when the family sat together for dinner (as they did more often than not), because it made the family feel whole, like a unit. Carol drove the dinner conversation, the same as she drove everything else in their lives. She had a way of keeping everyone on topic without it seeming too regimented, despite it in fact being very regimented. They will discuss their school days first, then check in on the business of the butchery, then onto the state of the house. Carol worked from home in an industry that Barnibus did not understand, a subject in which he could not gain better insight, as Carol, as a rule, refused to discuss her work with the family. Mostly the topic went unaddressed, but on the few occasions the subject was pushed, or the questions became more pointed, her demeanor would become cagey and evasive. Barnibus never understood why.

"I heard there was a fight down at the school today," Carol offered casually. "Do you boys know anything about that?"

Saga glanced over at Barnibus, hoping to take his lead. Barnibus gave nothing. Saga turned back to their mother, and now they were locking eyes.

"We saw something on our way out of school, yeah. I didn't know it was a fight, though…"

"Did you see who started it?" She had a tendency to ask questions she knew the answer to, like a skilled attorney. *Maybe she is an attorney?*

"Saga didn't do anything," Barnibus cut in.

"It's okay," Carol said, raising one finger to Barnibus, suspending him from the conversation.

"I was just walking by; I don't know how it started," Saga gulped.

"It's okay if you saw something you shouldn't have. You were just walking by, right?"

"Mark and Paul were going at it around the side of the gym," Saga spilled as he lowered his head to avoid his mother, "but I don't know what about." He glanced up to Barnibus, who shook his head lightly, cautioning his brother in how he proceeded.

"It's interesting that Mark and Paul would fight. I thought those two were fast friends." Carol moved forward with eating, giving her approach a casual air that both brothers found disconcerting. "Must have been something pretty personal to get between them like that. That's a shame."

Saga pushed the food around on his plate; the weight of guilt making even hearty pot pie unappealing.

"I told Paul that Mark had a crush on Kath," Saga said quietly.

"Did Mark tell you that?"

"No."

"So you just made up a rumor? For fun?"

"I didn't make it up."

"So Kath told you? Is it Kath or Kathleen?"

"Kath didn't tell me, but I didn't make it up."

"Hm," Carol mulled. "Mark didn't tell you, and nei*ther* did

Kath…"

Barnibus, well outside of his mother's laser focus, kept his eyes squarely fixed on her. He knew exactly how Saga knew what he knew, and was certain that he made nothing up. There were few things that Saga cared less for than rumors or gossip. And while his little brother did not traffic in lying or spinning yarns, Barnibus was lost as to what made Saga tell Paul what he knew.

"Knowledge is power. That power can be used for good, or it could be used as a weapon," Carol preached. "There is a responsibility in knowledge, Saga, and I expect you to exercise better judgement in how you wield it."

Here held the usual weight in the room when Carol's micro-sermons would come crashing into whatever wonderful child-like mess they would find themselves in. It was a regular, if not omnipresent, occurrence in their house, chalked up as yet another aspect of their lives with their parents that seemed simply normal and par for the course. And the thing of it was, she dropped it. Just like every other time they found themselves on the receiving end of Carol's righteous, albeit gentle and well-intentioned, admonishment, that was simply the last that Saga or Barnibus heard on the matter. She never checked in about it again, and as far as the family dynamic was concerned, it was as if this minor transgression had never happened. Lesson taught, time to move on. Carol did not hold grudges.

15

A ROAD TRAVELED

One foot after the other. Barnibus needed to remind himself how to walk — the mechanics of it — as every action felt arduous and unnatural now. His mind raced in a way that it had not in weeks, and the weight of the last few days felt crushing. *Just keep moving,* he reminded himself, trying to stay focused and control what he could. Puffs of dirt rose around him as his feet, heavy as boulders, shuffled along the path. He was confident that he would find his way back to the main road within the next couple of minutes, but he knew that such confidence stemmed from a best guess and less from knowledge. He wanted to find the road since the road would provide him direction, something that he sorely needed.

Barnibus felt electric. Strong. He ran through his conversation with his uncle in his head, having been urged to retrieve his dreams, to better control them and to harness what Uncle Ted called a gift. Barnibus had fought the very idea of it so ardently, but now feeling the power and strength in his mind again, something that he was unaware had been missing until this moment, he could scarcely understand how he had let himself get to that point. But while the excitement of possibility filled him with hope and vigor, he could tell that his grasp was tenuous without better practice. *Just keep moving,* he reminded himself again. *Get to Uncle Ted and do exactly as he says. He knows how to handle this; just let him teach you.*

"You shouldn't put so much faith in Theo," Carol's voice gave Barnibus a start. He jumped back, surprised both to have a partner on this hike and for that partner to be his heretofore missing mother.

"Mom! You're back!" He wanted to reach out and hug her. To throw himself onto her and ask her to carry him home. To feel protected. But something made him think better of it as she continued staring straight ahead as they walked, hardly paying any mind to Barnibus.

"Theo walked out of our family years ago. You shouldn't lionize him as some sort of hero." Carol was the only person Barnibus knew of who called Uncle Ted '*Theo*'. Each time it confused him, as it always felt so unnatural to him, despite *Theodore* in fact being Uncle Ted's full name.

"He knows what he's doing. I've seen it. If I do what he says, I'll be able to do it too. I just need a little practice."

"If all it took was a little practice, do you think he would live in that mess of a house? Probably not."

Barnibus thought about that for a moment. It was not a bad point. Being able to do what he can, why wouldn't Uncle Ted spruce up his house, make it into the ideal home? Instead, he's prepping to sell.

"No," he began quietly to himself, "no, I've seen him do it. He says I can do what he can. He can show me."

Carol laughed pointedly, and it cut Barnibus deeply.

"You shouldn't be out here by yourself," Carol said. "It's

dangerous. You're just a kid."

"It's dangerous back in town," Barnibus added absently.

"Don't argue with me," Carol hissed. "Back in town, you're a kid, too. You shouldn't be running around like this by yourself; you could get hurt."

"I'm not just a kid. I know how to take care of myself." He did not want to argue with his mother, something that he never felt comfortable or confident doing. He was simply too exhausted now to stop himself.

"I've never seen you take care of yourself before," Carol sneered, almost to herself. "Doesn't look like you could take care of your brother, either."

"Mom..." Barnibus pleaded. Carol gave no response to the call, just kept walking. "What are you doing out here?" Barnibus asked.

"Walking, but you'll have to tell me where."

"We're going home," he mused, unsure. "How did you get here? Where's Dad?"

"He's safe," she said through gritted teeth. "You don't need to worry about him."

Barnibus breathed a sigh of relief. He felt safe, recognizing in his mother the instinct to protect her children from fear, seeing her step in to reassure him that as bad as things might seem, they would be okay. She was here now, and his dad was safe, and some weight lifted from his shoulders. He watched her now as they walked in silence. She moved effortlessly, nearly gliding over the terrain. Before long, he saw the main road peek over the horizon, and he estimated they would get to it within a matter of minutes. From there, it would be another hour or more before they arrived back at their house. *How is Mom going to react to seeing half her house destroyed? Has she already seen it? Does she know what happened to the shop yet?* Barnibus shuddered as fresh worries rushed to replace old, as he felt his mind racing once again.

"You lost your brother," Carol said flatly.

"He's home now."

"You're just like your father."

"He's safe."

Carol scoffed. It seemed like every other thing she said to Barnibus was mocking him, and that realization made him feel small.

"He's safe," he repeated, "and he'll be excited to see you again. All of us together, we'll be able to go get Dad," his voice droning on more for his benefit now than that of his mother, "no problem." He picked up the pace, practically within spitting distance of the main road. Like a runner nearing the end of a marathon, he was more carried by momentum than direct action. He felt in equal parts like a boulder careening down a hill, and a feather floating on an airstream. *Nearly there now. Just keep moving. Just get back home, and we can all figure this out. Together.*

"It's funny that your brother was the one to get lost," Carol began, a few paces behind Barnibus now. "I always thought he was the one who was more resilient — more street smart — out of the two of you."

Barnibus kept focused on the road, intent on not letting his mother's barbs get to him.

"Resilient isn't the right word, I guess. Resilience is coming back from behind. Picking yourself back up when you get knocked down. Getting hit and hitting back. That's resilience."

"Let's just keep walking. We can talk this all out when we're all home."

"Neither of you has any resilience then, if that's the definition that we're using." Her tone was more biting than normal, which made Barnibus wonder exactly what she and his father had gotten into while they were away. If it was anything close to what he had seen in the last couple of days, he could hardly blame her for having a less-than-stellar verbal filter. But filter or not, there was a bluntness to this that Barnibus was not used to hearing from his mother. He weighed his options in being upfront with her about that and calling it out, but he was so glad just to see her, to know that she is safe, that it did not seem worth it to press the issue. "Shame it wasn't you that man took." Barnibus stopped in his tracks, letting his mother pass by him on the narrow path, hardly breaking her stride to so much as glance at him. He watched her pass, dumbfounded, frantically searching for the words to follow up. A sharp breeze pulled through the trees, wresting up a smattering of dead leaves and giving rise to a calamity of snapping branches, rustling leaves. As quickly as it came, the breeze dropped. The heavy silence would envelop Barnibus if he were not so enrapt in what his mother had to say. *What did she know about the Purple Man?*

"What do you mean, 'that man took'? Who took him? Have you seen the Purple Man?"

"Who do you mean?" She stopped, annoyed, to turn back to Barnibus.

"The Purple Man. You said, 'Shame it wasn't you that man took.' Have you met the Purple Man? Is he behind all of this?"

"I don't know what you're going on about," she chuckled. "It sounds like maybe you need to get some sleep." She began walking again. Barnibus needed to catch his breath, and drama aside, this was a good chance to stop moving and let his heart and lungs catch up with his legs and brain. "We both know it was you who did your brother in like that."

"Mom," he pleaded as he walked again, nearly chasing after her now. He was surprised at how quickly he resorted to groveling, and just as fast he recomposed himself. "I didn't do anything to Saga; you know I would never hurt him! And besides, you said, 'that man'." He paused, expecting her to own up to what she had said, or to offer anything in the way of an explanation, but she just kept walking. "Mom, please tell me what's going on."

"You're just a confused little boy; that's what's going on. A confused little boy who is in over his head. You're lucky I'm here now, because when you were left to your own devices, you lost your baby brother. What if he didn't come back, Barnibus? Your dad and I were missing, and so you just *threw your little brother away.* You're weak, and I should have seen that sooner. I suppose this is partly my fault, then. Happy?"

Barnibus let her comments hang in the air, not letting anything sink in through sheer willpower. Carol spoke again, but only a low, weak growl came out. She coughed, lightly at first, then with more vigor, before humming an even tone and beginning to speak again.

"When we get home, you and your brother are spending the next month in your room. This is totally unacceptable, Barnibus. *You lost your brother?* You're supposed to protect him. He's precious. You know he's fragile. This world can be too much for him sometimes."

Barnibus scoffed.

"Too much for both of you. That's something, huh? It's too much for your brother, so you need to be around to protect him. But who is around to protect you?"

"That's what you and Dad are for..." Barnibus muttered quietly, barely audible above the crunch of loose dirt and leaves under their feet.

"You'd think that," Carol said, barely letting the words escape Barnibus' mouth before addressing them. "But then where were we today? Your father and I."

Barnibus stopped and turned to his mother. He waited there for a moment, just watching, allowing her time to finish her thought, to reach some kind of point or conclusion to her own question, before he realized that perhaps the question was not rhetorical. Maybe his mother really was *asking* him where she was that day.

"Where... where were you... Mom?" Barnibus said slowly, trying to build the question as it took off. But Carol just chuckled to herself and then walked again, edging past Barnibus on the narrow path. Barnibus let her get a dozen paces ahead of him before he renewed his trek towards the road — *that damn road*, Barnibus thought. *How have we not reached the road yet?* He shook sweat loose from his brow, trying to stop any more from dripping into his eyes — a sensation he had become strangely familiar with in the last couple of days. Barnibus watched his mother, now out of arm's reach, and wondered what she had gone through, and wondered if she had the same question of him. He wondered, as he watched her focused, mechanical walking, why she had not asked him more about the events that had happened while she was gone. Even if she was unaware of everything that had happened, even if their disappearance really was completely unrelated to what he had been through with The Purple Man, should not she be curious about what happened, anyway? They were abducted, or something, and she seems completely unfazed by it, either for her own safety or for the safety of her children. This confused Barnibus deeply, but he did not know how to put a name to that confusion, or even how to describe the specifics of what he was confused about. He tried a number of times to proffer a question, anything to kick-start a conversation about the day they had, but anything he tried to say sounded immediately juvenile and narrow-minded the moment he spoke. Finally, he opened the conversation with a heavy sigh, how he had heard both of his parents do so many times before when they would talk at the end of a challenging workday. "Oh man," he began, "it has been a *day*." He let that juicy teaser hang in the air for a moment, expecting his mother to latch onto it the way that adults so often latch onto tasty morsels of complaints and gossip. But after a couple of moments, it became clear that Carol would not engage. She fundamentally, as far as Barnibus could tell, did not care about the minutiae of her children and her brother being taken captive by a man who travels by a magical train and dresses in a, frankly, irresponsible amount of purple. That was too pedestrian for Carol.

Barnibus soon had a new question in his head, which took some work to put together into an actual thought. The more he built onto it, and the more he tried to characterize what it was he was noticing, the farther away from the thought he felt. As it came into more focus, it just begat more questions, or more worry, or more... something. He could not tell what it was making him feel (having a hard time focusing on feelings now as his mind's races took up more of his energy and mental capacity). In time, he found the words to ask the question he wanted to ask, at least of himself: *Why don't I feel safe right now? Why don't I feel safe with my mother here with me?* As his eyes shifted from the back of Carol's head out to the main road — which he was supremely confident now they were not getting physically any closer to — he reached a conclusion that bothered him more than the questions it sought to answer.

This is not my mother.

The thought landed with a nearly audible thud in his mind. As soon as he put words to the thought, he felt himself a fool. *Why didn't I notice this sooner? How long have I been walking with this... thing... and not realizing something was wrong? What if I had trusted them? What if I had told myself to just look past it and move on? What if I—* he stopped himself short, noticing his mind carrying on much faster than his mouth — or his feet — possibly could. Worrying about it would not help him. Thinking the same questions and admonishments over and over would not make anything different. The only thing he needed to do now was to figure out who — or what — he had been talking to for the last few minutes, and figure out how to get away from it. He wanted badly not to let on that he knew something was amiss, but he knew he was not clever enough to weasel his way out of this unscathed.

"Hey," he began, as naturally as he could muster, "do you think we're ever going to get to the road? This is taking forever."

It kept walking.

"My legs are killing me. I feel like I've been walking for days. I could really use a rest."

"Stop over on that stump over there and rest your legs for a minute." It pointed to a decaying stump laid deep in the mud a few paces off the path. It did not break their stride and indeed did not pay particular mind to the stump itself. It stopped walking just as Barnibus did, and although they had both stopped and were now standing practically right next to each other, it did not bother looking at Barnibus. It stared, its eyes fixed in the middle distance, into the tree line.

"Yeah... yeah, maybe that's a good idea." He walked over to the stump, keeping his head canted slightly to watch this imposter over his shoulder. "Why don't you go on ahead and check out the road? I'll be right behind you. I just need a minute."

"I'll be right here," it said blankly, once again hardly letting Barnibus finish the thought before offering a retort.

"I'll be fine, really," he stammered. "It'll just be a minute, and I—I'm all out of breath anyway, so I won't be one for conversation." With that, it occurred to him that this person — this aberration — was not even remotely winded and seemed entirely at rest despite their trek through the woods. He reached the stump and quickly surveyed the area immediately around it. He was unsure of what he was looking for. Maybe a stick he could swing to defend himself, or maybe a rock of respectable heft, good for a strong offense. But as he arrived and lowered himself onto the stump, honestly relieved to get off of his feet, he saw nothing but fallen leaves and some well-decayed brush scattered about. Nothing worthwhile in the way of weaponry. Typical.

Barnibus knew what to expect, but he still could not help himself and gave in to the urge to look up toward the main road. It was just as far now as it had been when he began his journey. The burning in his legs and lungs betrayed how long he had in fact traveled, but he could not fathom an explanation for the delta between how he felt and what he saw. His breath was getting away from him now, and for a moment he could not help but feel amused that what had begun as a ruse to buy him time to escape his would-be attacker was now proving to be quite a valuable rest. He appreciated the opportunity to catch his breath, and as he watched Not-Carol paying him no mind, he felt the mental struggle between the growing sensation of a deepening Uncanny Valley, and the fact that was coming into focus in the back of his mind that he did not feel inherently *unsafe* with this person. He felt he could not *trust* them, but he did not feel in *danger,* nor that they meant to do him harm. While this realization should bring him comfort, he thought, it only raised more questions. Questions to which he did not know the answer. *Who is this person,* sure, but also, *why don't I feel like I'm in danger?*

"You don't want to sit?" Barnibus asked. "It's kinda looking like we're going to be at this for a while."

"Rest, sweetie. Mommy can keep watch."

Barnibus could not think of the last time anyone, not him, not Saga, had called his mother 'Mommy'. Saga had really never been big on what he called "parentaphilic rhetoric". Barnibus was at one time very close with his mother, following her wherever she went, up and down the hall of their house, into the bathroom, the garage, out to the store, everywhere. He called her 'Mommy' well into elementary school, and while that was something that he gave up nearing his enrollment in middle school, it was never something that Carol herself had reciprocated. She called herself Mom, and even that felt, at best, perfunctory.

"Mommy," Barnibus dared, "could you come sit with me, please?"

Not-Carol turned and looked at Barnibus sweetly. As it opened its mouth to speak, a twig snapped nearby, and they both turned with a whip to see if someone was approaching. The coast was clear. Barnibus turned back and found Not-Carol was gone, no longer standing on the path, no longer surveying the tree line. He sighed heavily, relieved, but also immediately reminded of how alone he felt.

"What is it you need, Barnibus?" Not-Carol said in a gentle, quiet tone. Barnibus turned with a start to find Not-Carol sitting directly next to him on the stump, their eyes glued emphatically to him. Barnibus felt an embrace, though this person did not move, and he felt safety and care as he looked into what he understood to be hollow, empty eyes.

"I'm scared," he whispered, surprised to hear the words coming out of his mouth. "I don't know what to do or how to stop any of this. I've never felt this lost before, and I don't know if I'm going to be able to find my way again. I don't know what to do, Mommy." Tears welled in his eyes, spilling over and down his face just as quickly as they came. The dam had broken, and the rush of everything that had happened came crashing down on him — the fear of having lost Saga, his uncle, the Purple Man, his parents. A weight that he thought he had known seemed to quadruple in his heart here in the woods as he let the thoughts and the fear wash over him. There was a catharsis in what he was feeling now, and while he felt like he should fight it back — *I know better than this!* — there was simply too much for him to hold back, and he let it all pour out of him there in the woods. He told Not-Carol about what had happened with Saga, what the Purple Man had said to them when he tied them up in the house, and how sinister and determined his eyes were when he burned down the deli. Every single thing he saw and had hoped to keep buried boiled to the top of his mind. Just as quickly as the thoughts came, he blurted them out, sitting there on the stump with Not-Carol, sitting an arm's length away, but herself offering nothing in the way of comfort. There they sat bolt-straight while a child wept next to them. Before long, his torrent of emotion ceased, and the tremendous weight that had precipitated it retired into a dull tension, a black cloud that, while lofty, felt like a manageable companion. Barnibus caught his breath as he felt his mind relax, and his vision clear from tears. Not-Carol offered no guidance, no reassurance. There they sat for a moment before Barnibus broke the silence. "What do you think I should do?"

"Oh, I don't know," Not-Carol shrugged. "I can't tell you anything that you don't already know. So. I guess that's kind of it. You said it."

"What do you mean?" Barnibus asked as he wiped his arm across the underside of his nose. Not-Carol held their gaze as Barnibus suspected he saw a glint of sympathy.

"Barnibus," she offered. "You know."

Barnibus sniffled as he refused to look away from what he desperately wished was his mother. He knew. He did not want to, but he did. After a moment, he looked back up toward the road and saw that it was, at best, twenty yards away. Much closer now than when they had sat down. He got up, taking a moment to get his legs under him and taking a mental inventory of just how much his body ached. He walked a few steps over the brush and joined Not-Carol, who had somehow passed him without his noticing and was now waiting on the pathway.

"Just keep going," Not-Carol said. "Get back to the house, and you can work through this together."

Barnibus felt his throat catch, but he quickly squelched it. He would box that up to deal with it another time. He turned back to the tree stump now to see it missing. In its spot was just more brush, and the footprints he had left in the mud — just a single set — on his way there and back. The sun was breaking through the trees as it crept over the horizon to kick-start the day.

"Just keep going," he heard his mother say. When he turned, he found himself once again alone in the woods, with the main road just up ahead.

"Just keep going," Barnibus repeated to himself.

* * *

The rest of Barnibus' walk home was, mercifully, uneventful and solitary. He considered trying to conjure Not-Carol again, having found some retroactive comfort in having at least a facsimile of his mother there, within arm's reach. But try as he might, like flexing a muscle you have yet to train, as much as he strained, he saw no results. He noted, however, how empty the streets around his home were as he descended deeper into his neighborhood. Not that they were routinely bustling with activity, but a standard din of homestead activities and passing cars had been the norm, something he did not realize until it was gone. He wondered how many people had really been affected. How many of his friends might be missing their families as well, or how many families may be missing their children. The thought alone was enough to stop Barnibus in his tracks on more than one occasion, and as he paused and let his mind race, he would feel the ground beneath his feet tilt, his footing growing increasingly unsure, like a false door was bound to open at his feet and the earth would swallow him home. As the ground would shift and he would stumble from where he stood, he would snap back into reality, the ground would seem to right itself, and he would carry on. He decided after the second or third time experiencing this within only a couple of miles that it would be best to keep himself focused on his own family. Trying to wrap his head around the full magnitude of what appears to be a mass casualty or mass disappearance event would only blind him to what was immediately in front of him, and what he could, presumably, control and respond to.

It was late morning by the time he arrived back at home, and when he cracked open the front door (climbing in through the missing wall felt too familiar, even for his own house) he was relieved to see Saga laid out on the couch. He had been there, sleeping soundly, when he left. But considering how quickly he had disappeared the last time, he was not confident that his brother would continue to stick around, no matter how much they both might want it. Uncle Ted peered excitedly from the kitchen when he heard the front door latch disengage, and it was plain to see the disappointment on his face when he saw it was Barnibus and not Carol returning home.

"Eh, er, Barnibus, thank goodness you've returned," he stammered as he fumbled with the bag of coffee beans he held unnaturally in his hand. "Where have you been? Not to sound like a cliché, but we've been worried."

"I was fine," Saga deadpanned from the couch, not bothering to look over at Barnibus in the entryway. "I don't worry about you. Or anyone."

"He doesn't mean that," Uncle Ted offered in a hushed tone.

"I did what you suggested," he said to Uncle Ted, without taking his eyes off Saga. He wanted to run to Saga, to give him a big hug, to tell him he had seen their mom, but after a moment he remembered, obviously, that it was not their mother that he saw. Instead, this made him want to talk to Uncle Ted even more. "Can I talk to you in the kitchen?" He signaled Uncle Ted into the next room, as Saga scoffed and rolled his eyes.

Barnibus moved so quickly into the kitchen that Uncle Ted nearly tripped over himself trying to keep up with him enough to follow. They moved to the far end of the kitchen and got close together so they could talk quietly enough to keep the contents of their conversation out of Saga's ears. Barnibus felt like he had so much to say, so much to apologize for, so much to tell him and to ask him and to get off his chest. He did not know where to start, and for once the racing in his mind told him he was on the right path. Whatever was going on — with the Purple Man, with his mind, with Not-Carol — was too much for him to wrap his head around. If he did not feel like he was brimming with a million questions, then, he figured, he must not be paying close enough attention. Him not knowing what to lead with actually brought him some comfort, the realization of which was enough to invite a small smile to creep across his face. In that split second of lightness, he led with his vision of his mother.

"I saw my mom earlier. About an hour ago, maybe two." He offered this information as if it were plain intel, with the matter-of-fact bluntness that one might use to say they saw a passing car. It was true, and plain as day, as far as Barnibus was concerned.

"You saw her? My God, Barnibus! Is she okay? Where is she now?"

"I have no idea."

"Well—what happened?" Uncle Ted stammered, trying to keep his voice low.

"I *saw* her!"

"That's great! That's huge; that can help us. Where did you

see her?”

“In the woods, I was on my way back.”

“Okay!” Uncle Ted exclaimed. “Okay, that’s good! That’s good. That’s a starting point. Okay. Your mother is in the woods. We can work with that.” Barnibus could see the gears already turning in Uncle Ted’s head, thinking a step or two ahead now. Before long he’d have the whole night worked out. “What were you doing in the woods, anyway? You never told me what you were getting up to.”

“I followed your advice! I went out last night and got my dreams back. Found where I had put them and dug them up. It took a while to find the right rock — the right place! But I got ‘em, and I really—I feel fantastic.”

“Oh...” Uncle Ted said, deflated.

“What’s wrong?” Barnibus asked, concerned. “This is great news! You told me to go get them back.”

“No, no, you’re right, my boy.” He patted Barnibus on the shoulder. A little too hard, Barnibus thought. “You did well. That was brave, what you did.” He exhaled. “But whatever you saw out there, it wasn’t your mother. I’m afraid that was quite literally a figment of your imagination.”

“I already know that,” Barnibus said too loudly, hardly able to keep his excitement contained. Uncle Ted took a moment as he regarded Barnibus, searching both the boy’s face, trying to understand where he was coming from, as well as his own thoughts, trying to think of how to respond. His excitement felt mismatched with what he was describing, and while he was acutely aware of that duality — which confused him likely just as much if not more than it did his uncle — he could not contain the excitement he felt now that his mind was back to life. To say that the possibilities felt endless would be an understatement, a total disservice to how invulnerable and powerful he had grown to feel on his walk home. Socially, he knew, on some level, that normally he would hide how he truly felt. Underplaying his excitement out of, he did not know, maybe a sense of embarrassment? Whatever it was, he could recognize what would be his normal operating mode, and there was a weightlessness now to feeling untethered by it. Unmoored from reality, he thought.

"You have a really weird energy right now," Uncle Ted said slowly. "I'm afraid I'm not entirely sure how I should approach this." He paused for a moment before reaching past Barnibus and pulling a chair away from the table. He planted it firmly next to Barnibus. "Maybe you should take a seat here. How does that sound?" He placed his hand on Barnibus' shoulder, urging him towards the seat. "Yeah... yeah, that sounds good," said Uncle Ted in reply to his own question.

"No, really, I'm fine," Barnibus enthused as he took the offered seat. He sat very much on the edge of the seat, poised to spring back into whatever action might come next. "I know how this sounds, *trust me*, but I know what I saw."

"I know what you *think* you saw, Barnibus, but you have to believe me; it was just your imagination. What you saw wasn't—".

"It was my imagination. It was a construct of my mother based on my picture of her in my mind. I know that; I just said that a second ago."

Uncle Ted hesitated again now, really drawing out this conversation with unsteady footing. Barnibus could see in his eyes the slightest glint of fear, and for a moment his own confidence stumbled as he worried that what he saw, or what he was saying, was scaring him. Or worse, simply breaking his heart. He tried to place himself in his uncle's shoes, and a swell of sadness came over him as he tried to picture what it would feel like if, while Saga was missing, someone came to him and insisted they had just seen him. That is what he is doing, he reminded himself. His mother just so happens to be his uncle's sister, as is so often the case in these instances. And before Ted was his uncle, he was just a person with a sister. As the swell of sadness grew, he could feel a hint of tears begging to well hot in his eyes. The lights in the kitchen dimmed. Uncle Ted's sole focus on Barnibus wavered, broken by the energy that seemed to overtake the room and, in fact, the whole house. The lights dimmed, and a slight chill entered the air. As he surveyed the room, Uncle Ted quickly shot his gaze back to Barnibus.

"Barnibus," Uncle Ted called softly. Barnibus did not respond, his eyes beginning to glaze over, lost in thought. "Barnibus," he repeated as he gave his nephew's shoulder a little shake. Just enough to snap him out of it.

"Uh? Sorry. I just had a thought," he offered as the lights came back up. Back to normal now. The shift was slight, unlikely to have been noticed even by Saga in the next room, but Barnibus knew what had happened, and he knew, without conferring with his uncle, that he knew as well.

"Are you okay?" Uncle Ted asked as he got back to work, searching Barnibus' eyes.

"I just—I was thinking about—I know what it must have sounded like when I said I saw Carol." It felt unnatural for him to call his mother by her name, but it was important to him to appeal to his uncle as a human, not just by his familiar title. "I didn't mean to get your hopes up or anything like that."

"It's okay, Barnibus," he said with a heavy sigh. "You have nothing to apologize for. I just want to make sure you're fine."

"Yeah, no, it's fine. I can... I'll keep it under control."

"I don't just mean right now," he said, checking over his shoulder to keep an eye on Saga in the other room. "I mean, generally. That sounds like quite the night you had, and that would be a lot for anyone to shoulder. Especially a kid."

"I'm not just a kid."

"You are. I'm not saying it like it's a bad thing or anything, but you are very much a child." Uncle Ted's voice raised, not a lot, but enough to get Saga's attention in the other room. He sat up a bit and tried to see into the kitchen, while still trying to remain aloof. Listening, but not. "Both of you are still children, and children under my care, at that. We can't forget that." Barnibus could not help but think that the last bit was more for his uncle's benefit, a reminder for himself, than it was for him and Saga. "I need to keep the two of you safe. And when you disappear all night without telling me where you're going, or what you're doing, it feels like I have failed at that, and that something horrible has happened to you. You *scared me*, Barnibus. This isn't fun and games. This isn't some fun pretend scene that you and your friends are playing at recess." Saga walked over to the doorway of the kitchen, making no secret of his interest in their conversation. "We need to be in this together. That means working together, but also keeping each other safe. Respecting each other." He turned to see Saga standing, watching intently from the door. "That goes for both of you. Understand?"

Barnibus and Saga both nodded. Sheepishly at first, before that reluctance melted away into genuine acceptance. Their uncle was right. They could not argue with that. They had been acting like children because it's true: that is what they are. But they needed to work as a team, and that meant respecting their uncle's role in that team. And if they gave that respect, Barnibus reasoned to himself, they would get a similar degree of respect in return. The idea of being treated as equals excited the Jones brothers, who had spent most of their short lives quite under the thumb of their parents.

Silence hung in the air. On the surface, the conversation had stopped. Come to a close. The hammer fell, and that was it. They remained there, Barnibus sitting eagerly in his chair, Uncle Ted hovering closely in front of him, and Saga there in the doorway, perched watching.

"Now," Uncle Ted broke in. "Tell us exactly what you saw. Every single thing."

16

EVERY SINGLE THING

It felt like another long night to Saga, only this particular long night happened over a couple of hours in the late morning. He listened with rapt attention to Barnibus' tale of the night before, how he had retraced his steps to find his dreams, how long he searched to find them, past-Barnibus having nearly outsmarted present-Barnibus. How the Purple Man had, in one way or another, helped Barnibus find hidden treasure, paraphysically or not. And how he had talked to their mother again, though he knew immediately and without question that it was not their mother at all. He recognized this as Barnibus' version of their mother, much less his own interpretation of her. But most of all, he listened with great interest to how *alive* his brother felt now. This was the Barnibus that he remembered from before, now turned up to eleven. When finally he finished spinning his tale, Saga followed up with one immediate request, which confused Barnibus and brought him back down to earth.

"Get the light for me," Saga said.

"What?" Barnibus asked, as he looked at the light switch

practically right next to Saga's right arm.

"From there. Get the light for me. I saw what you did earlier. With the lights and the... turning down the AC, I guess."

"I don't think that's how this works."

"Oh, it is," Uncle Ted reassured the boys, "but I don't think Barnibus is quite there. This is all very new, my dear Saga."

"You don't have to tell me; I've been here with you guys for the past few days, living this whole new thing," Saga said, before adding venomously, "*dear uncle.*"

"What I'm trying to figure out," Barnibus began, to Uncle Ted.

"Oh, wait," Saga cut in. "That's right. I forgot for a second there. I *haven't* been here with you guys this whole time." He feigned embarrassment at his artificial taboo. "How silly of me! There was that whole thing, you know, where you *sent me away.* Teleported me right out of the room and sent me to a whole other place entirely. I don't know how I forgot about that. That's so weird." He chuckled to himself. "Anyway, sorry, you were telling me about how you can't turn a light on and off — like you did just a few minutes ago — because, I guess, that would be *too complicated* or something?"

Barnibus looked embarrassed. He could not tell if that embarrassment was genuine, even to himself, but he knew that whatever he felt, he wanted to show deference to his brother. Because Saga was not wrong, he knew that. It was his biggest question at this point. The one thing confounding the confident power he felt otherwise. Why was he able to do something so extraordinary like, as Saga put it, teleportation, but could not muster something as comparatively simple as flipping a switch? He thought of all the things he had watched his uncle manipulate back at his house — his suit, his hair — and how effortless it looked to be to him.

"I won't pretend to understand how any of this works," Barnibus began.

"I'm afraid even I'm unsure right now," Uncle Ted said. "There's some sort of system here, and I'm still trying to work it out myself." He paced as he mused. "As far as I can tell, the things that Barnibus *has* done with his gift all seem to stem from his emotional state. He's not reaching out with his mind and flipping a switch because that's what he wants to do," he said, miming flipping the light switch on the wall. "He's not setting out with the stated purpose of sending anybody away. No, that's not it. The lights from earlier didn't turn off. They dimmed. The air conditioning didn't turn on earlier. The house itself, on its own, got colder. He's not *doing* these things, for lack of a more elegant way to put it. They're *happening.* Does that make sense?"

"No," Saga said flatly. Barnibus shook his head emphatically.

"Okay, let me—" Uncle Ted looked around for something to help him illustrate his point, but nothing immediately around him looked like it would be of much use to explain the pseudophysics of a young boy manipulating reality with his mind. Sometimes that is just what luck you have in these situations.

"It doesn't feel like I have any control over what happens," Barnibus begins to explain to Saga. Always trying to solve problems.

"Because you can't control it," Uncle Ted said, pointing excitedly at Barnibus, finding his way back on track to an explanation. "At least not yet." He got back to work pacing about the room. "You're not controlling what's happening. At least not in the sense that you are choosing what happens.

In these instances, you were in a state of heightened emotion, right?"

"That's all it's been these last couple of days," Barnibus nodded.

"And in those instances, when you're overcome by those emotions, your reality, and by association, *our* reality, bends, matching those emotions, or bending to aid in the fundamental *goal* of that emotion."

"Do emotions have goals?" Barnibus asked, still genuinely confused.

"Not in the traditional sense," Uncle Ted continued with near-manic excitement. "It's not that your... reticence wants to go grocery shopping."

Saga could not help but chuckle at his uncle's quite stilted choice of example.

"But emotions have things that they seek to accomplish, to a degree. You're angry because something that is happening around you, or to you, or to someone you care for, feels unfair. And you want that thing — whatever it is — to stop. Or you're *scared* because your mind is trying to find a way out of a situation that feels unsafe. That's an extraordinarily narrow, surface-level way to look at emotions, but for the sake of this explanation, that's all we need. Back at the deli, you didn't think '*okay, I'm going to send Saga away from this place.*' What happened, I believe, was that you were scared, and wanted, at an emotional level, for your little brother to be safe. So, your mind sent him to safety. The lights here earlier, the heat you were talking about when you were being held by that Purple Man before, those were tied to sadness, and to *anger*. If I were to venture a guess, I'd say this gift of yours is rooted in your emotions — how you feel, and what you're thinking in those areas quite literally shapes the world around you."

Barnibus nodded deeply as he thought through this well of new information. Saga, who by now had taken a seat on the floor just inside the doorway to the kitchen, searched emptily about the room, his eyes focusing far off into the middle distance, as he put the puzzle pieces together himself.

"What am I supposed to do with that?" Barnibus finally asked.

"Now *that's* the question. That much I don't know. I can't do what you do — never have, thinking back practically as long as I can remember. Never been able to get the world to bend to me the way you can. I know I said before that you and I are a lot alike in this regard — and to a degree, I certainly still believe that to be true! But this is... this is unique, to be sure." He thought for a moment before adding quietly to himself, "Extraordinary..."

"Fat lot that's going to do for us if he's just over there throwing things around all over the place just because he's frustrated or whatever," Saga said, annoyed. "No offense or anything, and I know how that sounds, but come on..." He held Barnibus' gaze, knowing that his brother was likely thinking nearly the same thing.

"Frustration, anger, sadness — there is a lot to harness in those feelings, and we shouldn't be so quick to dismiss them," Uncle Ted urged the boys.

"When that happens... whatever it is... it feels like I'm not in control. I'm not making these things happen. They just sort of do," Barnibus said.

"Some philosophers believe that man himself is the center of the universe, and that we draw our power directly from nature — from the universe itself! Such tremendous power... how else would we harness that kind of power besides powerful emotions?" Uncle Ted's pacing became more rapid, his glee barely masked.

"The Purple Man is... I don't know what he is, only that *he's* powerful. What are we supposed to do?"

"We'll get there," Uncle Ted reassured them. "We're just beginning to unravel this. And it feels like we're close. It really does. Right now all we can do is pull on the loose threads as we find them and see how this whole tapestry unwinds."

"And if I just get scared? I don't want to let anyone down, but Saga is right. The Purple Man is something. Something we don't understand. Anger and sadness — I think I can get a handle on those. But just... fear? What then?"

"People often dismiss fear, or talk badly about the idea of being afraid. But fear, boys... fear is a powerful tool." Uncle Ted's tone shifted from optimistic to grave, foreboding. "It was fear that kept Odysseus tied to the mast in Homer's Odyssey, ultimately saving his men. You need to know how to harness it. You control your fear by not letting it control you."

"Easier said than done..." Barnibus lamented to himself.

"Easier said than done," Uncle Ted could not help but agree. The weight of the task once again descended onto the room as Barnibus spun the wheels on how to stop his mind from racing. The irony was not lost on him that his fear fed on itself, and that his mind racing was the thing that he most feared as he felt control over himself slipping away. The idea of keeping that under control only snowballed onto itself as he was afraid of the consequences of failing, which in turn made him more afraid. To add to this, his finger was throbbing like crazy, something that had been mercifully kept at bay until this point. He had, with surprising ease, adapted to functioning with two of his fingers tied together. But the dull throbbing was growing louder. At first it was agitating him, but when that agitation became distracting, becoming the object of the ire on his mind, he welcomed it. It was nice to have something to focus on that felt more immediate and physical. More time spent thinking about that meant less time available to fret about what was going to happen next, or when the next train would arrive, or through which wall it would be arriving. Before long, he noticed the faint thwump thwump thwump sound pulsing throughout the kitchen. The sound of his foot bobbing up and down on the floor, manifesting his anxiety. He caught himself and steadied his leg. As best as he could tell, his fidgeting had gone largely unnoticed, but he still thought it best to change the subject to throw them off his trail, just to be safe.

"What about Mom?" Barnibus asked broadly to the room.

"Don't worry, we're going to find your parents," Uncle Ted said emphatically. "How they fit into this, I'm still not sure, but—"

"No, I mean, not-Mom. The thing from last night. I know it was a figment of my imagination, or whatever, but if all of this is tied to my emotions, what was that?"

"Can you do it again?" Saga asked.

"I mean, not if I don't know how or why it happened to begin with. I've spent my whole life keeping it from happening, and now I don't know if I can let that go."

"Well," Saga thought for a moment. "How do you stop it from happening? Maybe if you could figure that out, you could just – I don't know – do the opposite?"

"It's like," Barnibus began as he searched for the words. "If I just don't look right at it, it can't have any power. You know?"

"I don't know, no," Saga said, mildly annoyed.

"Like if I don't acknowledge whatever it is I'm thinking about – I just let it hang out there in the corner of my mind – then it can't be real. It's just there, right? But sometimes... a lot of the time... it's not something that I can avoid looking at. And it becomes all I can think about, and it's overwhelming. That's when I get into trouble."

"We can harness that! Tell us what you were feeling at that moment with your mother," Uncle Ted said, like a teacher coaching a pupil through a new equation.

"Alone. Lost. It was quiet then. Not many people are out in the woods in the middle of the night. I was trying to find my way home. I thought I knew my way back, or at least thought I could make it up enough to figure it out, but I definitely felt alone in trying."

"Who helps you when you're feeling lost?" Uncle Ted urged him.

"A lot of people, really."

"Okay," Uncle Ted chuckled.

"Structure," Saga muttered. Barnibus looked to him expectantly. "Mom gives us structure. When you're lost, you need directions."

"Mom is our compass," Barnibus nodded.

"We can use this," Uncle Ted said enthusiastically. "I don't know how yet, but that's a big step forward. You created a construct who — while unable to themselves directly impact reality — could inform you, or could..." he thought for a moment, "reveal to you information that you have, but cannot call upon."

"I thought I had it," Saga said as he blearily lowered himself back down to the floor, "but now I'm lost again."

"She couldn't tell me anything I didn't already know,"

Barnibus said, smiling. "She told me that herself."

"Clever," Uncle Ted laughed. He chuckled as he walked over to the kitchen window, reflecting and admiring, with the renewed appreciation of a new dawn, the mid-afternoon daylight, warm and heavy, casting growing shadows across the yard, birds fluttering by quickly, insects trilling. He cracked the window open to let the fresh afternoon air into the room. Barnibus thought it strange, given the open wall nearby, but he counted it among his uncle's many quirks. And for the first time in days, the boys felt optimism. The water had long since risen over their heads, but now they felt they could see the surface, and before long, they would be able to find their way out. "We keep chipping away at this," Uncle Ted began. "I think we can have a real idea — a real plan! — by nightfall. We're close now. We can do this." He breathed the fresh air deeply. "It will just take a little time."

In the distance, a low rumble. A plume of smoke rose steadily from the direction of the school. The shadows of the afternoon disappeared from the canvas of the backyard as the thick smoke blotted out the sun. Time was not something on the side of the Jones brothers.

17

THE FALL OF THE HOUSE OF ANNA TUTHILL HARRISON JUNIOR HIGH

There were three bunnies on the side of the road. Or four. Saga could not be sure. It was not a high number for a boy of his age to count to, by any means, but around the second bunny he found himself distracted trying to remember what differences, if any, there were between bunnies and an honest-to-goodness rabbit. Was there a difference? There must be. Bunnies are... something. Fake? Like a narwhal? Wait, that's not right. Narwhals are real and fantastical. That was something that always caused Saga to second-guess his perception. Narwhals, toothed whales with a spiraled tusk on their upper jaw: real. Unicorns, horses with a similar ailment: that of legend and fairytale. As they walked along, he casually convinced himself that bunnies, rather than rabbits, were of a similar ilk; very close to something that does in fact exist, but in itself a wholly fictitious being. Saga, of course, had every capability necessary to find the answer to this quite easily, but such was the mind of a child; caught up in trivialities as a means to fight off boredom. And that was, somehow, despite everything that they had gone through, what Saga was in this moment: bored. Sure, he had seen a great number of terrible things in the last couple of days, and whatever lay ahead of them was most assuredly, he knew, death. But right now, he was just walking. Again. There had been a lot of walking, and he was at this point rather sick of it. So, in order to numb himself to that fact, he debated bunnies and their validity.

Not questioned, however, by anybody but Barnibus, was why there were bunnies — which very much existed and were the same thing as rabbits, simply called something different — on the side of the road to begin with. They were still well within their suburban development, and rabbit sightings were hardly commonplace. But they were this evening, because Barnibus had made it so. Inadvertently at first, with the first bunny arriving because Barnibus saw a fallen tree branch which, to his mind, resembled a bunny sat surveying the horizon. Once he thought about it, *pop*, there it was. He tried at first not to draw attention to it. But the little fella was harmless enough and just hopped along next to him, his brother, and his uncle, gently enough that he let it pass with little worry or trouble. Before long it amused him, and he pictured a few more to join his little friend and create a little bunny convoy, which, to his mind, made the whole trek more bearable.

"Barn," Saga called forward from the back of the group. He had taken to calling Barnibus 'Barn' in order to avoid 'Barney' but still sound familiar and close. It was the type of calculated move Saga was known to make, even well-intentioned. "How are you feeling?" He knew more than he was letting on, the irony of which was that Barnibus and his uncle knew Saga was well-aware of whatever was waiting for them at the school.

"Tired, but I think okay," Barnibus replied. "I just want this to be over."

"We'll be there soon enough," Uncle Ted cut in, trying to keep his young wards from spiraling down a wormhole of worry.

"Too soon, if you ask me..." Saga mumbled.

"We're going to be okay," Barnibus called quietly over his shoulder. Uncle Ted was taking point on this expedition (Barnibus was also growing tired of the amount of walking he had done in the last couple of days), and he was careful to keep their conversation between him and his brother. Uncle Ted, who of course could hear their quiet voices chirping a few feet away, paid them no mind, giving them their privacy as he kept watch of whatever was ahead.

"It's bad, Barn."

"I know," Barnibus said reluctantly. "What did you see?"

"I don't want to say..." Saga trailed off cautiously.

"It's better if we all know what we're heading into. Remember what Mom said: knowledge is power. You know what's up ahead, and that puts you at an enormous advantage. If we could all get to where you are, it would help us a lot."

"It's all gone."

Barnibus thought for a moment.

"How do you mean?"

"The building is still there, I guess, kinda, but everything inside, the people, everything that makes it... I don't know, a school? Whatever happened there is ugly. I don't know how else to describe it."

"Well, what happened?"

"That's the thing; I don't know."

"Just over this next hill here, and around the corner. Not

much farther now," Uncle Ted called over his shoulder with theatric volume, trying to change the subject and distract the children.

"It just starts when I — when *we* — get there. I keep searching for what precedes that, but it's just... it's blank. We arrive and it's like that's the start of it."

"Like we're inevitable," Barnibus offers.

"That's better, right? Like — is this what we're meant to be doing? That must mean that we're doing the right thing," Saga says, near pleading, to his older brother.

"We're doing the right thing," Uncle Ted says, unable to continue playing the unaware fool any longer. "We're going to be okay. But no matter what happens, this is where we need to be at this exact moment. Life, it turns out, plays out exactly in the order and with the intent it was meant to. No amount of posturing or guarding can stop that. I hate to say it, boys, but whatever happens from here — everything that has happened in these last couple of days — is meant to be."

"Heavy," Saga says flatly.

"It's true, boys," called Barnibus Sr. from the far side of the road, his brow heavy with sweat and his butcher's smock caked in the day's viscera. He concluded with striking enthusiasm, "Whatever happens from here on out was simply meant to be. To try to avoid it would be a fool's errand."

"Dad!" Saga exclaimed.

"It's not—just don't worry about it," Barnibus said bluntly. "Nobody pay any attention to him," he called out. "He's just going to walk with us for a bit, but it's—it's just me thinking out loud? I think?"

"That's nonsense!" Barnibus Sr. walked in line with the boys now, practically bounding with enthusiasm. "I'm as real as those bunny rabbits over there, and I'm here to help y'all really kick some butt!"

Barnibus Sr. was not one to say 'y'all,' Saga knew. The down-home country slang of that sort is characteristic of how Barnibus himself would talk about their father — a key ingredient to his impression.

"Wow..." Saga gasped, weighing the sheer power on display — and from his own brother, no less!. "And you can just... *do that?* You just brought Dad here like *that?*" He said, snapping his fingers.

"That's not your father, Young Saga," Uncle Ted cut in with great urgency. "That's little more than an anthropomorphized idea that your brother mused, brought to fruition on our mortal plane as an aberration like one might find in a ghost story or other such fantasy. It's just your brother thinking about your father, that's all."

"Sorry..." Barnibus said sheepishly.

"Not at all," Uncle Ted said with a wave of his hand. "This is good! Although I wish we had more time to work on it, this shows a tremendous amount of potential!"

"That's the spirit, Teddy!" Barnibus Sr. exclaimed. Uncle Ted shuddered.

"Seems pretty real to me, I suppose," Saga said as he studied what he was certain was his father walking along beside them.

"I don't know how much I'll be able to add to what you boys have going on — I admit I'm a bit out of my depth here — but whatever you need, I'm here!" Barnibus Sr. said as he synched up his smock with the cold confidence of a warrior heading into battle.

The menacing husk of their school, tattered and dark against the night sky, crested over the horizon as they turned the corner, their destiny now within plain view.

"How does this work exactly?" Saga asked. "You just send Dad wherever we need help, and he's just sort of... there?"

Barnibus Sr. was no longer there. Barnibus' vision had ended, either because Barnibus had moved onto other plot holes or blind-spots in his plan, or because, he worried, he did not think even his father would know what to do if he were to find himself in a situation like this.

Saga had not told him much, but Barnibus could see plainly right in front of him that his little brother had been right. The school lay empty as a husk. The sun was setting now, and he knew that even on a normal day the place would be devoid of activity or occupation, but what he felt striking about it was the particular *type* of emptiness. Everything that could be void was void. There was no sound; there was no movement aside from the flickering of light and flame along the hallways just inside the torn-open doors. Barnibus wondered, the closer they got, why they could not hear the fire alarms. He had been through enough public school fire drills to know how piercing the sound was (indeed that was quite by design, he understood), but now, their moment to shine, so to speak, they were silent. He wanted to find it poetic, trying desperately to find some aspect of what they were approaching that was free of abject terror, but he just could not muster the artistic presence of mind to find this anything but foreboding. Barnibus swallowed deeply as his foot left the curb and set onto the school's parking lot. It was only a couple dozen hours earlier that Barnibus and his brother had first met the Purple Man, and he hoped now would be the last time they would ever need to see him again, for better or for worse (but hopefully for the better).

"Which way do we go in?" Uncle Ted asked Saga, his voice

trembling.

"I went in through the front, and I didn't run into anyone... We could try that way."

"We could *try*?" Uncle Ted shot back with uncharacteristic snark.

"If that's what you saw," Barnibus said, "that's what we'll do." He gave Saga a light squeeze on the arm, something that the two of them had found each other doing more frequently in recent days. A quick reminder that *I'm here for you, brother.* "What do we need to look out for?"

"The main hallway is a mess — the classrooms are destroyed, and whatever ripped through there did it quickly and violently."

"Sounds like we're running into some stuff you boys shouldn't see. You two wait out here. Better let me go ahead first and make sure the coast is clear," Uncle Ted said, trying to muster what bravado he felt he had left in the tank.

"It isn't," Saga said bluntly. "This coast isn't clear; this coast is the Bay of Pigs. This coast is Normandy." It always tickled Barnibus when his brother nonchalantly tossed around anachronistic analogies. Uncle Ted did not find it quite as amusing.

"That's a touch macabre," he cautioned his young nephew with a tone bordering on outright admonishment.

"Anything we're going to see in there, I've already seen," Saga said. "And anything we *could* see, Barnibus can invent with his mind. I think if there are any two children in the world best suited to walk through that door right now, it's my brother and me."

"My brother and I," Uncle Ted corrected.

"No, he's right," Barnibus interjected.

"Boys, I don't think—".

"It's '*my brother and me*', not '*my brother and I*'," Barnibus continued. "If you were to take away the first subject in that sentence, '*my brother,*' you wouldn't say, '*It is I*', unless, I guess, you were a supervillain revealing yourself from the shadows."

"Whatever is in that school waiting for us just caused a whole lot of mayhem against a whole lot more people than just the three of us. This isn't a game right here, my dear children. This is real life — as hard as it is to believe. And if that..." Uncle Ted searched a moment for the name, "if that Purple Man is in there, he means serious business. He wouldn't do all of this if he weren't trying to get us specifically to walk in there right now and try to save the day. Now he knows we're coming, he's in an extremely defensible position, and he means to hurt you. This grammar lesson right now is beside the point."

"But it isn't. You corrected my little brother because you assumed you were right and he was wrong. You assumed he was wrong because he's a child and you're an adult and you know better than he does." Barnibus turned to look at Saga. "And right now, before we walk in there, the number one thing that each of us needs to understand is that Saga is the only one — the *only* one — of us who knows what we're walking into." He paused a moment to make sure the lesson landed on his Uncle, before addressing Saga. "If there is anything at all that we need to know going in there, either we need to know it right now, or we need to know it while we're in there, you need to shout it out. Shout it loud, make sure that we hear whatever you need us to hear. Don't be afraid. If we all know what you see, we'll be able to help each other through it, okay?" He squeezed his little brother's arm again. "Remember that knowledge is power."

"And that knowledge can be a weapon," Saga continued.

There was an old stairwell immediately to the right of the main entrance to the school. It was considered 'old' to the students of Anna Tuthill Harrison Junior High because it was disused and always chained shut. In the minds of children — at least bored and curious children, the type you may find wandering the halls of any junior high school — anything that they do not use, or they do not see being used immediately in front of them, is considered old. A thing of the past. A relic. Barnibus himself had taken to calling it '*the old abandoned stairwell*' some mornings on his way into school. The old abandoned stairwell was open now, the double doors disjointed, with the left door dislodged from its hinge, now hinging instead about mid-mass, dangling by the now ineffective chain meant to keep both doors shut. As they made their way slowly towards the front of the school, the boys did not dare to peer inside. There was an unknown evil within the school, but at least they were on home turf. The stairwell, however, was already a foreign landscape. They stayed back cautiously as Uncle Ted stuck his head in the open doorway, first looking down, then craning his head farther in to see up towards the roof.

"Water," he called back to the boys. "A lot of water. It looks like there's a hole in the roof—" he strained as he leaned farther in. "Yeah, I'm seeing moonlight up there. Must have cut through the fire sprinklers, causing the stairwell to flood." He nearly lost his balance pulling himself out, and as he walked the short distance back to the boys, he straightened out his suit with his hands, while his hair, collar, and lapel righted themselves. Barnibus was nearly certain he saw sweat disappear from his brow, and something about that he found inspiring.

They reached the main door to the school, and where Uncle Ted was moments earlier the brave member of the party to first scout the stairwell, this time Saga approached first, eager to see if what he first laid his eyes on fell in line with what he had seen before in his vision. He took two quick steps into the front door and gazed down the hallway. His expression, were you to be positioned well enough to survey it, betrayed no reaction whatsoever. He digested everything he saw for a moment before he turned and stepped back outside, joining his brother and uncle just outside the door, posed on either side, ready to roll like the world's least effective SWAT team.

"Yep," Saga nodded, "this is it."

Barnibus once again sighed heavily. They were unavoidable for Barnibus in moments of stress, given to deep exhales to cope with his rattled nervous system. He hoped that his companions had instead taken this to be a sigh of relief.

There they stood, motionless. They had come this far, but these last couple of steps, the ones that would bring them over the threshold and into the school, felt the most daunting to each of them. Saga watched his older brother, and Uncle Ted stared into the door and down the hallway, his eyes focused in the middle distance.

Barnibus was the first through the door. Then Uncle Ted. Finally, Saga.

Blood. A significant amount, both boys thought. As much as it pained them, and as much as they did not particularly want to see any of this, they still felt compelled to survey the hallway and the classrooms as they passed, looking for anything — anyone — that they could identify, or anyone that they recognized, out of a morbid curiosity that they both in equal parts recognized and felt embarrassed by. But as they marched with trepidation onward, they mercifully saw no bodies. Blood, damage, fire, destruction, but no corpses.

"Torture..." Barnibus mumbled quietly to himself as he gave into musing on what must have happened here before they arrived. Distant screams rose from further up the hall, and just as Barnibus tensed up, readying himself to see something that would stick with him well into adulthood, they disappeared, just as quickly as they came. He snapped out of it and kept walking.

Saga was uneasy, now that they were inside, by how familiar it felt, and how he had a strange sense of home. He had felt this sensation a couple of times before when he had gone on to experience events or locations that he had visions of beforehand, and he hoped now that it would be something he could use to his advantage. But those hopes vanished quickly as he surveyed the destruction. It was just as he had seen before, but more visceral and concrete. Terror filled the air. Not just theirs, but the reverberation of what those caught in the wake of all of this felt in their final moments.

"Do you think this is because of us?" Barnibus asked.

"We can't think like that, my dear boy," Uncle Ted whispered. "Do not think like that. Someone who would do this... well, they were going to do it, anyway. It wouldn't matter what we had done."

"But we could have stopped it," Barnibus said quietly, almost to himself, as he looked around. "Back at the shop, we could have... I don't know, but we could have done something. This didn't need to happen."

"Yes, it did." Saga said. It hung heavily in the air.

"He's right. I hate it too, but no matter what we did, this was going to happen."

"This was inevitable. We played our parts in the lead-up, but our parts in that were scripted. Destined, whatever you want to call it." Saga said, stepping over a large section of the ornamental pillars that bookended the old trophy case, now lying across the main hallway, blood pooled on either side.

"I don't like not knowing what to do," Barnibus said. "Any time I try to think of a plan, I can't help but second-guess myself. Like... is this the pre-destined thing to do, or am I picking – somehow – the wrong destiny?"

"That's not how destiny works," Saga chuckled. The break from his often stoic brother caught Barnibus by surprise, and he could not help but snicker as well.

"What would your mother say?" Uncle Ted asked.

"You should be in your room finishing your studies by now!" Saga mimicked through laughter, his brother also giving in to the infectious, nervous energy once again. A couple of doors down the hall — the science room for the eighth graders — there were two loud pops as a couple of beakers burst from heat exposure. The sudden noise shook the boys loose of their giggles and snapped them back to reality. The return to their present circumstances left them flush as they remembered that none of this was particularly funny.

"I meant that as an honest question," Uncle Ted said patiently. "Barnibus, what would your mother have to say about this? Right now. If she were here... *right now.*"

"Oh, I don't..." Barnibus trailed off, slightly embarrassed that he had seemed to have lost track of his role in all of this. "I don't know how to, exactly, make anyone... like, how to make her... appear...?" Barnibus still felt deeply uncomfortable talking about his gift — in fact he particularly hated calling it a *gift,* as that felt ceremonial and self-important to him.

"Don't try," Uncle Ted said as he stopped and turned on the heels of his impossibly clean loafers. "If you're thinking about *doing* it, it will not happen," he said, turning to Saga, "whatever *it* is," he added with a wink. Both boys knew their uncle turned to charisma as a defense mechanism if he felt uncomfortable, and while they found it annoying on principle, it was strangely effective, especially right now. "If you think, '*Oh, I need to do this thing,'* what you're thinking about is the doing. You're not thinking about the *result,* and thus the result does not happen." He started pacing laterally across the hallway, as he was wont to do when waxing philosophic about topics grounded in a patently dubious reality. "Don't think '*how can I do this'* either. Just think about the thing. Whatever it is you want to have happen. And then let's... see what happens," he finished with a shrug.

"You boys should not be here," Not-Carol called from a couple dozen paces back down the hallway. "You should both be in your rooms finishing your studies before it gets too late."

Saga stifled a snicker as Not-Carol shot him a startlingly authentic motherly glare, which stopped him dead in his tracks. Just like Barnibus' vision of their father, Saga knew this was nothing more than an aberration, but he still could not stop his breath from catching. He wanted to run over and give his mother a hug, to hold her tightly so she could not get away from him again, and with that he would feel safe... but he knew that was not how it would work. Quickly he settled himself, repeating in his head that what he saw was nothing more than a figment of his brother's imagination. He was no longer snickering.

"Hi Carol," Uncle Ted called with a near-sincere amount of

warmth and affection. "I was hoping you might join us this evening."

"Theodore, what did you get my boys into?"

"I'm afraid I'm but a spectator on this one," he said lightly. "Helping where I can, but it feels more and more like I'm just along for the ride."

"Hm," Not-Carol said, regarding Uncle Ted for a moment before turning to Barnibus. "How are you getting along?" she asked.

"I'm afraid," Barnibus replied quietly, shaking loose of the fact that he was doing little more than talking to himself. "I don't know what I'm supposed to do, and all of this... it's a lot."

"It *is* a lot," Not-Carol said, nodding as she looked around the hallway. "That is a lot of blood. Does that seem right to you?"

"Nothing seems right in any of this. I want to make sure these people are safe... wherever they are."

"That's one thing I love about you, Barnibus," she said warmly as she placed a hand on his shoulder. His skin crawled with expectant goosebumps anticipating a comforting maternal touch, but was left wanting as no such sensation arrived, as if someone had instead placed an old glove onto the outside of his coat. "You want to protect people, to keep people safe. I admire that." She held his gaze for a moment longer. "But where do you suppose all the people *are?*" she asked as she went back to looking up and down the hallway. "I would think with this much blood, we'd be seeing all sorts of people around needing, at a minimum, pretty urgent medical attention."

"Right..." Barnibus agreed, looking more closely at a pool of blood nearby on the floor. It was there; he could see it plain as day. The look, the smell... it was definitely blood; he held no qualms about that. But what became of that blood's owner?

Another series of loud cracks and snaps rang from the far end of the hallway, down towards the cafeteria, followed closely by a low rumble, the type of which Barnibus expected to precede a major explosion. But before long, the low rumble tapered off, and no explosion came to follow.

"You know what that is?" Barnibus asked Not-Carol.

"I know, honey..." Not-Carol mused as she brushed Barnibus' hair from his eyes.

The rumbling began again, this time growing louder than before. They turned towards the cafeteria, this time expecting to see a crumble of debris, or a clattering of terrified people running for their lives, but once again they saw nothing. As the rumble grew closer, the trick of echo and reflection fell as Barnibus realized, only a moment before his brother and their uncle, that the commotion this time was approaching them from the entrance to the school, back where they had just been moments before. They spun around again, just in time to see the entrance to the school and the first few classroom entrances off the hallway snap shut with a violent, sudden fury. Then, silence. Save for the faint trickle of small rocks and pebbles settling into their resting place, there was nothing more to the event. No screams, no secondary tremors, nothing. There were other exits from the school ahead, Barnibus assured himself, but without knowing what truly lay ahead of them deeper into the school, he could not help but feel trapped. It felt like everything was closing in on him, and his every minor move felt laborious and sloth-like. His breath quickened and grew shallow, and though he tried his best to keep his panic at bay, to keep it from his brother and be his powerful protector, there were some clues that were unfortunately unavoidable.

"Quicksand!" Uncle Ted called out as a caution to the Jones brothers. "Keep your feet up! Move! Quickly!" Barnibus' eyes widened at the realization that the quicksand — he was fairly certain — had come from him. "It looks like it's clearing up ahead! We need to keep moving!" The boys, their not-mother long vanished, lifted their knees high to follow their uncle further into the hallway, which seemed to grow dimmer the farther in they ventured. After several laborious, trudging steps, the quicksand thinned, and their movements became much easier and less labored.

"Guys," Barnibus panted, "I'm sorry."

"What for?" Saga said, similarly struggling to catch his breath.

"The sand," he replied. "I'm pretty sure that was me. I couldn't help it. I'm sorry. I just—with the hallway closing, and the—and the lights, it was just a lot and my mind kind of got away from me," he continued in a series of starts and stops.

"Don't worry about it," Uncle Ted offered reassuringly. "Just slow down. Stay focused. Something is amiss here... aside from the obvious in all of this... I mean something more-so. I can't put my finger on it yet, but whatever is going on, we're going to need to concentrate and take it all in to understand it. That goes for you too, Saga. Slow down, take it all in, and think about what you see — what you *have* seen!" He crouched now, lowering himself to the boys' level. "I know that this is a lot, and you're going to be fighting the instinct to look away. But it is imperative that we not shy away from studying our surroundings."

"He's right," the call came from the far end of the hallway, "this place is a real mess, but you'll want to drink it all in, because boy does it go down smooth." Barnibus was the first to turn with a start, as Saga squeezed his eyes shut, desperately refusing to get drawn in. There just outside the cafeteria doors stood the Purple Man, proudly, defiantly, half shadowed by the harsh light of flickering flames bouncing off the side of his face and body. He was a good distance away, which brought Barnibus an immeasurably small amount of relief. But something of that distance, or perhaps a trick of the eye, made him look impossibly tall. Barnibus remembered how he had felt as the Purple Man towered over him, and now tried to parse their interactions to put together a mental image of his opponent. But as he quickly flipped through the events of the last couple of days, particularly the times the two of them had crossed paths, he realized with some embarrassment that he did not have a real definitive picture of the Purple Man in his mind's eye. Aside from the fact that this person was always adorned in purple trappings, he could not get a handle on their actual stature. At times they seemed of average height, no larger to Barnibus than his parents, or the adults he would cross paths with when out running errands or at school. But at other times, the Purple Man was oppressively tall, much taller than a person should reasonably be. And that lack of reason, that impossibility kept Barnibus (and he was sure the same could be said for Saga) on his back foot; playing catch up in any situation, without realizing it, because he was spending so much mental energy just trying to grapple with what he was seeing, who he was talking to. There now before them was this same impossibly large Purple Man. Even at such a great distance, he easily towered over them, appearing large enough to reach right out and pluck Barnibus right from where he stood. Barnibus did not like this feeling of vulnerability, and though it felt unpleasant, its arrival did not strike Barnibus as a surprise. Vulnerability was the succinct description that Barnibus hated to use with such accuracy, but it washed over him and overtook every sense.

"We're going to be okay," he said shakily to Saga, repeating a bit louder for Uncle Ted's sake as well.

"I didn't see him before," Saga whispered, his voice trembling. "He wasn't here. I could feel him, but I didn't see him. I don't know what he has planned." He was breathing fast, eyes darting around across the ground. "Barnibus, I don't know what he plans to do with us."

"You boys stay low," Uncle Ted said as he arose and took a couple of contemplative steps towards the Purple Man. "Stay low and stay put. I'm going to have a chat with our friend here." Barnibus pulled Saga close, both of their legs shaking, beginning to drop the pretense of hiding their fear from each other. They lowered themselves into a crouch and watched, near-frozen, as Uncle Ted walked in silhouette towards the Purple Man.

"Theodore! Apple of my eye — it's been a while, hasn't it! How have you been?" the Purple Man called jovially, his arms stretched out wide as if he were inviting a hug. "How's the family?" His arms dropped to his sides. "Oh, ouch. Right. You have no family. Well, aside from your sister, who is missing, and your two nephews whom you've brought here to die. That's awkward. That's on me. I apologize for bringing it up." He turned to call over his shoulder into the cafeteria, "Sorry everybody, that's my bad!" When he turned back to Uncle Ted, he kept his head tilted gently to the side, as if in deference to Ted's poor position. "I don't think they mind much, but you know I hate making a fool of myself in front of *anyone*, but especially in front of helpless victims. It's just so *unbecoming*, you know? Helpless victims really need to feel that you're in charge. Helps give their impending demise a sense of purpose."

"Let's talk, you and I," Uncle Ted called out, now about midway between the boys and the Purple Man. "Enough theatrics, enough of whatever this is. You let those people go — you let my family go — and you and I can just have a conversation. We can talk through this, and I can help you get whatever it is you're looking for." As he walked down the hallway, he gingerly waved his hands at his sides as the lockers he passed swung shut, closing gently beside him. A show of force, however small it may be. Reminding the Purple Man that he's not the only one who has tricks they can play.

"What is that? What are you doing? Are those lockers *closing on their own?* My stars!" the Purple Man feigned terror, making a meal of his exaggerated fear. "But how can that be?" He dropped the panicked hysteria affectation as quickly as he adopted it, his rubber face dropping into blank folds of displeasure. "Enough theatrics," he said flatly, barely above normal speaking volume. With a slight flick of his wrists, two banks of lockers pulled from the wall with a loud SNAP and crumbled to the ground in front of where they had spent decades standing. They had narrowly missed Uncle Ted, but Barnibus still flinched, certain he had seen the tails of Uncle Ted's suit whip as the lockers nearly hit him.

Something in the close call made Barnibus' broken finger throb as he realized he was wrapping his other fingers, as best he could, around the field dressing he was still wearing to help stabilize the break. It reminded him of the stakes of Uncle Ted heading out on his own to face the Purple Man, and while he had been fearful until this point, he found himself overcome by another emotion at this realization: embarrassed. He was letting his uncle — who, granted, is a much older adult and therefore is probably more deft in a situation like this — fight his battle for him. Letting him walk right into danger and pain that Barnibus himself understood first-hand. He pulled Saga up to a stand, and together they walked towards the banks of lockers that had just crashed to the ground, Saga following without question, entrusting his brother to make this decision on his behalf. As they reached the lockers, Barnibus' grasp on his brother slackened, and he broke off.

"Barn, wait, where are you going?" Saga pleaded with his brother.

"Uncle Ted needs my help. I'm going over there."

"You can't leave me here alone," Saga cried, betraying a side of himself that he worked hard to keep hidden from the world. "What am I supposed to do?"

"You'll be okay — *we all will!* Just stay here and stay low. I'll be right back." Barnibus climbed up and over the bank of lockers, his tennis shoes landing on the floor with a light, barely audible *tap*. His climb over the lockers was astonishingly smooth and certain, which gave him a jolt of confidence. But as soon as his shoes touched the ground, he second-guessed his decision. It is easy to say you're going to do something, Barnibus often noticed throughout his young life, but quite a bit more difficult to follow through on actually *doing* the thing. Now he needed to do the thing and, darn it, he was not sure how to do that. How to do it, or even, frankly, *what to do.* But he had committed, and now he needed to move forward. He was just about to put one foot in front of the other (he would figure out a plan on the way, he figured), when he heard a light, barely audible *tap.*

Saga bounded over the bay of lockers with a measure of confidence and certainty that even rivaled Barnibus' entrance. The two brothers locked eyes, and while they knew each of them was scared and uncertain, and that whatever they were about to do would need to be made up on the fly — indeed, this part had not appeared to Saga in his dream — they knew they had an exponentially better shot at this together. One foot in front of the other, or in this case, two feet in front of the others as they approached in nearly lockstep. *Tap. Tap. Tap. Tap. Thap. Thap. Thap. Thap. Thud. Thud. Thud. Thud. CHUD. CHUD. CHUD. CHUD.* After a few paces, Barnibus and Saga could feel their footsteps growing loud and commanding, like the weight of a thousand men crashing down on the floors of Anna Tuthill Harrison Junior High, the building practically shaking with the rhythmic pulsing of their march. *That's what this is,* Barnibus thought to himself, *we're an army — the opposing force marching into battle.* Barnibus felt big, and bigger still as they kept walking. The Purple Man, who until this point was holding a laser focus — one Barnibus knew all too well at this point — on Uncle Ted, adjusted his eyes back to see the young Jones brothers approaching, and Barnibus watched as his eyes, at first filled with fire and determination, softened and widened as the boys came into focus. The Purple Man's feet, his rock-solid foundation, shifted almost imperceptibly.

"Well, isn't this a lovely trick," he said with a smirk. "But no. Uh uh. That's not how this goes. Not with your little friends there." He sighed the heavy sigh of a disappointed parent. "This is between us. I'm disappointed in you, Barnibus," the Purple Man shouted with a vague annoyance as he turned and moved quickly towards the cafeteria, snapping his fingers and filling the narrowing space between him and Uncle Ted with a crashing of debris as the ceiling came crumbling down, effectively sealing off the hallway from the cafeteria.

Barnibus and Saga stopped dead in their tracks. The hallway, albeit much smaller now with both ends sealed shut, felt at once massive and empty as the commanding thud of their approaching footsteps came to an abrupt stop with them.

"Little friends? What does he mean, Uncle Ted?" Barnibus asked loudly, still a way behind his uncle.

"I'm afraid I don't know," Uncle Ted replied as he surveyed the debris in front of him. "I'm not sure why he seemed surprised by the two of you being here. He had just addressed you moments ago. I don't know why he would—" Uncle Ted turned towards the boys and leapt with a sudden start, enough to startle Barnibus and Saga, making them both jump and land with a cacophonous *CHUNK*. "Boys!" Uncle Ted exclaimed.

Barnibus searched Uncle Ted for an answer before he followed his gaze over his own shoulder, turning to see – if he were to venture a guess – about a hundred Barnibuses (*would the plural of Barnibus just be 'Barnibus'?*) and Sagas standing in a flying V formation behind them. The duplicates all remained looking steadily forward, but the movements of their bodies mirrored the Prime Jones Brothers precisely.

"Holy Christmas!" Saga was beside himself, quite literally.

"Phenomenal," Uncle Ted said in awe. "Oh, this is great work, Barnibus. Really impressive beyond belief," he said as he pulled his glasses out of the breast pocket of his suit. As he put them on, just as his eyes quickly adjusted to his corrective lenses, the army vanished with little fanfare. "Tsk. Okay, well. Still a good step forward."

"How..." Barnibus asked quietly, more to himself than his

uncle, "... did I do that? Did *I* do that?" He searched around the hallway, hoping his army had simply adopted a tactical stealth position, but alas, they were gone.

"I'm afraid you did that, yes," Uncle Ted said with a proud smile.

"That was pretty cool," Saga said. "An actual army. You commanded an actual army, Barnibus!"

"For a second, yeah..." Barnibus said, still in shock. Though the path forward was blocked, they could still hear what was happening in the cafeteria. Crashes, odd minor explosions, or popping sounds. Knowing that there was still something ahead of them was enough to snap Barnibus back into the present. "What are we supposed to do now?" He asked Saga.

"I didn't see any of this before," Saga said, shaking his head. "I would have mentioned an army of us'es." He looked up and down the now very short main hallway, bookended completely by rubble and carnage. He saw a classroom door lying on the ground in the doorway. "Maybe we could get around if we cut through the science classroom, through to the lab, and then back out to the hallway. If we can still hear what is going on, then this pile must not be too thick."

"Looks like that's the only option we have now," Uncle Ted said. "I'll take a look and you two stay—" Before he could finish his thought, Barnibus stormed past him with a renewed sense of confidence, striding with great certainty into the science room, Saga following closely behind him as if pulled into the wake of a mighty ship.

They made it through the science room with little trouble, and into the separate lab space once Uncle Ted 'jimmied' the lock by smashing the knob off the door with an old 1960s microscope ('*This thing weighs more than my old Buick,*' he complained). Back out in the hallway now, they found themselves in a maze of destruction: more lockers pulled from the hall, bags and paper everywhere, and blood. Barnibus wanted badly to look away from the tremendous amount of blood, but he recalled his uncle's advice, *if you could call it that,* to survey everything and resist the urge to look away. He could not avoid his first thought upon a closer look, which was, understandably, '*boy, that's a lot of blood.*' He was not quite sure how constructive that observation was, but he figured it was in line with what Uncle Ted had asked for, so he offered it up.

"Boy," Barnibus began, "that's a lot of blood."

"It is..." Uncle Ted said absently, the gears in his head clearly turning as he took in their surroundings.

"There's a lot of blood, but I'm still not seeing any bodies..." Saga added.

"I don't think I could take a dead body right now," Barnibus said. "And honestly, I'm a little worried that dead bodies may rain from the sky or something if we see bodies around here." He felt what he hoped was just air lurching up from his stomach. "Like a self-fulfilling... whatever," he eked out before abandoning the thought.

"Or that the bodies we see are just something that you conjured up," Saga said with a half-serious laugh.

"Yeah..." Barnibus said, considering the loop of that potential snake eating its theoretical tail.

"If we're just seeing things because we thought of them and they're not even real... we'd be screwed. We'd be trapped here forever," Saga said as the three of them ducked below a fallen array of flagpoles formerly displayed proudly by the school's Model U.N. program. As he arose, he stopped in his tracks, his eyes fixed on the trophy case, torn asunder and brutalized in the middle of the hallway. Glass littered the floor, and the remaining jagged scraps still attached to the case itself were covered heartily in blood and tattered clothing. "I've seen this before," Saga said coldly. "We're back on the right track now." The mood among the group shifted as the conversation halted and the serious, back-on-track mood regained control of the boys and their uncle.

"What comes next?" Uncle Ted asked finally, more at peace with the idea that young Saga knew best which approach to take. They stood only a few feet from the entrance to the cafeteria now, and while the loud concussive noises had all but stopped, there was an indistinct murmur emanating from the doors, which still hung intact and open. As the silence settled after their conversation, Barnibus began to make sense of the noises that he was hearing from within. Voices. A lot of voices. Adult voices.

Barnibus stepped carefully into the doorway, his body square and vulnerable against whatever waited inside. Chairs bordered the center of the room in a circle, like Barnibus had seen done before in group counseling classes that had come through a couple of times. The chairs all faced inward, so everyone in the group could get a good look at everyone else in the group, prepped for everyone to take a turn speaking their mind or telling their story. In those chairs sat people, most of whom he did not recognize, and as he scanned the group, who were still unaware that the Jones brothers were watching them from the doorway, he picked out some of his friends' parents. He must have seen half a dozen familiar faces before he spotted them. Across the circle, on the far side from Barnibus and Saga, sat Barnibus Sr. and Carol.

18

PARTICIPATORY THEATER

"Ladies and gentlemen," the Purple Man called over the PA system, the crowd flinching and cowering at his voice. These people have been hurt, Barnibus realized. Recently. And badly. "You are tonight's entertainment!" In an instant, the house lights snapped off just as a spotlight shone in the dead center of the circle of imprisoned parents. There, absent just a moment ago, stood the Purple Man in full purple military parade dress, holding a microphone. He knew how to make an entrance. "I would say welcome, as a gracious host might, but of course you've all been here for quite some time," the Purple Man chuckled, "so let's forego those pleasantries, shall we?"

He did not seem to notice Barnibus in the doorway, now joined at the door's edge by Saga. Saga continued to scan the crowd, having not yet seen his parents. Barnibus was so enraptured by the presentation — The spectacle! The showmanship! — that for a moment he had hardly even noticed his brother also in the small audience alongside him. It was only with a moment to spare, just as Saga's eyes landed on their mother, bound to a metal folding chair there in the school cafeteria, that he snapped back into big-brother mode and sung himself over to cup a hand over Saga's mouth before the small yelp of recognition could leave his mouth. They both fell to the floor just outside the door, Saga struggling to get back up for another look as Barnibus used his virtually insignificant bodyweight to keep him pinned down, quietly shushing into his ear. Uncle Ted peeked his head around the edge of the frame to see what was happening, though he could hear the ongoing narration by the Purple Man thanks to the surprisingly robust school PA system.

"I know what a lot of you are wondering: '*Oh God! When will this nightmare be over? Why won't this lunatic let us go? Will I ever get to see my family again? My God!*' And listen: I get it. But to answer those questions as succinctly as possible: I don't plan on letting you go, to be frank. Listen, it's nothing personal. Just that once I commit to a plan, I really commit to it. You understand, you're all professionals." He honed in on one parent in particular, a single father named Justin, who trembled so badly that his metal folding chair was clattering across the floor. "Shhh, shhh, shhh, it's okay. It's okay. You stop that now, do you understand?" Justin, averting his gaze as his drooped head caused sweat to pool on the lenses of his glasses. He struggled not to look directly at the Purple Man and continued trembling, now whimpering to go along with it. "You already know the drill. If you don't stop that racket, I'm going to kill your son. It's that simple. We've been through this. It's like you didn't even pay attention at the read-through." He turned now to loudly address the empty space at the far edge of the room. "Ugh, I swear! It's like you can't even find blameless victims anymore!" Justin stopped trembling now, but as he drew slow, metered breaths, he could not help but make a whimpering sound. After a moment, he took a chance and looked over the rim of his glasses, under his sweat-dripping brow, directly into the eyes of the Purple Man, eagerly awaiting just a few inches away. "Splendid, thank you," the Purple Man said gently. "Now, I'm going to loosen the rope that is tied around your right leg, okay?"

Justin nodded.

"Great. And don't try anything, obviously, because again: if you do that, gonna kill your kid, blah blah blah, like a broken record over here," the Purple Man said like a standup comedian trying out new crowd work. The crowd was not interested.

Again, Justin nodded.

"Super duper." The Purple Man knelt down and loosened the knot he had placed around Justin's right ankle just enough that Justin could lift his leg up and down, but not enough that he could pull his leg forward or up and out of the rope. "Feel that?" the Purple Man asked.

Justin nodded, wordless, with a smile of relief creeping onto his face.

"Kinda feels like if I were to do the same thing with the other leg, you'd be able to stand right up, huh? March around the room with a chair strapped to your back?" the Purple Man said, and he pantomimed Justin waddling around the room.

Justin slowly nodded, the smile fading.

"Now, I want you to take that right foot of yours, the one that feels all footloose and fancy free there, and I want you to kick yourself backwards in your chair as hard as you can. Okay? Do you understand?"

He shook his head *no.*

"Justin," the Purple Man cautioned, "don't be like that. I

know you understand. You've already shown yourself to be such a good listener." He stood and turned about to address the entire circle. "You all have!" As his full turn brought him back to Justin, without taking the time to kneel back down, he stated flatly, "Do it."

Justin kicked his right foot down into the ground with enough force that Barnibus could swear, if he were to have time to examine the moment in his head, he heard Justin's knee dislocate with a loud *POP!* But Barnibus, unfortunately for him and for Justin, did not have that time to examine that singular moment, because the severity of the popping sound of Justin's knee dislocating (it had in fact dislocated) was immediately supplanted in Barnibus' mind by the bluntly final sound of the back of Justin's head slamming against the floor. As immediately as he hit the ground, he stopped moving. The only sound, faint enough to evade an echo, were the immediate, unavoidable gasps scattered across the crowd.

The lack of sheet panic gave Barnibus the impression that this was not the first exhibition of this sort that the parents had seen over the last couple of days.

"Do you know that man's child?" Uncle Ted whispered to Barnibus and Saga. Barnibus shook his head no, while Saga gave little response at all. "We should be sure to find out. Tell them their father died a hero."

"There are no heroes here," Saga whispered.

"Did you see this, Saga? Before?" Barnibus asked.

"Not this. I showed up after," Saga said. "I don't know what comes next," he continued as he crouched low again to peek around the side of the doorway into the cafeteria. After he looked for a moment, "just that there is a lot more of it." He settled back down, tugging on Uncle Ted's jacket to get him out of the doorway as well. "Unless we stop it."

Barnibus sat on the floor, his hands on his knees as he felt the energy drain from his body. They were here now. The big showdown. He was not sure what he expected, but he knew damn well what was expected of him: save mom and dad, save the world. He actually was not sure if the world itself was at stake here. In fact, no one had told him directly what the broader stakes were in this, and he was not shy about admitting that this was his first time doing something like this. But he had looked into the eyes of the Purple Man, and those eyes told him he had something big planned. Something big and very bad for a lot of people.

Barnibus was too young to comprehend evil. If you asked Saga, he would say that he understood that kind of darkness, and hell, if you were to ask Barnibus, or Carol, or Barnibus Sr., they would say the same thing about him as well. But his understanding of evil — of true, baseless hatred and anger expressing itself in such a boundlessly cruel way as to rise to the definition of '*evil*' — was not something that he had truly experienced. Dark visions, of course. Some of life's worst droogs like you may run into on a particularly tense day in the lunar cycle, yeah, more than his fair share. But with world-defining evil, the kind that leaves a black mark on all of humanity, Saga was just as out of depth as his brother. Barnibus wondered what he could do, what would possibly bring him to match the Purple Man, whose power seemed boundless and overwhelming, and in fact he asked both his uncle and brother that very question. *What do we do?* But the only answer he got back was more of the same. *Great question,* they seemed to say. *What **do** we do?* Although only a couple of minutes had passed, Barnibus was rooted to his spot on the hallway floor, leaning barely far over enough to watch his parents inside. They were scared. Bruised. They had seen some things. Of that Barnibus was sure. But aside from those minor afflictions, he was happy that they were mostly unscathed.

"Saga," Barnibus called in a harsh whisper. His brother perked up and came scooting over to where Barnibus sat. "Do you think we could get a message to Mom?"

"I don't see any way into that room without him seeing us, and at that point the message won't be arriving."

Barnibus kept watching.

"What do you think Mom would do?" Saga asked.

"I would have thought she'd talked her way out of this by now. I don't think I've ever known Mom to sit somewhere she didn't want to be for more than a couple of minutes," Barnibus said with a vague smirk.

"We could ask her," Uncle Ted interjected flatly, as if he was only half involved in the conversation, the other half involved in keeping watch on the events transpiring in the next room.

"We were just saying that we can't get a message to her in there," Barnibus said. "Besides, if we could, I don't think she would appreciate the message from the outside world to be, '*Hey, how can we help?*'"

"We can't talk to Carol," Uncle Ted said patiently, "but we've seen already that we have access to the next best thing." He gestured towards Barnibus, who took a couple of beats to register what he was talking about.

"I don't think I can just make it, you know, happen," Barnibus said.

"You just did not too long ago," Saga said, sitting up as he got more excited, relieved to see any idea being kicked around.

"I know you can do this," Uncle Ted said. "You just need to

concentrate."

"She won't be able to tell us anything that Barnibus himself doesn't already know," Saga said with true realization, the wind beginning to drop from his sails.

"Yeah," Barnibus said, pointing to Saga. "I don't know what we're going to get out of her... of... it... that we don't already know."

"Precisely," Uncle Ted said. "We will not learn anything new. That ship has sailed. We're in the big show now, and I'm afraid there isn't any time for practice and rehearsal." He let this point sink in a little before he continued, "but getting another set of eyes... at least, I guess, a second set of your eyes, can't be underestimated. There is something we're missing here — some other option or loophole that we haven't picked up on yet."

"If this is the kingdom of heaven," they heard the Purple Man begin in the other room, "then let God do with it as he will. You all know that quote?" Barnibus and Saga whipped over towards the door so they could see what he was up to now. Something about the volume and severity of this new sermon caught their attention. "It's not important if you don't. We can all just pretend I said it. It's original to me; I'm quite remarkable." He held for applause here, and when none came, he paid that fact no mind. "What I'm saying is that you've entered my kingdom here. This is my dominion, and I can — and will — do with it as I please. That's just the fact of the situation here. I hate to break that to you."

"Call her," Saga said to Barnibus, whispering out the side of his mouth. "Call her *now*."

"I can't just call her. It's not like picking up a telephone and ringing the operator," Barnibus said, the stress and panic beginning to bleed into his voice. Sometimes when he was trying to mask his panic, Saga noticed minor details of what he said would feel quite antiquated and out of touch. Barnibus' emotions were getting the best of him, as the sight of his parents — so close and yet so far away — was getting to him. *They're right there,* he reasoned with himself, *just run out there and get them. Run to them and they will run to you. They will protect you.* He felt bad about how quickly his mind had turned from altruistic thoughts of saving his loved ones from harm's way to self-preservation. But he reminded himself of a simple fact which he had lost sight of throughout this whole adventure: he is just a child. A parent's role is to protect their child, and *by defaulting to wanting to be protected,* he told himself, he *was simply playing his evolutionary role.*

"You're going to need to grow up eventually," he heard Not-Carol say softly. He smirked at the fact that he thought he could not tell the difference between Not-Carol and honest-to-goodness Carol, but the feeling faded as he found that Not-Carol had a programmed, precise cadence, which sounded markedly different from Carol's natural, precise cadence; big difference. At least to Barnibus.

"I need you," Barnibus mumbled, certainly not loud enough for Not-Carol to hear from feet away. But a conversation exchanged between two figures of one mind tends to help bend the possibilities of how sound and light travel, how ideas are conveyed and understood.

"You don't need me," Not-Carol said softly, now right at Barnibus' side. "You want me, and you feel safer now that I'm here." She stroked Barnibus' hair, something that always brought him immediate peace and comfort, ever since he was barely more than a baby. Saga crawled over to Not-Carol and snuggled into her, nestling between his mother and his older brother, cocooning himself against the world. With her other arm, Not-Carol squeezed Saga tightly as he breathed her in.

"There's no way this isn't real," Saga said, fighting back frightened tears. "There's just no way this isn't Mom."

"Do you feel safer now, boys?" Not-Carol asked her not-sons.

"Yes," they both answered.

"I missed you," Barnibus continued.

"Well, if this feels safer, then I suppose there's an argument that this *is* real. I'm here to protect you, and at least for now — at least for this moment — it feels like I'm doing that job." She spoke softly into the boys' hair and into the group hug they shared there in the middle of the debris-ridden hallway. She turned and looked over at Uncle Ted, who watched them with tears in his eyes. He was older still, and had much more experience with these types of things, but it still was quite the trick of the heart and mind exactly how well it worked to put him at ease seeing his sister safe again. They held each other's gaze for a moment, both smiling softly, communicating with just a look that they would be okay.

Here, for now, in this moment. They were okay.

"We need to think of something, some plan or some way that we can get you and Dad out of there — safely — without getting anyone else hurt," Barnibus said as he composed himself. He was focused on staying grounded in what was happening in the next room, and for a moment he kicked himself, feeling that he had let his guard down by being coddled by his imaginary mother.

Not-Carol nodded her head towards the cafeteria, urging Ted to take a look inside. The circle of parents had disbanded, and now were building some sort of structure, a monument out of assembled ephemera and mismatched materials, with a long platform on one side, suspended outward from the main body a couple of stories into the air. In the intervening few moments, they had pulled out the bleachers from the side way and constructed a relatively stable-looking... something... as they moved with slow, droning precision. The blank looks on each of their faces made Ted uncomfortable. He turned back to Not-Carol, who nodded and gave an expression that seemed to say, *It's time to get back to work.*

"It's good to see you're alright, Carol," Uncle Ted said with a smile. It was performative for the boys' sake, and they each knew this in their own way. But all still appreciated the gesture, as it helped them shake themselves loose from the preposterous situation of talking to an imagined person while also showing that they were not alone in how they felt. How they felt about this aberration.

"You need to get back out there," she said sternly to the group. "You will not help anything by sitting around here in the hallway. Get in there and make some waves. Get loud. Get big."

"We can't get bigger than he is. There's nothing we can do to counter anything he throws at us," Barnibus said. "He's too powerful. You haven't seen what he's capable of."

"Haven't I?" Not-Carol said. "After all, I'm just you, right? Whatever you've seen, I've seen."

"Yeah," Barnibus said sheepishly, "I guess that's true."

"So really, you don't need me here anyway, since I can only tell you things that you already know. I can't add any new information or give ideas that aren't already yours."

"No," Saga says, suddenly alarmed. "Please don't go!"

"Sweetie," she says as she hugs Saga tightly. "I'm not going anywhere." She turned to look up at Barnibus as he climbed back to his feet and paced, something that would surely remind Real-Carol of her brother Theodore if she were here.

"How can we go big?" Barnibus asked Uncle Ted. "What's bigger than what he can throw at us?"

"We don't really have a way of knowing what he can do until he does it," Uncle Ted says. "He's unpredictable."

"He has that train... and he ripped the side of our house, burned down the shop..." Barnibus enumerated.

"Did he?" Not-Carol asked.

"You were there," Barnibus replied, slightly annoyed. "You just said you've seen everything that I've seen.

"True..." she said, "I've seen everything you've seen. Did you see him burn down the shop? Him specifically."

"What do you mean?"

"I don't know," she shrugged, exaggerated. "I know the shop burned down, and I know he was there when it happened. And I know the side of the house blew off, but I don't know what caused it. Do you?" She asked Barnibus specifically, but looked at the entire group, prompting them to think for themselves.

"I guess I don't..." Barnibus said, as he searched his memory.

"The side of your house?" Uncle Ted asked, his head contorting with confusion.

"That's what happened to the kitchen, remember? The back wall of the house."

"Looked fine to me...?" he trailed off, as if searching his own memory now. "Inside was a mess, but I went around back to get in, and I didn't see anything the matter. Some paint was peeling," he shrugged, "but nothing much beyond that."

"What are you talking about?" Barnibus asked incredulously.

"You were right there! You must have seen it! You asked about our homeowner's insurance!"

"As a joke," he chuckled. "I meant because it was a mess in there. Whatever you boys did, it was a doozy."

Barnibus, trying to make sense of this, turned to Saga. He did not offer much help beyond his own confused look, twisting his face trying to pull an understanding from the dried well of his brain.

"I guess it's just weird that we've never seen him do anything. We've seen things *happen* while he's around, and we've seen some things that he's made appear..." she trailed off for a moment as if trying to get Barnibus to pick up the thread himself. He did not take the bait. "Don't you think it's weird that he barrels a train through the front of a school, or down a quiet street, and no one says anything? No cars or other houses get damaged?" There's a smattering of slight nods and thinking noises around the group. "You'd think something like that would cause a big stir. Or at least raise a few more questions."

"You're saying like an illusion? Like he's making us see the things that he wants us to see?" Saga tried to reason.

"I'm not telling you anything, remember. I'm just a reflection of what your brother thinks. That's all," she said with a heavy shrug.

"But that wouldn't make sense. The heat, the shop burning down. I mean, the fire department showed up for that, that happened," Barnibus argued.

"Did they? Did you talk to the fire department when they came? They must have helped you with your finger, right?" She stared at Barnibus, allowing realization to wash over him. As he thought, a low commotion shook Barnibus from his concentration.

Inside the cafeteria, groups of three parents at a time climbed the structure they had since finished assembling. Climbing the back of the bleachers three abreast, they reached the top near the arm they had craned out of the side, and there they stood waiting. After a moment, the next group of three scaled it in the same manner and, upon reaching the top, took their place in line and waited. So it continued until each parent, paired off with two of their cohorts, was patiently — and absentmindedly — queued up along the backside of the platform.

"I've grown bored with this, boys!" The Purple Man called loudly from the cafeteria. "I'm putting on quite the show in here, and I'd be lying if I said it wasn't for your benefit!" He turned himself around expectantly, looking at the far walls of the cafeteria for Barnibus and Saga. "Save these fine people a lot of pain and just walk yourselves in here. I promise I'm not going to hurt you."

Barnibus leaned over the edge of the doorframe to look at what had been set up while they had been running through their notes with Not-Carol. He saw the makeshift structure with the parents lined up, staring blankly ahead. Somewhere in the middle of the crowd were their parents, although he could not see them specifically beyond the occasional glimpse of an odd piece of clothing. The longer he looked, the farther he could see past the blank obedience in the faces of their parents. They stared ahead absently, but their bodies trembled, their brows growing heavy with sweat. These people were prisoners in their own minds.

"Okay," the Purple Man said finally. "I think that was a fine amount of time to wait. If you will not come on stage on cue, we're just going to need to improvise until you're ready." He turned back to his group of captives. "Isn't that right, gang?"

The group let out a smattering of small whimpers, the most it appeared any of them could muster. Some rogue tears rolled down cheeks, betraying the anguish of their owners.

"You all know the tune! Let's go with our first line!" Right on cue, with the practiced polish of a military parade march, the first group of three parents stepped to the edge of the platform. "And a one," he began, "and a two, and a three—"

Perfectly in time, the two people on either side hoisted the person in the middle over the edge of the platform. The person kept their arms at the sides and their chin up as they were thrown about five feet outward before falling, pencil-straight, directly to the ground twenty or so feet below. They landed with a heavy thud — like a trashcan full of rocks — and immediately upon impact their composure broke. Blood-curdling screams filled not only the cafeteria but reverberated coldly out into the hallway. Barnibus jumped backwards at the sight, unsure of what he had expected, but horrified at what he had seen. He shuffled backwards into Not-Carol and Saga, just as Uncle Ted shifted over to look at what happened.

"Off to a great start! Beautiful! You really know how to put on a great show, I'll tell you," the Purple Man called up to the two other parents remaining on the platform. After a second, they turned in opposite directions and descended the stairs to wait patiently at the bottom. The next set of three people took their place, and as they stepped up, Uncle Ted finally put together the mental image of what must have transpired a moment ago. He turned to look back at his family, his eyes welling with tears for Barnibus having needed to witness such a thing.

Barnibus, shaking in the arms of his not-mother, grappled with what he had seen. *It can't be real,* he reasoned. *Just like with the other things, we didn't see him do anything. What if this is another one of his illusions, if that's what they are?* He brought his hand up, his finger still wrapped in a splint lashing it to another finger. He gingerly touched it with his other hand, wincing immediately. *This is real. This I feel, and I know this is real.* He could not come to terms with how those two things could coexist. He thought back to that night in the butcher shop, how simply and plainly the Purple Man had spoken, beckoning him quickly and authoritatively to break his own finger. He could hardly even question it. It was so immediate, so definite and absolute that it seemed, despite how opposed to it he was, that it was destiny.

"Oh," Barnibus said lightly, "oh no..."

"Yeah..." Not-Carol added with a pitying tone.

"What's happening, Barnibus?" Uncle Ted asked urgently.

"Barn..." Saga added.

"Everything is absolute. He shows you something, tells you something, and you take it as the truth," Barnibus said slowly as he assembled his thoughts in real time.

"He's just... a really good liar?" Saga asked.

"No, it's not that. It's like he puts a thought in your brain — incepts an idea into your consciousness — and your brain accepts it as the singular truth. The train, the heat in our house, all the things we've *seen*, but also *this*," he added, holding up his broken finger. "He made me do this. By putting the idea in my head, it was no longer an option. It was inevitable. It wasn't a request or an order; it was as if he were predicting the future to me, and all I could do was allow it to play out as destiny." He got up again to look into the cafeteria, just in time for the next victim to take the plunge onto the floor far below, their screams seeming to arise precisely at the moment of impact.

"And those people too...?" Saga said as he arose to join his brother at the door.

"That's why they're so silent while they're waiting, but can't help but scream once they hit the ground. The pain shakes his grip loose as the brain takes over, panicking and reacting to the pain."

"Maybe the people we see in there are all images that he's showing us, too!" Saga exclaimed excitedly.

"Oops, no," Not-Carol interjected. "Sorry. They're very much real. Including me—well, out there, that Carol. Very much real people, and the ones screaming are very much in real pain."

"They need our help," Barnibus mused to himself.

"You could send in the army again," Saga suggested, his mind twinging at the idea of commanding an army of real, life-size toy soldiers.

"No, not like that. Even if I could do that again... and I don't know how... but if I did, he'll just bring the room down around us, or maybe — I don't know — turn our army against us or something. No, he needs to think that he's won. That's all he cares about is winning. Once he has that — has *me* — he'll let his guard down."

"We need a distraction," Saga continued on his brother's train of thought.

"Something to draw his attention," Barnibus said, their minds nearly working as one.

"While he's not looking, we can get to Mom and Dad, and—"

"Not just Mom and Dad," Barnibus cut in. "We need to save all of those people."

"Hold on now, I can't let you boys do that," Uncle Ted said as he shuffled himself back to his feet, back over to the Jones brothers. "I'm here to protect you, and that's what I'm going to do. You tell me what I need to do, and I'll do it, but I'll be doing it alone."

"You can't," Barnibus said. "He wants something from me. He told me specifically back at the butchery that he and I are alike — like you and me — but that I can do something that he can't. He wants what I can do, because he knows all he can do is make people *think* things. It seems like I can make people see things, but also make things happen — to make things change."

"That's all the more reason to keep you safe," Uncle Ted said, more sternly now. "Can you imagine what that monster would do with a power like that?"

THUD. More screams. Another jumper.

"We don't have time to argue about this anymore," Barnibus said, practically already walking through the door. "We need to help them. Now."

As Barnibus strode confidently into the cafeteria, Saga following immediately behind him, the whole crowd, minus the heap of horribly maimed people just below the platform, turned in unison to look at them, their eyes locked with mechanical precision, following them as they moved.

"Ah," the Purple Man sighed, relieved. "The guest of honor has arrived. And he brings with him his young ward — how exciting!" He clapped a modest clap of joy before waving a hand dismissively at the crowd still assembled on the bleachers. "You all take five." As he waved, the crowd relaxed, their knees buckling, a heavy sigh arising from the group along with yelps of pain and whimpers of terror. While they remained locked in place, their feet rooted to where they stood, they collapsed as best they could into each other's arms.

"Let these people go," Barnibus shouted. "You want nothing from them. You just want me. Here I am."

"Don't be such a cliché," the Purple Man said, annoyed. "I know I don't want anything from them. You're not convincing me of anything there." He rolled his eyes exaggeratedly. "I don't *want* anything from them, but I sure do *need* something from them. They're an excellent motivational tool — honestly one of the best money can't buy." He bounded over to the bleachers, gesturing to the structure and its inhabitants like someone showing off a new model at a car show. "Case in point," he exclaimed. "You and your little brother there would have kept cowering in the hallway if I hadn't hurled your friends' parents at the ground, snapping their legs and lower vertebrae. And that," his tone taking a grave, serious tone now, "would have been," he continued, "pretty annoying." He snapped out of his faux-serious performance and back into his showman mode. The persona, Barnibus was noticing, that he seemed more comfortable in.

"Then they've served that purpose. You can let them go now," Barnibus said, as he suddenly became very aware that his own parents were in the ground. He held his head rigid to stop himself from looking over at them, from picking them out of the crowd, as he knew that would make him lose his focus, would break him and bring him back to that feeling of wanting to be protected. Now was his turn to be the protector.

"That is so rude of you to assume that they're all used up," the Purple Man scoffed. "Are you saying that they're useless? How. Dare. You." He turned to the captive crowd. "You two," he called, pointing to Carol and Barnibus Sr., "do you care to explain yourselves for the type of child you've raised?" Their mouths opened, and their cries erupted as if they had broken through a heretofore unseen gag.

"Barnibus!" Carol screamed.

"It's going to be okay, buddy!" Barnibus Sr. continued.

Barnibus remained rigid. *Keep it together. You can't give up now. You're too close.* He would not budge as his parents kept pleading for his attention through their words of encouragement. He knew he needed to be strong. The Purple Man, having only allowed this to continue for a brief moment, snapped his fingers, returning the gag to both of their parents.

"Okay," Barnibus said, trying to maintain his composure. "If you have my parents, why do you need all the rest of these people? You can let the rest of them go."

"Well, that's the fun part," the Purple Man said as he bounded back towards Barnibus, stopping out of arm's reach. Barnibus could not help but note the distance between them before the Purple Man continued. "I didn't know those were your parents." He made a performance, scamp-like shocked face for good measure. "I knew you — whatever you are — lived in this town, and I knew you were a kid, roughly however old you and your friends are, but I didn't know which one of you vile little pukes was the one I was looking for. So I just did what any reasonable person would do in that instance and simply kidnapped a broad cross-section of parents and other adults affiliated with the school, knowing that it would invariably draw you out." He waited for a moment, a look of faux guilt parading on his face. "Fact is that I didn't know those two useless husks were your parents even just then when I called on them. I thought you looked an awful lot like that schlub," he said, pointing at Barnibus Sr., "so I took a gamble. Matter of fact," he added, turning back towards Carol and Barnibus Sr., "you, schlub," he waved his hand once more. "What's your name?"

"Barnibus," Barnibus Sr. added, his voice shaky and weak. The Purple Man waved his hand violently now, and Barnibus Sr.'s gag returned once more.

"Gah, now I just feel lazy for having not just asked any of their names. That would have saved... honestly, that would have saved a lot of time and effort." The Purple Man thought for a moment. "Oh well! That's a lesson for next time, I suppose."

"There will not be a next time," Barnibus said, trying to be as stern — as menacing — as he could muster. "This ends tonight, just you and me. Let the others go."

"I'm confused why you think you're dictating terms right now, *Barnibus,*" the Purple Man sneered. With a snap, the next group of parents in line stepped up to the platform. "Come here," he said firmly to Barnibus. Barnibus, without hesitation, stepped forward and closed the gap between them, the Purple Man's radiating heat and sour breath enveloping him. The Purple Man did not break his gaze with Barnibus as he once again snapped his fingers, and a split second later, **THUD,** followed by pained, terrified screams from the person who had just taken the plunge. "Shut up," the Purple Man uttered over his shoulder, and with immediate effect, the screaming ceased.

"You didn't need to do that..." Barnibus pleaded.

"But you see, I did. Because you're still unclear on what exactly is going on here." The Purple Man leaned in closer now. "This might have been fun, this little cat-and-mouse game we had going on — I know it was for me! But that game is over now. You have lost. I have won. And now I'm going to get my prize."

"You have me. Let them go," Barnibus tried again. "There's

nothing left to gain by keeping all these people here."

"Maybe I was unclear the first few times. I know it can be hard for kids to understand complex concepts like torture and mutilation." With that, the Purple Man held his hand up for a moment and then waved it lightly, beckoning the next set of people to step forward onto the platform. He hesitated for a moment before twisting his hand to wind up for a snap.

"Wait!" Barnibus exclaimed. "Just my family. Let my parents go — Saga, my uncle — you can keep me, you can keep the others. But don't make the rest of my family go through this," Barnibus said coldly, distant. In the crowd, Barnibus' parents twisted against invisible binds, tried their best to call out to their son, but nothing came out. Others in the crowd began trying to defend themselves, to call out objections, but no one could make a sound enough to convey a complete thought.

"Barnibus, my dear boy," the Purple Man said, charmed. "You little scamp! You would do that? For me? Gift to me all these innocent people, all so—what was it again? *Your* family doesn't get hurt?" The Purple Man sneered, "You really are no better than me. My God, we're a perfect match, you and I." He looked Barnibus over, for a moment giving Barnibus the impression that his deal had worked, or that he was getting through to the Purple Man. But after a moment, "No. No, I don't think I will. But hey, it's a bonus — for me — that these fine people know that in your final moment — and make no mistake, these are your final moments — you will throw them in the trash." The crowd erupted now in full-throated screams and vitriol, all directed squarely at Barnibus, as his head fell, defeated. After about five seconds of chaos, the Purple Man held up his hand, and all sound ceased. "You can't imagine that type of power." He turned to face the crowd once again as he spoke to Barnibus. "To have this many people waiting on your every word. Willing to do *anything* just for you. Whatever I ask, they'll do it," he chuckled. "Imagine what you and I could do together."

"Please..." Barnibus said weakly as he looked up at the Purple Man, a tear falling loose from his eye.

The Purple Man moved swiftly back over to Barnibus, getting so close that Barnibus was sure their faces were about to touch. He'd been here before, a sense of familiarity and almost comfort washing over his face as the Purple Man's hot, putrid breath and fiery eyes invaded his nose and eyes. He had lost, and the Purple Man was here to take what he had come for. Barnibus, here in the middle of the cafeteria, in front of the families of his friends, held captive with varying degrees of injury, had attempted to bargain with the Purple Man, a conceit so patently absurd that it strikes one's mind as *lazy*, or a wholly shallow attempt at a climactic ending. *Why*, one would be driven to wonder, *would Barnibus just wander out into the cafeteria and just ask the Purple Man to stop?* And here in proximity, that absurdity showed on the Purple Man's face, in his crooked, broad smile. Barnibus was just a boy, and he had been outclassed.

The Purple Man had won.

* * *

At the far side of the cafeteria, just beyond the reach of the Purple Man's spotlight, behind the crowd of people rooted in place watching the Purple Man's performance, Barnibus moved swiftly from one pile of debris to the next, as two movements behind him, Saga darted from one stack of chairs to the next. As he would break cover, he would sneak a glance at Not-Barnibus and Not-Saga, partly to make sure everything was still working as he had hoped, and also, he was not afraid to admit that he was simply proud of himself. It had been a long time since he had felt that sense of pride in something that he had done, and although the stakes in this current moment were impossibly high, he wanted to take that amount, fleeting as it was, to bask in that feeling.

They reached the back of the crowd, who, much to the benefit of the Jones brothers, could not give any reaction to seeing them weave through their ranks as they made their way to the middle of the crowd, to their parents. They moved quickly and quietly, Barnibus keeping an ear towards the Purple Man's monologue at his doppelgänger (if he could call it that. He still was not sure about what it was he was doing when this happened). When Barnibus and Saga reached their parents, Saga squeezed his mother tightly as Barnibus hugged their father and began taking inventory of any binds they had. He was surprised to see there were none, and while he understood why that was, it complicated their escape somewhat. While they had hoped to untie or otherwise free the captives, to take them out of the equation with dealing with the Purple Man, they would now have to settle for their parents knowing that they were there working to rescue them. Nothing more, at least not yet.

"We're going to get you out of here," Barnibus whispered to his parents. "All of you," he clarified as he turned to the other captives immediately around him. "Don't listen to that me out there," he said, himself sounding confused as well. "That's— that will take some time to explain. But we're going to get you out of here. You'll make it out of this." He turned back to his parents. "We have a lot we need to talk about."

Barnibus and Saga heard another snap come from across the cafeteria, and the next set of people took two steps forward before stopping again just shy of the platform's edge. This time, from his vantage point among the crowd, Barnibus noticed something otherwise masked by the spectacle of people following command hypnosis. When the Purple Man snapped his fingers, a signal to the person (or persons) he was commanding, other people under his control momentarily — *for an instant!* — moved of their own free will. The Purple Man was not as powerful as he wanted to be seen, and the limits of his power only allowed him a finite grip on the people he controlled. And the grip was growing weaker. Barnibus had found his in.

"Did you see that?" he whispered to Saga.

"They flinched," Saga said.

"On their own, they flinched. I think when he moves to command someone, he needs to loosen the grip he holds over everyone else in that moment."

"He's not so powerful now, huh?" Saga taunted.

"I think when he does that, he needs to get everyone back under his hold. There's a break there where that happens... If we can stop him from being able to do that — from regaining that control — we can get these people out of here."

Saga shut his eyes for a moment, gently swaying his head in a near figure-eight, as though he were looking about the room. After a moment he opened his eyes again, looking first at his parents, then turning to Barnibus.

"If we make a move now, he'll know we're here and he'll snap these people's necks," Saga said matter-of-factly. "Or at least have them snap each other's necks." Barnibus thought for a moment as he tried to avoid picturing that inevitability (it was still too risky for him to let his mind wander without careful supervision).

"He doesn't need to know *we're* here," Barnibus says. "He already has us," he adds as he points towards the main show.

* * *

"Open your eyes," the Purple Man spat at Not-Barnibus, whose eyes shot open with immediate obedience. "I want you to show me how you do that wonderful thing you do. I promise you this will not hurt."

Not-Barnibus trembled, making a great show of how much he was fighting the Purple Man's commands, how much it pained him to lose. His eyes widened as the Purple Man leaned in closer still, their noses practically touching.

"That's good," whispered the Purple Man. "I'm glad you've finally come to your senses. There's just no use in resisting. That was a waste of time." The fire in his eyes grew as he delved into Not-Barnibus' mind, searching for the tools — the triggers, the pathways — he had that the Purple Man did not. His eyes flickered as he grew frustrated. Not-Barnibus did a serviceable job of selling the anguish he was meant to be feeling in this moment; trembling, tears running down his face, but with his eyes locked obediently to the Purple Man's. "Where are you..." the Purple Man mumbled as he searched.

"It's not going to work..." Not-Barnibus taunted through gritted teeth. "With all your power... here's something you can't do."

"Silence!" the Purple Man shouted. He stumbled, and for a

moment there was movement in the crowd; a shift, a shuffle, a murmur. As he regained his footing with Not-Barnibus, so did he regain his footing with the crowd, once again lashing them back into his control.

* * *

"There it is again!" Saga exclaimed quietly.

"Drat," Barnibus whispered to himself. "It means he's getting weak. But we need to know it's coming in order to make our move..."

"What is our move exactly?" Saga asked.

"I was hoping you'd tell me," Barnibus said uneasily. "Was there anything else you saw when you came to the school earlier? Anything that could help us know how this ends?"

"When I walked through, it was already over. There was no ending for me to see."

"Oh..."

"What is it?"

"Do you think the absence of an ending means we die? You didn't see what happened because we cease to exist in that timeline?" Barnibus said slowly, grappling with the implications of what he was saying.

"Not today," Saga shook his head emphatically. "Not like this."

"How can you be sure?"

"Not today," Saga repeated. Saga's eyes narrowed as he avoided matching Barnibus' gaze.

"Saga," Barnibus began slowly, "have you seen how we die? How *you* die?" Carol, unable to hold on to her children or comfort them in the singular time in their lives that they absolutely needed it most, trembled and mumbled, trying as hard as she could to be there for her youngest child as tears continued to flow from her frozen, terror-filled eyes.

"There was ice. At the school. Or I guess after... outside the school? It wasn't here. But when I saw it, there was a flash of ice. Like, endless ice, outside. It was nighttime." Saga pieced clued together as best he could.

"Ice?"

"Lots of it."

"Here? In town?"

"It didn't look like anything we have around here," Saga said. Another shuffle from the crowd snapped the boys back into focus on the Purple Man and his assault on Not-Barnibus' facsimile of a mind. They could see clearly, even from their far vantage, that he was growing increasingly frustrated, his movements fidgeting and erratic.

"I have an idea," Barnibus said in a haunted tone. "But you're going to want to look away."

* * *

"You minuscule piece of filth," the Purple Man hissed. "You're not the destination, you're a stopover. You and your brother are a bus stop. This is not where I come to hang my hat, this is where I stop to take a leak on my way to the big show." Sweat was dripping from the Purple Man's forehead, and Barnibus — by way of Not-Barnibus' up-close-and-personal view — was taken by this clear sign of weakness from this monolith of villainy.

"Just let him go," Not-Saga warned. "This doesn't end well for you."

"I've grown especially tired of *you*," the Purple Man sneered at Saga. "I don't even understand why you're here. Are you two some sort of package deal? Is that the idea?" He turned back to Not-Barnibus, "Seems like you two are pretty inseparable, huh?" He relaxed as he pulled away from Not-Barnibus, shifting his attention from the laser focus on the unknowingly shallow and empty proxy mind Barnibus had hastily built into his own effigy before sending it into the trenches. Not-Barnibus sighed heavily as he struggled to catch his breath.

"Leave him out of this," Not-Barnibus shouted. "You don't want him, you want me."

The Purple Man moved lithely towards Saga with staged elegance meant to convey suave confidence. Everything about the Purple Man, even now, is designed and calculated for projection.

"Hey, no, hey!" Not-Barnibus pleaded frantically. "Over here! Eyes on me!" He struggled to move, but was held in place, still under the Purple Man's spell, same as the rest of the trembling captives. "Get back here and finish what you started!"

"Let it go, Barnibus!" Not-Saga shouted. "He's too weak to do anything," he taunted the Purple Man. "Look at him," he chuckled, "he's pathetic."

"Saga, no!" Not-Barnibus scolded. "Don't do that!"

"Couldn't even beat two kids," he said to the Purple Man, now standing right in front of him, his nostrils flared, breathing heavily and seething with anger. "That's gotta feel pretty demoralizing."

"Saga, please!" Not-Barnibus shouted.

"No," the Purple Man said as he held one finger aloft. "Let

him finish. It sounds like he has something *really important* he needs to add to the conversation."

"I've read this word sometimes in books," Not-Saga began, "*pomp.* I'd read it in different stories — I like to read a lot — but I never knew what it actually meant. *Pomp.* It's fun to figure it out now, though. That's what you are. *Pomp.* Just circumstance. Just show," he shook his head mournfully. "There's nothing more to you. You don't scare me anymore."

"That's really unfortunate," the Purple Man said softly, confidently. "I'm sorry that you feel that way." He turned back to Not-Barnibus, "Is that how you feel as well?"

"I swear, if you touch him..." Not-Barnibus growled through gritted teeth.

"I won't. I would never! Barnibus, I'm not some sort of *monster!* Is that what you think of me? That I'm just some impeccably dressed monster, out here hurting children? That really hurts me, Barney. It does. Here I thought the three of us were really bonding. Tsk. What a shame."

"You *are* a monster," Not-Barnibus said.

"I'm sorry, I couldn't quite hear that," the Purple Man said. "Mind coming over here for a second?" He beckoned Not-Barnibus, who once again obediently approached and stopped directly next to Not-Saga and turned abreast with his not-brother to face the Purple Man, who towered over the two Jones brothers menacingly. "You say I'm a monster, and yet your brother seems to think otherwise," he began. "What do you suppose we should do about that?"

Not-Barnibus, his eyes locked squarely on the Purple Man, gave no response.

"That's what I thought," the Purple Man said, annoyed. "Now I'm afraid we have to move on," he said with a sigh.

"Barnibus, snap your brother's neck."

Not-Barnibus hesitated now, a little flourish he could add here as Barnibus' projections were not subject to the Purple Man's whims.

"Barnibus, no!" Saga shouted.

"Cute," the Purple Man said, before adding flatly, "Do it."

Not-Barnibus reached over with both hands, placing one on the back of Saga's head and the other cleanly astride his chin, and with one quick, definitive swipe, he snapped his brother's neck with a loud POP.

Thunder; a loud roar which shook the entire school. Sustained in power and volume, shaking the Purple Man's concentration as panic filled his eyes. It came first in a light dust, snow dropping from the rafters as it gained speed and grew more dense. Within barely even one second, Not-Saga's body having hardly even hit the floor, the thunder growing deafening, a blizzard erupted here in the halls of Anna Tuthill Harrison Junior High. The crowd of captives split in every direction as the prisoners, now free from their shackles, scattered as best as their beaten, tired bodies would allow, desperately seeking whatever cover they could find. The shaking peaked in violence as the floor of the cafeteria tore open below the Purple Man, swallowing him in an instant before it closed once again.

Just as quickly as it began, it was over. Silence. The Purple Man was gone.

Saga — who had escaped with Carol to the hallway where Uncle Ted had gathered the survivors — closed his eyes. In a moment, a wry smile spread across his face as he surveyed the Purple Man's fate. Where he went, Saga reasoned, he will not be a problem any more. He opened his eyes as he heard Barnibus approach, helping a limping Barnibus Sr. to safety.

The hallway, which they had traversed not long ago, navigating around piles of debris and carnage, puddles of blood borne from immense violence and suffering, was clear. Indeed much of the destruction and hazard they had seen when they arrived, their hearts and minds taken by the staggering violence and potential loss of life had been manufactured. The Purple Man had projected, as a show of strength and of pomp and flair of theatrics, everything that they had seen. In the cafeteria, however, remained the platform from which some prisoners had been made to jump. While the Purple Man could not invent items in truth — and remained now unable to do so having not extracted what he needed from Barnibus — he could convincingly command others, and in this case he succeeded at that. While the destruction of their school had been a projection, the violence the boys had witnessed themselves was all too real, the Purple Man having influenced the actions of the other parents, driving them, outside of their own volition, to walk the plank. The lack of control, the terror, the torture — these were all tools which the Purple Man brandished quite willingly, and with pure elation.

Through the crowd, stumbling about trying to make sense of what had happened, Barnibus saw Mr. Calhoun. His clothes were in shambles, and deep dark bags hung heavy under his eyes. Barnibus, once one to snap-to when faced with even the smallest degree of authority, now felt nothing for his science teacher. He saw him now for what he was: a human being. Barnibus felt as though he could taste the terror that Mr. Calhoun had felt, simply by measuring it on his face. Fittingly, on the wall just over Mr. Calhoun's shoulder was a poster for the upcoming *Eastern Mid-Sized Middle School Science Conference and Jamboree.* Barnibus chuckled at the glimpse into what he would soon consider to be his old life. The pressure of something as quaint as a glorified science fair felt hardly worth much concern, and he found it hard to imagine why he had spent much mind at all on such trivialities. Of course, knowing himself as Barnibus now did, he knew that, were he to imagine it, that pressure would become quite real once again. So he thought better of it, and did not pay it much mind. As he watched Mr. Calhoun wobbling his way onto his feet, Barnibus turned back to his parents, hoping that his newfound perspective on the world, and of Mr. Calhoun as a person and not a monolith, would extend to them as well, and he would see them as people, not mythical beings of authority and omniscience. But alas, as he regarded his mother and father, he knew that was not the case. Barnibus felt larger than life; a builder of worlds, a commander of an army which stood and fell at his command. But what he wanted now was to be protected. He leaned in close to his brother. Carol and Barnibus Sr. held their boys, reunited as a family.

"Barnibus," Carol began, her voice trembling and hollow, "who is that?" She pointed towards a group of other parents tending to their wounds, helping those who had taken the plunge off of the Purple Man's high-dive. There among them, helping Walter's father, was Not-Carol.

"Right," Barnibus said. "About that."

19

EPILOGUE: AN INTRODUCTION

Barnibus Jones was a boy who dreamed. At first, too much to handle, and then not at all. But as he found his way out of the dark, as light and image re-entered his mind and illuminated the machinations and musings inside, he dreamed once again. First a little, and then a lot, and in time, he would grow to dream at a scale he could scarcely fathom; entire worlds would rise at his whim, civilizations developed in a vacuum. Some with expressed purpose and others simply developing and falling as they may. Worlds bending to the will of one person would have tremendous consequences; the implications on both sides of the equation are quite too much to discuss here. That is a story for another time.

Beyond Saga's eyes lay totality. Possibility. An endless expanse of everything the universe could forge, branching in every direction, and from every direction of those directions, and so on and so forth. There was hope here now, in the mind of Saga. It was not without its darkness, of course, much like the world itself and the realities that fell into the Jones brothers' timeline. And make no mistake about it, this was, and continued to be, the Jones brothers' timeline. Saga would fear to admit it, recognizing exactly how he and his brother were shaping the world around them. It felt to him how it felt when he and Walter would build their world out there in the woods before his passing. Whatever they needed in that moment, they could fabricate effortlessly. And that ease of discovery, abundance of innovation and prosperity felt boundless and free, until Saga felt the branches in the farthest reaches of his mind wilt, to darken with rot, twisting and gnarling with decay. That, too, is a story for another time.

And there, on the outskirts of the farthest reaches of the world, devoid of civilization, or communication, or life of any kind, the Purple Man remained. Looking out over a lifetime of ice and, for any other being, certain death, he had all the time in the world to contemplate what he could do and how he could do it, and how gleefully free he would feel when he exacted his revenge once he returned from exile. But without the trappings of living creatures, without their simple, moldable minds, he had no avenue to travel, no way to escape, no means to an end. Of course, with time and in the harshest of elements, even something as vile and self-serving, a being of such singular purpose and drive, must too evolve. And what once seemed to be final, what once seemed to be inescapable and exacting, a curtain call for the Purple Man, would too become another scalable obstacle. There he remained for now. This, too, unfortunately, is a story for another time.

THE END

www.ingramcontent.com/pod-product-compliance
Lightning Source LLC
Chambersburg PA
CBHW021807130726

47987CB00010B/3049